THE PLAYING FIELDS

THE PLAYING FIELDS

Stella Cameron

**SEVERN
HOUSE**

First world edition published in Great Britain and the USA in 2021
by Severn House, an imprint of Canongate Books Ltd,
14 High Street, Edinburgh EH1 1TE.

Trade paperback edition first published in Great Britain and the USA in 2022
by Severn House, an imprint of Canongate Books Ltd.

severnhouse.com

British Library Cataloguing-in-Publication Data
A CIP catalogue record for this title is available from the British Library.

ISBN-13: 978-1-78029-123-9 (cased)
ISBN-13: 978-1-78029-821-4 (trade paper)
ISBN-13: 978-1-4483-0559-9 (e-book)

All Severn House titles are printed on acid-free paper.

MIX
Paper from
responsible sources
FSC
www.fsc.org   FSC® C013056

Typeset by Palimpsest Book Production Ltd.,
Falkirk, Stirlingshire, Scotland.
Printed and bound in Great Britain by
TJ Books, Padstow, Cornwall.

BEFORE

I *deserve what I've got. I earned every bit of it. Thinking about the ones who were so big, so looked up to all those years ago, used to make me angry. Now I'm so much more than they are, and I know they're jealous of me and I pity them. That's not true, the last bit, I hate their guts for being too weak to really come to something in this world. Nobody ever gave me anything. Nothing I did was good enough before, but it is now. What they don't understand is that they can't stop me from making my good things happen. I'm in charge of karma.*

God, that makes me laugh.

It's understanding how weak they are and what they're missing that bubbles up inside and makes me laugh like that. I don't make any noise, don't have to, I'm in control and there's my power.

I study them, you know. That takes a long time. We can't have mistakes just because impatience leads to haste. There isn't much I don't find out about them, and I use it. If they looked around them, really looked, they might notice me, but I doubt it. Self can make a man, or woman, blind.

When the kill was done, I felt like my feet didn't touch the ground, like I was on the moon, sort of, and leaping along or maybe bouncing. Inside I was hot. I shook then and I'm shaking now just remembering. If I laughed aloud it would come out like one of those kitchen mixers, vroom, vroom, bursts that would rattle my jaws. Must not laugh out loud.

All of this, the planning, the studying, the records I keep, they have kept me happy and I don't want the feeling to stop. When I think about the happiness going away so the dark, flat place comes back, I roll up my eyes, far back as they will go, to stop me thinking like that. It's my trick to stay in control – I mean to keep controlling what happens. CONTROL IS MY THING!

ONE

Richard Seaton collected himself, took two steps on to the gravel drive in front of his house and stopped walking. Underfoot, the stuff sounded like birdshot sprayed on glass. He made a sideways leap to the grass and looked up at the bedroom window. Still dark and no twitching curtains.

Winter stinks. These snappish cold nights almost make me feel like hopping into bed. Alone. And there's the rub – let a woman in your life and your bed is no longer your own – what you do and when you do it is definitely not entirely up to you. Thus, all this sneaking around.

In his study on the ground floor of the house, faint reflections moved, flickered against the closed blind. His mythical alibi watched television. Fortunately, Kelly found it 'rather sweet' that he had designated the room as private. She had never discovered that it was often empty during his late-night absences from her side. Thanks to enough sleeping pills to turn her into the living dead, she no longer woke up with one of the hysterical panic attacks that had plagued their earlier years together. She went to bed at nine, or even before that if he was lucky, and soon after he could count on eight or more hours of freedom.

Kelly protested his parking the Nissan Navara beside the road rather than in the garage, especially when, as she repeatedly pointed out, their high hedge meant they couldn't see it and thieves or vandals would have an easy job. Kelly was obsessed with lurking miscreants, intent on doing her harm. She had inherited a fat pile when her father died and had never known want, but she guarded what was hers with manic attention. Richard gritted his teeth. She made him a sizeable allowance but also saw him as one more of her possessions. He allowed her that, encouraged it even – he couldn't afford to cut the satin ribbons that tied him to her, not yet.

He walked on the cold frosted lawn to the gates and slipped outside. Clouds drifted in swathes across the moon, playing with an icy shimmer on the road. A deep breath seared his throat and chilled his lungs. Abruptly, the moon went out, fine, piercing rain hit his face and almost instantly became a pelting squall. When he got where he was going, after making a quick stop in Folly, there would be a hot toddy, a fire and some interesting company. In other words, like-minded men and women with their eyes on expanded horizons.

The sheepskin jacket he'd picked out tonight was a good choice. He turned up the collar and thrust his hands deep into the pockets. The Nissan was just around a bend in the road – by design, not necessity.

Headlights and a car engine approached from that same bend and Ricky drew back against the hedge. Their neighbors weren't usually nosey, but there was no point risking inconvenient comments should he be sighted leaving home in the dwindling evening like this.

For an instant the lights hit him fully and he shielded his eyes.

The car slowed and Richard heard the passenger window roll down. A man's voice called out, 'Ricky, is that you?' He walked to the curb as the car drew up beside him. 'It is Ricky, isn't it? We met at the Royal Chestnut in Gambol Green. Malcolm, Malcolm Loder. We hadn't met for years before that. Remember?'

Did he remember that name . . . vaguely? Ricky laughed easily. 'Yeah, I do, Malcolm. What brings you around here?'

'This isn't my patch. Never been through Bishop's Cleeve before. I took a turn too early. I think, anyway. On my way to the Rum Hole – at Mill House. Whatever that is. Never heard of it before but I'm told it's the only place to be. All the people making things happen around the area, and elsewhere, go there.' He gave a snort. 'Sounds like one of those places to see and be seen. Not that I'm opposed to that if it can be useful and the company's good.'

The Rum Hole was fashioned after the rash of London speak-easies and not designed for casual drop-ins, although there were the occasional people who wandered in after eating at the Mill House Restaurant. Seating was precious, and recommended guests were usually introduced by someone of standing who accompanied them, at least on their first visit. That was not broadcast, but it was understood. They had no reason to advertise.

'Ever heard of it?'

'Ah, yes, yes I have.' Shit, and this had to happen when he wanted, needed, to establish an excuse for his absence from home – should that become necessary – before moving on to a couple of blessed hours to decompress. As far as Kelly was concerned, he occasionally ventured out to a pub. That was it. If she knew he frequented the Rum Hole, thought of as a clubby establishment for those who wanted to make new contacts, she would probably have a lot of questions he did not want to answer.

'God, am I the lucky one? You on your way there now, by any fabulous chance?'

He wasn't about to let this man in on his game by saying he was going to the Black Dog in Folly first. That was his own business. But if he lied, then ran into this one at the Rum Hole later . . . 'Yeah. Probably I'm going.' That sounded daft. He hadn't had enough practice at deceit on the fly.

'That's *fabulous*. Jump in. Damn, this is brilliant. If I hadn't taken a wrong turn, I'd never have run into you.'

'I ought to drive myself,' Ricky said, wondering if he should bag it for tonight and turn back.

'Rubbish. Get in and show me how to get there. As soon as you're ready to come back, I'll be glad to leave, too. I'm only going out of curiosity.' The door swung open. 'Dome light's broken. Hope you're not scared of the dark.' His laugh irritated Ricky.

Still, he hesitated, but he didn't want to look like a fool. 'OK. Thanks.' He got in and Malcolm started pulling away, scraping the door over the curb before Ricky could yank it shut. Old Major Stroud wouldn't be happy at being stood up at the Black Dog, but that couldn't be helped tonight. There was no question of turning up there with someone else in tow, not when Ricky wanted to touch Stroud for a contribution to the drama group. He'd been working on the man for weeks and could feel success getting close.

'Look at this fucking sleet. First rain, now this. I hate the bleeding crappy winter weather.' The man leaned forward over the steering wheel to peer through what was, indeed, sleet. He waved a hand. 'Sleet mixed with snow. Would you look at that? Fasten your seat belt.'

'When did we meet?' Ricky asked, clicking the belt buckle into place. The car, something low-slung and sporty he hadn't identified before getting in, screeched with Malcolm's angry acceleration.

'It was sometime back. At the Royal Chestnut in Gambol Green, if I remember rightly. I went in one night while you were there with a motley bunch after some rehearsal for a play – or something like that. Shakespeare? I don't remember.'

That could have been any one of a number of occasions. The local amateur drama group went to the Royal Chestnut after some of their rehearsals. 'Sorry,' he said. Honesty could be the best solution. 'I'm not sure I do remember you.'

Malcolm laughed again, a laugh that skated up high this time, almost to a feminine giggle. 'Isn't that the way? We meet people we don't notice and can't remember even if they remember you. I know what you mean. Not to worry. I remember you. Which way to Mill House? The club's upstairs there, isn't it?'

Ricky wanted to tell the man it wasn't really a club, more a comfortably trendy bar for movers to go to when they needed to get away and be with their own kind. Malcolm wasn't promising to be anything like Ricky.

The Rum Hole was in several comfortable rooms at the top of Victorian Mill House. The restaurant was on the main floor. The Rum Hole was popular, and pricey, with décor reminiscent of the below-decks of a cask-filled galleon. Drinks were pricey. So were the upmarket menu items, but at least Kelly was generous when it came to money and Ricky. He hadn't made it on the stage, other than as the leading light in the local Phoenix Players, and working as an accountant in a boring Cheltenham firm didn't bring what he was worth, but he did all right financially. What rankled would always be the way he'd been passed over for parts in plays where he could have shone. But, hell, the West End still shimmered in his mind and he wasn't dead yet.

Resigned to arriving at the Rum Hole with Malcolm, he swiped at condensation on the inside of the window. 'We're about out of Bishop's Cleeve. Turn right at the main road and keep on until I tell you to make a gradual left. We skirt Underhill and Folly-on-Weir. The place we're going is off the beaten track, but not that far. It's actually closest to Underhill. You know Underhill, don't you?'

'A dump,' Malcolm said shortly.

Why hadn't he given directions, then taken his own car to go wherever he felt like going, or better yet, not gone at all? He could have avoided Kelly by ducking into his study for an actual tele session.

'You sure you don't remember me?'

He felt rather than saw Malcolm aim his face toward him.

'Keep your eyes on the road.' Ricky laughed. 'By the looks of things, it could really snow. If it does, it's going to get slippery – or worse. Not this way!' He raised his voice as Malcolm jerked a hard left and threw him against the door.

'We can get where we need to go from here,' the man said, turning down what was little more than a pathway between dry stone walls.

'What happened to you not knowing the way?' Ricky didn't even remember the gap was here. He pressed forward to see through the windscreen and the seat belt sprang undone.

Predictably, Malcolm gave one of his curdled laughs.

'No, we can't go this way.' The belt would not stay buckled. 'We'd miss it this way. We need to turn around and carry on toward Folly. Then—' A howling screech of the brakes shot him forward and Malcolm threw a protective arm in front of him. Ricky straightened sharply. The seat back collapsed completely under his weight. Feeling ridiculous, he struggled to haul himself up, to keep a grip on the door with the fingertips of both hands.

'No need to get up for me,' Malcolm said, sniggering.

Again, the vehicle howled away, tires juddering and slipping.

'Remember me now?'

'No,' Ricky shouted. 'I don't know you at all, dammit. I think you're pulling something here.'

They surged from the pathway between dark trees and Malcolm hit the brakes once more. The car slewed to a stop.

'Now, do you remember?' The laugh turned into a squeal and Malcolm grabbed the back of Ricky's neck, crushed his face into the dashboard.

'Yes,' he yelled, lashing out uselessly. 'Yes, dammit.' The shock seemed to blind him, and so did the pain in his face.

The man landed a punch high between Ricky's shoulders. The next blow crashed into the base of his neck. So hard. For seconds there was nothing, nothing but the blood that spurted from his nose into his mouth, and the clawing fear in his belly. His eyes wouldn't focus. He scrabbled to push himself up and to fend off this attack. Getting away was all he had to think about. Something wedged behind his back, low down. The doors locked loudly, just as he reached for a handle to throw himself out of the car. With each suck of air, blood bubbled at his lips. Terror flooded him.

Knives of pain blasted from his spine and through his head, like electric shocks.

The maniac was climbing on him, cursing, jamming a knee between his shoulder-blades. There was no room to fight back.

Grabbed by the hair, his head ground sideways. He tried to twist free of the arm that hooked under his jaw, the elbow bent in a paralyzing grip on his neck. *Headlock.* He thought it even as his sight failed completely.

He could not scream.

TWO

'Another shoe's going to hit the fan, I know it is,' LeJuan Harding said through tightened lips. 'And I know I'm mixing metaphors, but I need both of 'em.'

Detective Chief Inspector Dan O'Reilly studied the broad back of the man standing by the conservatory windows. His sergeant had been uptight since they arrived at Dan's cottage – uptight for most of the day, come to that.

'Don't try and guess how I know more trouble's coming our way,' LeJuan said. He looked into deepening darkness, toward the River Isbourne. 'I feel it in my bones. Let me work it out for myself.'

'And when you've done that, you'll share it with me, I'm sure,' Dan responded, joining the other man. 'Don't suppose you could force down some good French Merlot?' He dangled two glasses by their stems and carried the open bottle in his other hand.

LeJuan took the glasses and held them while Dan poured, then set the bottle aside on the windowsill.

'Tasty stuff,' LeJuan said after a hefty swallow. 'Unfortunately, I drink wine like pop so I'm not a cheap dinner date. You want my conclusions now – about my hang-ups over what happens next in the Edward Coughlin brained-with-a-cricket-bat mystery?'

'Sounds like a schoolkid yarn,' Dan said. 'Yes, I want to know what you're thinking. Try sipping the Merlot. Savor the taste.'

LeJuan rolled his darkly expressive eyes. When he was working a case with Harding, Dan could easily feel invisible in his black partner's dramatic presence – which was sometimes useful if he wanted to observe a suspect's reactions in near privacy.

'It's been more than six weeks since the Coughlin murder,' LeJuan said. His London roots colored his deep, rumbling voice in a way the female officers called *yummy*. 'I've never seen as much *absolutely nothing* useful on an open case before. Every day at the station I'm waiting for snide digs about flogging a cold case. That and I'm dealing with my own doubts at the same time. What if we've really bolloxed things up this time and any moment there's going to be another killing by the same offender? That's what keeps me awake at night. What if we've missed leads and this schmuck isn't a one-off like we've about persuaded ourselves he is? Thinking he's beaten us could make him decide to have another go. Shit! It's taking too long, and we've got almost nothing.'

'We're in a hard place,' Dan said. 'Caught, whichever way we go – maybe. Is that the prospect that's eating at you? If so, how right you are – at least from the way I'm thinking. The Super's whining in advance about cost overruns. His term, not mine. Like we're doing a kitchen remodel rather than chasing after a killer. He's making noises about how we must be wasting our time. As if he knows what we're doing with our time.'

They both faced the fading scene outside. Rain had threatened most of the day but had yet to put in an appearance. At least it was not quite as cold as the forecast had promised and there had been no repeat of last night's snow.

'Do you think the Super's about to pull the plug on this one and send in interference?' LeJuan asked.

'I'm pretty sure he's thinking about it. If he does, he'll regret it – or that's my take. Like you, I'm picturing this bastard chortling behind some corner just waiting for the coals to cool before he lights everything up again. And I hate it.'

'I know you do.' LeJuan chuckled. 'You sound even more Irish when you're ticked off.'

Dan ignored that. 'You got a hot date tonight?'

'Nah – unfortunately.'

'Good. I want to go over what we've got. *Again.* We could be getting stale already – or convincing ourselves we're jumpy for nothing and Coughlin was a definite one-off after all. Tell me again why we think our man – or woman – might kill again?'

'First, we're sure it's a man.' LeJuan held his glass at eye level, squinting into it as if he might find answers there. 'The body was moved after death and the victim was a big chap. That took a lot of strength. So did smashing that bat – or whatever bat he actually used – smashing it hard enough to make that much of a mess.'

'Or just a lot of adrenalin and . . .' Dan let that hang. He believed their killer was male, too. 'Yeah, you're right. And there's no reason not to believe the murder weapon was a cricket bat, even if not the bat found at the scene. Molly's got questions about lack of hair and tissue residue – and what she thinks should be more evidence of blows to the wood at the supposed point of impact.'

'The scene was staged,' LeJuan said. 'Showy. Bat handle clean as a whistle. But the business end propped against the head the way it was. Like the whole thing was arranged for a painting. Still life.'

'Or a photo,' Dan said. 'That doesn't fit with a crime of passion. Whoever did it had the patience to stick around a bit after the initial deed was done. Like it was important to make some point to whoever found the body. Or to us. You hungry?'

LeJuan nodded.

'How would pizza be – or kebabs? There's Chinese. We can get delivery from Winchcombe. I'm not living totally in the sticks out here.' The village of Gambol Green did not run to fast-food delivery, but they were only a few miles from Winchcombe, which was considerably larger.

'You know how to do a fast topic change,' LeJuan said, wiggling his empty wine glass. 'I'll sip the next one. Promise.'

Dan nodded toward the windowsill. 'You pour. I'll order pizza. Anything against pineapple?'

'You know the answer to that. Not on my pizza.'

'Right, half-and-half so I can have my pineapple. Did Longlegs say he'd drop by on his way back from Folly?'

'Said he might,' LeJuan said of Detective Constable Longlegs Liberty, an indispensable officer who frustrated Dan and LeJuan, among others, because he refused to sit his long overdue sergeant's exam and none of them could figure out why.

'I'll order enough for him. That means another whole pie. Vegetarian. That skinny man eats like he's got two hollow legs.'

'No – just long.' LeJuan laughed at his own brilliance.

'Very funny.' Dan smiled. 'Keep entertaining yourself while I order. You get to put on some suitable music. Just no rap – not that I have any.'

He phoned in their order to a pizza place in Winchcombe that did a quick turnaround of orders, and went into the kitchen to scrounge up paper plates and napkins. Canal Cottage had become his only six weeks earlier, as stacks of still untouched packing boxes affirmed. The former owner had left what had been a centuries-old guesthouse used for her friends in wonderful condition, but Dan wanted the kitchen made more functional. The one full bathroom upstairs, and a pokey little loo that had been added to the downstairs years ago, also needed facelifts.

The coincidence of picking Gambol Green out as the place he wanted to live – and finding Canal Cottage – still blew him away, but he already loved the place.

Dan recognized some Dave Brubeck coming from the sitting room. LeJuan was a jazz man, almost any jazz. He also listened to a lot of opera. The rap dig was a running joke with the team.

'We'll pass on the silver service this evening,' he said, returning to the conservatory. 'It'll look great out here once I get it filled up with plants.'

LeJuan looked dubiously at a single stalked rubber plant that Dan had brought from his previous home, the house he had sold in Gloucester after his divorce. 'I've got to start over. That rubber thing's the only one I didn't manage to kill with neglect. Corinne always looked after . . . well, anyway. History.' His ex-wife had remarried and lived in Dublin now, as did their son, Calum, most of the time. 'Pull up a pew.'

LeJuan slid a large box aside and shunted a rattan couch closer to the coffee table. Cushions with faded palm leaves on their covers had seen better days, like all the mismatched pieces in the conservatory. But it was a comfortable enough place, and Dan didn't intend to make many changes in too much of a hurry. The adjoining sitting room would also do as it was for now. In retrospect it might not have been such a good idea to give Corinne first choice of all their joint possessions.

The conservatory table, topped with chips of green stone embedded in a thick resin, grated on Dan's nerves, but he set down the plates and napkins and grinned at LeJuan. 'Knives and forks? Or fingers.'

'It's pizza, man. Real men don't eat pizza with knives and forks. Does Calum know all about your move?'

'Oh, yes.' Dan picked up his wine and sat down. 'When you have a fifteen-year-old, you'll find out how attached kids become to the familiar. At first he said I was selling *his* house, but he sounds about over that phase now. He chronicled all the Christmases and the barbecues, and his first this and first that. Almost had me in tears. I hope Corinne doesn't pull another stunt this Christmas. She and her husband booked a trip to Spain last year and Calum ended up going with them, even though it was supposed to be my turn for Christmas.'

'You could have insisted on sticking to terms.'

'I could, but sometimes it's better to keep the waters smooth. Then, when I want something, I can point out what a sterling ex-husband I am. What an incredible father.' He didn't enjoy this topic, even though his boy was rarely too far from his mind.

'D'you think he'll like it here?' LeJuan asked.

'I think he'll love it. Once he has a chance to see what a great place it is. The whole area, as well as the cottage – and Gambol Green.'

'He'll probably like it better once he can drive.' LeJuan shrugged. 'Not that I'm suggesting he'll be a pain in the neck when he visits. Wanting to be chauffeured around, I mean.'

'We'll work that out,' Dan said. 'We always have.' The probability of warring schedules wasn't new to Dan, but he would rather not have it pointed out that a homicide detective could be hampered by sole responsibility for a teenaged son.

A rap sounded at the door. Going for his wallet, LeJuan got up, but Dan waved him back to his seat. 'My shout. You can get it next time.'

The pizza delivery person was almost bowled over by a beagle with a bossy attitude who brushed past the man's legs and dashed into the cottage. 'He's fine,' Dan called to LeJuan. 'Belongs to some neighbors but wants to move in here.' The dog wagged his flagpole tail and nether end hard enough to dislocate something.

Dan tipped the man from the pizza place and went to set the boxes on the table. 'I'll put Longlegs' food in the kitchen. If he doesn't show up, it'll get eaten tomorrow. I'll take it in to the station.

'The dog's Busybody, alias Busy. He belongs to my neighbors in the big so-called farmhouse behind me – Ham's Plat, they call it.'

'How could I forget?' LeJuan said.

LeJuan cleared his throat to continue, but Dan interrupted what he expected to hear next. 'And yes, it has reached me that some of the lads think I moved to Gambol Green because I'm obsessed with this case. I may be obsessed with it, but I moved here because this is where I want to live. Finding this place was incidental. And if anyone wants to know, I first saw this cottage and fell for it more than a year ago when it wasn't even for sale – and Edward Coughlin wasn't a murder victim yet.'

'Fair enough,' LeJuan said. He opened the pizza box and shifted a large piece on to a precariously floppy paper plate. 'I defend you, y'know, boss. I tell 'em you chose this place over the one by the old cricket club. You could have been really close to the murder scene there.'

'Thanks. There wasn't one near the club. Just fields and woods.'

The phone interrupted LeJuan's laughter.

Dan pulled out his mobile, checked the readout and mouthed, 'Lamb,' indicating his friend and former partner Detective Inspector Bill Lamb was the interruption. 'Hey, Bill. What's up?'

He looked at LeJuan while he listened. Busybody approached the coffee table from different angles, feigning disinterest in the food while his nose and whiskers twitched.

'Bloody hell,' Dan muttered, looking toward the glass roof of the conservatory. Rain drummed in earnest now. 'When and where?'

Scant moments and he told Bill, 'Yeah, I think you're probably right. Good thinking. Good of you to call me direct, Bill. LeJuan's with me. We'll be right there.'

LeJuan closed the pizza box on Dan's pineapple and ham – cooling nicely, he supposed – and with Busy at his heels, carried it to the kitchen where he slid it on top of the refrigerator. 'Let's have it, boss,' he said shortly once he got back to the conservatory.

Dan shrugged into a raincoat. 'It could be that shoe you were talking about hit the fan.'

THREE

Alex Duggins tried not to look as if she was watching the door.

She *was* watching the door, darn it. Where was Tony?

'Funny night,' Hugh Rhys said. Hugh managed the Black Dog, Alex's pub in Folly-on-Weir. 'Quiet, but like we're waiting for something to happen.'

She gave him a sharp glance. This was a bad moment for mind-reading, but Hugh did seem to have a way of sensing when she was disturbed. 'I hope Harriet and Mary are all right,' she said. 'It isn't like them not to show up all evening. It must be too late for them to come now.' The Burke sisters' regularly reserved table sat empty before a cheery fire that flared and spat its way over the blackened chimney breast.

'Major Stroud's in one of his obstreperous moods.' Hugh gave the counter several unnecessary swipes with a wet cloth. 'He's got that look. As if he's hoping someone will say just the wrong thing and give him an opening to get in a nasty comment.' He bent his head but glanced up at the major who was working through at least his fourth double whisky of the night – following a customary opening pint. Or two. Watery eyes flat and sunk deep in flabby pouches, his thin lips were set in a line beneath a gray moustache trimmed with military precision. His gaunt face was flushed dark and he already rocked on to his heels and back slightly. The more drink the man imbibed, the more sharp-tongued he became.

'What time is it?' Alex asked. The question was automatic and superfluous. The clock on the stone mantel over the Inglenook fireplace read 10:30.

'It's 10:30,' Hugh said. 'I thought Tony was coming in by now. This is turning into a night for no-shows.'

That was the last comment Alex needed. 'Tony had an emergency at the clinic. It must have gone long.' Tony Harrison, her as yet publicly unannounced fiancé, was the respected vet for small and large animals in Folly-on-Weir and the surrounding farms.

He should have been there hours earlier. Alex had already made a surreptitious call to his clinic and Tony was not there, but she had felt the need to come up with an excuse for his absence. She had particularly asked Hugh to stick around after closing and have a drink with them. And Lily – and Doc James Harrison, Tony's father, who was the local GP. In addition to being Alex's mum, Lily ran the inn and restaurant on the other side of the Black Dog building. Now that Alex thought about it, Lily and Doc had also been absent from the main bar most of the evening.

She crossed her arms tightly – as if she could contain the jumpiness she felt. If she had not pretended to be busy with orders when she talked to Tony about them getting together tonight, 'Just for good times' sake. We need to catch up. It's too easy to lose touch with friends, even when you see them regularly and you believe you know all about them,' well then, if she hadn't been concentrating so hard on hitting just the right breezy note, she would have paid more attention to what he might have said about any existing plans that could make him late joining the rest of them.

Oh, he must have been delayed at one of the farms and had not had a chance to call. Tony took his work so seriously. He was one of those rare, wonderfully transparent people who didn't have secrets and who expected everyone else to be just as straightforward and accepting as he was.

So, where was he? And that wasn't all.

'Where's Lily?' Alex turned her back to the room and leaned against the counter, the better to see Hugh's face. 'Do we still have diners in the restaurant?'

'Don't think so. I'll go and check.'

'No, don't bother. It's not important.'

Major Stroud, decidedly unsteady, attempted to saunter as he approached the bar. 'Thrill me with something interesting,' he said, his speech slurred, and placed his glass very carefully on the counter. 'As long as it's interesting mind you.' The words slid together.

If she had not felt fractured, Alex might have mentioned the dangers of overserving, but the aggravation of dealing with his ire would not be worth it tonight. Better to give Stroud a lift home – an increasingly frequent occurrence.

'Cun't rely on anyone these days,' the major said, resting his elbows on the counter and leaning forward. 'Know what I mean?'

Hugh placed a single shot of Lagavulin in front of Major Stroud. 'Lots of good people in the world, Major,' he said. 'Look around you. We count ourselves lucky here at the Black Dog. In Folly generally. Good people.'

'Hogwash.' Stroud took a swallow of his fresh drink. He planted his feet and studied the ceiling. 'Your hops are looking a bit faded, old thing,' he said of garlands looped from dark beams. He coughed and sneezed.

Alex took a self-protective step backwards. 'Are you peckish, Major? We've got some lovely rare roast beef. How about a sandwich?'

Stroud took another swallow, eying her blearily across the rim of his glass. He jutted his considerable jaw but made no comment about her offer of food.

'Quiet tonight,' Hugh said, polishing the counter yet again. 'Emptying right out already.'

Major Stroud snorted and slapped his glass down once more. 'I taught my sons t'be reliable. I'll tell you that. If they make an agreement, it's an agreement. On the nose. None of this forgettin' to show up. Least he could do was give me a jingle last night. Not a word. And not a dicky bird today either. He needn't think he'll hear from me. Damned if he will. Bastard's taking advantage, that's what it is. Thinks I don't know what he's angling for. Wants money for that tatty tithe barn of his. Well, s'not getting it now. Not from me. He'd better make up to that toffee-nosed wife of his. Jumped-up no-personality piece if ever I saw one.' He tottered toward a chair where he had left his coat.

Alex wondered who had offended the major, she assumed by failing to show up as promised the previous evening. Asking was out of the question, but offense had obviously been taken and had simmered all day. She also couldn't help remembering that Stroud's younger son – Harry – was probably still in jail for embezzlement. Peter, the older offspring, had followed his father into the army and rarely appeared in Folly, although his name was frequently invoked in glowing terms.

'I'll give him a lift home,' Hugh said. 'Chat him into waiting a few minutes, will you? Just while I bring a car around.'

He went between the ceiling-high walls of spirits bottles and into the kitchens beyond. Staff cars were parked behind the building.

Alex hurried to join Major Stroud. 'I keep meaning to ask how Mrs Stroud is,' she said. Making conversation with him was not easy.

'Is that right?' Stroud said. 'Can't imagine why. You don't like her any more than she likes you, if I remember rightly.'

There had been an unpleasant incident around the time when Harry had got into trouble, but it was history to Alex now. She had mostly filed away memories of attempts to pressure her into speaking up for Harry, attempts that went so far as to lock her into the Strouds' dark house at night and leave her there. 'Is she still an avid ballet buff?' When the occasion demanded, a person did what a person had to do. The man could not be allowed to drive in his current condition, and she would talk to him about anything that would keep him from leaving before Hugh could get back.

'Bloody ballet,' Stroud muttered under his breath, rhyming ballet with Sally. He was having difficulty buttoning his tweed overcoat.

The last few customers began to straggle out, bundled in warm coats and most wearing boots. Winter lay thick in the air and pressed down on the land with ever colder purpose. Alex looked toward the front windows. Sleet slanted past the colored fairy lights along the rooflines and slashed against mullioned windows. Air close to freezing roiled up from the ground in foggy-looking white swirls. There had been talk of snow threatening again tonight, but so far no one had reported the threat becoming reality.

'I'll take another for the road,' Stroud said with a sniff. 'Make it a double, there's a good girl.'

Alex heard the front door of the pub slam open, caught by the wind, no doubt. Even in the bar, a rush of cold air reached her. The same air that brought Tony into sight. His damp, dark blond hair had been blown curly, but it was his frown that caught Alex's attention. He walked directly to her and put an arm around her shoulders.

Tony was almost never demonstrative in front of others.

'How are you sweetheart?' he said.

'Very well now you're here,' Alex said with a smile. For an instant she wondered if this was her night for drunks, but Tony's eyes were clear and focused steadily on her face. 'I'm great. The weather's getting worse, isn't it?'

'It's horrible. Biting. The kind of cold that cuts to your bones. You can't go out there without a warmer coat than the one you've been wearing lately. Have you got another one upstairs?'

'I don't know. The one I'm using is very warm.'

'I'll take a look at it before we go home.' They shared the house that had been Tony's – on the hill above Folly, dropped down into a shallow valley affectionately dubbed, The Dimple. Alex's house was on the market and there was a sale pending.

'In fact, we're overdue to take you shopping,' Tony said, brushing her short dark hair away from her face. 'I know you say you don't care about clothes, but you wear them well. A new winter wardrobe for you would make us both happy.'

There was something unfamiliar about his manner. 'Let's talk about that another time,' she said.

Tony pressed his mouth shut.

Her stomach tightened. He wasn't one to fuss – and he definitely didn't do overprotective and overbearing.

He frowned deeply. 'Where's Hugh? I thought you said he was joining us for a drink. You're not here on your own, are you?' He gave the major a quelling glance.

'Let's go over here.' He pulled her back toward the bar.

'Just a minute.' Alex stood still, holding his hand with both of hers. 'We're about emptied out. Once Hugh brings a car around to drive Major Stroud home, we'll close up and go into the snug. I think Mum's doing something in the restaurant so, no, I'm not here alone.' She frequently was and never thought anything about it. Should she need it, help was rarely far away.

Hugh appeared from the front door and waved as he bore down on Major Stroud.

'What's all this about – this gathering or whatever?' Tony asked. There was no annoyance in his voice, but neither was there anything Alex recognized. That was it, Tony didn't sound like Tony. 'You said something about friends getting together. Who's going to be here?'

'Come with me.' She took him by the hand and towed him toward the passage that led from the main bar, past the snug to the restaurant and a flight of stairs to the upstairs offices and guest rooms. 'Mum,' she called, going into the restaurant. 'There you are. Could you watch the bar for a while? We'll be in the snug. Hugh's taking the major home. Round up Doc and I'll give you a shout when we're ready.'

Her mother knew what Alex had planned and she grinned. 'James is on his way,' she said, with a suspiciously moist glint in her eyes.

Tony turned away so rapidly that Lily was left where she stood while he whisked Alex into the snug and closed the door.

'What is it, Alex? What's going on?' Now he looked close to irritation – and he definitely was confused.

'My turn first. Why were you so late getting here? You knew I'd made arrangements for a little party.' She deliberately avoided calling it a celebration.

'I had a frustrating evening. My emergency took a long time getting to the clinic and Radhika had to leave before we were done so I had to finish up on my own. Radhika will go back and check on the patient in an hour or so.'

Either he was concocting a story or there was a problem with his phone – and Radhika's – and the clinic phones. She took a shaky breath.

Tony took off the Barbour he wore unbuttoned over thin cotton scrubs. He hardly looked dressed for cold weather himself. 'I had an errand to run, too, and it took me three times as long to get where I was going as it should have. The road out of Winchcombe. Not on the way to Toddington, more heading southwest. There were several police and emergency vehicles. The road was clogged. I think they were heading toward the Underhill area where all those fields are. There aren't many buildings out there. A farm or two. The tithe barn. And that short golf course. It didn't look good, but for once it's not our business.'

'Thank goodness,' Alex said automatically. Which was his

supposed excuse . . . a long clinic session or a mysterious errand? She added, 'I wonder what was going on. That cricket club where . . . where a man was killed. That's out there, too. Not that there has to be any connection.'

Tony looked troubled, but then he smiled a little. 'We'll hear soon enough if it's anything important. Alex, I have to talk to you. Sit with me.'

A naturally calm man, Tony was almost constantly gentle. He exuded quiet confidence – not anxiety. Did he realize how uptight he seemed tonight?

She leaned away and pulled out a chair. 'OK, we'll sit down. Are you OK?'

'Of course, I am. Why would you ask a thing like that?'

'Because I've never seen you like this before, but if you say you're fine, then you are. You've had a long day. Would you like a drink?'

'No.'

Good.

'I'm sorry, sweetheart. I've been thinking about this for days – more than a week now. Forgive me for coming off like a mad man but I'm starting to feel like one.' In the subdued light of the snug, his dark blue eyes were near black – and the emotion there was close to desperation. And what did he mean, he'd been thinking about their future for more than a week? It had been at least two years since they had known they wanted a future together.

'OK, Tony.' She managed a smile. 'What's up? I thought everything was going along well with us. My house looks as if it's sold. We're making some wonderful changes to yours—'

'Ours.' He cut her off, raised his voice. 'It's our house now. That's the agreement. I've made an appointment with old Barstwick in Cheltenham to deal with the paperwork. Getting my will the way it needs to be is important, too. I can't delay that any longer.'

'There isn't a hurry, is there?' she said, trying for a measured tone. 'We've got plenty of time and a lot to think about first. I've been so happy. I am happy. I thought you were, too.' He was making her nervous.

'I want the legal stuff taken care of,' he told her, more

forcefully than needed. 'And there is a hurry for me. I don't deal well with uncertainty.'

Shock tactics might be just the thing to bring them both down to earth. 'What do you think about New Year?' she said, stuffing her hands in her gilet pockets and hunching her shoulders.

He studied her face, his expression blank. 'New Year?'

'For us to get married,' she said. 'A small, intimate thing. Our families and close friends and villagers. And anyone else we really want. What do you think?'

'New Year is only weeks away,' he said, and she saw him swallow hard. 'It's an incredibly busy time of the year for you, isn't it? Is there time to plan properly?'

'What matters more?' She held his hands and he gripped hers back, too tight. 'This place or our marriage? We've waited a long time, Tony. I thought you wanted this as much as I do.' If he hadn't pushed for marriage, she wouldn't have taken this step tonight.

'I want it,' he told her, but she did not like his hesitation – or the way he made her feel she was dropping her idea, her plan, on him. Please let her not be making a horrible mistake by pursuing this. She could find a way to back out gracefully, but not if she waited much longer.

'I know how much I want us to be together for good, Alex.' His grip relaxed just a little, but she took the opportunity to delve into a pocket again and pull out the ring box he'd given her months ago.

'I brought this with me. In case you want to put it on my finger. It's probably getting moldy in the box.' Her laugh did not convince even her. 'I know I've held back. I'm not holding back anymore. I know what I want. Tony, I want you and I hope you still want me. And I want to tell the people who care about us that we're getting married.'

He took the ring from the box and threaded it on her finger, diamonds and green stones in a band. It was beautiful, but Alex could not get excited about those things. She had once, but the first time she had taken a man's ring had ended in disaster and this time what she wanted was different.

His fingers were icy on her skin.

No matter how hard he tried to persuade her that his reactions were normal, they were not.

'Emeralds because of those eyes of yours,' he said, and finally his smile was soft, his look intense in the way she loved. 'I want you to wear it for me.'

He *was* subdued. She couldn't make a scene out of asking him for an explanation of his behavior, not now. But she would have to get the truth out of him soon. 'What a beautiful thing it is.' Looking at the ring, she touched it softly. 'And it fits. I won't ask how you managed that.'

'I pinched one of your rings from your jewelry box.' He was open and joyous again; he was the Tony she loved and understood. 'What do you think?'

'I think I love you as much as I already knew I did,' she told him. 'And, yes, I'll wear it – for us, not only for you.' And she wished the shaky feeling inside would go away.

'Thank God,' he said, and closed his eyes for a moment. Then he got up and paced back and forth across the small room. 'Please be patient with me, with what I'm going to tell you. It doesn't make any difference to us – it won't. But it could mean some inconvenient hurdles to get over, even a delay. I don't want that.'

Forcing the words past a dry throat, she said, 'Neither do I. Just tell me what's happening, Tony.'

The bar hatch from the snug opened and Hugh put his head through. 'The major is safely delivered home . . . again.' He was laughing. 'Is it time for that good champagne you've been hoarding, Alex? Or is the blushing groom too weak-kneed to toast his bride?'

Alex had an urge to cry. She looked at Tony and he took her in his arms. 'It's all right,' he murmured. 'Leave it to me. Give us more time, Hugh, my man. We have more talking to do first.'

'Right,' Hugh said after a brief, awkward pause. 'More time, it is. We've got as long as it takes.' He withdrew rapidly and closed the hatch again.

'I'm going to get this out fast,' Tony said. 'You know Penny disappeared while we were in Australia. More than eight years ago. She'd gone diving. Her body was never found.'

She watched his face. 'I do know all this.' Penny had been his first wife. 'Something's changed, hasn't it? Is everything up in the air again? Oh, Tony, I'm so sorry. How awful for you.'

'I don't have any details other than . . . Recently I got an email from a woman calling herself Penny Harrison. She said there are things she wants from me – things I never expected to confront. She doesn't really threaten me but it's implied. You and I need to make some decisions about our immediate future. I'm sure she has no claims on me, but I intend to do more footwork before thinking about legal action – which probably won't be necessary at all. Logically, I don't think there's anything she can do. The death declaration should arrive any day.' His fingers threaded together with hers and she felt how he trembled.

'So, we'll stay calm and deal with it, Tony. Carefully.'

'If this isn't a hoax, it's possible she can make our lives diffi-cult,' he said, and added hurriedly, 'but it won't be anything I can't get under control.'

Sweat broke out along Alex's spine and she was hot and cold by turns. 'You need to tell me everything you know. And every-thing you think.'

He bowed his head. 'I'll understand if you don't feel you can come back to the house with me tonight,' he told her quietly.

'There's nowhere else I intend to be.' She stood up. 'Let's get the dogs and excuse ourselves from the others. They'll understand when we say we've got a problem we can't talk about yet. We have to decide what we're doing next – if anything – before we say much to them.'

'My dad knows something's going on,' Tony said. 'He's angry, but that's another story.'

'Come on,' Alex said. 'We'll tell them we'll get together with them soon. Then we'll go.'

FOUR

The Phoenix Players' tithe barn stood in a clearing amid extensive woods not far from Folly. When Dan had first come here, heavy foliage still hid the old building from a wide track that threaded toward it through gentle hills where sheep grazed. In the weeks since the Coughlin killing, and with the help of lashings of rain, all that had changed. As LeJuan drove closer on this wet winter's night, lights pricked at them from between the dark trunks of mostly bare deciduous trees.

The closest community would be Underhill, Folly-on-Weir's neighbor, both villages lying to the southeast of Gambol Green and Winchcombe. Out here buildings were scarce; open fields stretched in all directions.

'We're not that far from the cricket ground,' LeJuan said, glancing sideways at Dan who chose not to comment on the obvious.

'Just saying . . .'

'Yeah, I know.' He felt tight. His scalp and spine felt tight. It would not be long before the superintendent, or worse, the chief constable, pointed out that this second killing in the area would look really bad to the public. Or that they, the police, were now likely to deal with freshly rapacious media and panicky locals. Damn, but he hated the thought of facing TV cameras to beg for tips and parrot supposedly calming platitudes. He could already feel his gut clench at the thought of babbling voices demanding answers he would not, could not give.

'This one doesn't have to be ours,' LeJuan said of the corpse that awaited them.

'No,' Dan agreed. 'But it could be and we both think it probably is, don't we?'

The track opened on to a field used as a car park in front of an ancient tithe barn. A white SOCO van already stood in a blaze of brightness from the building's wide-open front doors. Police and emergency vehicles stood at angles, and personnel moved briskly in and out of the barn, sloshing through puddles that shone slick in torchlights.

'Bill Lamb's assuming this is more of the Coughlin killer's work,' Dan said. 'He knows what he's seen here – and what he saw after Coughlin died – so he's probably right. Let's get in there.'

LeJuan whistled through his teeth. 'Scene of the crime at the Phoenix Players' tithe barn, no less.' The right front wheel of the Lexus dropped into a mushy dip and he swerved to a stop. 'Tell me people don't use this place in winter for fun. Looks like somewhere to keep pigs happy.'

'The barn's something else.' Dan pushed the passenger door open and sat sideways in the seat to pull on the ancient pair of Hunters he'd thought to toss in the car. 'We did have the place checked out early in the Coughlin case, remember, but that was just to tick a box. No leads found. None of the Phoenix members had ever heard of him or, if they had, they said they hadn't. May have to look closer at that story now – if it turns out we're looking at the same killer.'

The skies had turned truly vicious, dumping sluicing torrents on the already soaked landscape, and the moment Dan stood up, mud squelched to his insteps.

Minus boots, LeJuan trod gingerly around the bonnet towards him, the collar of his coat pulled up to his ears while water dripped from his hair and down his face. 'The forecast said there'd be snow in places,' he said. 'We'd need a plough if it was coming down here. It's a good job the stuff from last night melted instead of freezing.'

Side by side, they walked toward the barn entrance. As LeJuan had said, this one didn't have to be theirs.

Officers standing guard recognized them. Their warrant cards got cursory nods and they passed from a bare lobby, through swinging doors into a cavernous area – the auditorium – where rows of folding metal chairs fanned both ways from a central aisle. Beneath the arching timbers of the roof, small windows pierced thick stone walls.

'Only a hundred and fifty seats, you think?' LeJuan asked quietly.

'Hundred max. What difference does that make?'

'Trying to figure out how popular the place would be.' He took out his notebook and a pen. 'If there's a connection between the victim and the scene – who knows, maybe he or she's a cast member. Could have a lot of people to question.'

'And could have about no one if our current luck holds. We don't even know if there's been a show on recently. See to finding that out as soon as you can. The place doesn't look as if it's being used. Chairs and everything are all over the place.'

'And it smells fusty,' LeJuan added.

The stage wasn't large and only about three feet above the rough and dusty stone floor of the barn. At first glance, they could have been seeing part of a production. SOCO arc lights cast a stark white glare over a slow-motion choreographed tableau.

DI Bill Lamb jogged sideways toward them between two rows of seats. 'Sorry to call you out on such a rotten night but I think you're going to want to take a look at this one. If you see it the way I do, it's going to be yours anyway.' Cold as it was inside the barn, Bill had shed his suit jacket and tie. As usual, his shirtsleeves were rolled up. 'On the stage,' he said, 'scene suits ahead,' and he led the way with LeJuan.

Molly Lewis, the pathologist, stood there with the crime scene manager, Werner Berg. Their heads were close together, and Molly didn't look as furious as she usually did at a crime scene. Bill's blonde, long-legged sergeant, Jillian Miller, paced the area, notebook in hand. Dan tried to like the woman, but she was too sharp for anyone's good; besides, she continued to gift him with her attentions, which had become an annoyance as well as making him the butt of department jokes.

Hopping on one foot then the other, LeJuan struggled into a scene suit. 'Shit,' he said loudly enough to get Molly's attention. 'Look at that.'

He vaulted on to the stage with Bill close behind and strode to look down at the body of a man, draped face-down over a trunk, and with a knife handle protruding from his back. Dan followed, minus the Hunters. The rock floor prodded his feet through booties and socks and did nothing for his athletic form.

Molly joined them. 'Might be a good idea to keep your voices down,' she said. Her blonde bob gleamed, and she was as commanding as ever despite her small stature, but there was no mistaking an added intentness in her blue eyes. The lighting was cruel. A web of lines on Molly's face seemed more marked than when he had last seen her. Speculation about the police pathologist centered on her occasionally unreliable balance. She drank too much, was one explanation put forward. Dan was pretty sure that was wrong, but he didn't have an alternate explanation that rang true. Arms tightly crossed and feet planted apart, she stood silent, removed. In a moment her face tilted up and her full attention was on him again. 'I might want to talk to you later, Dan. Maybe in the morning. We could have a different kind of trouble.'

'That's news?' Dan said and immediately regretted the question. 'You know what I mean, Doc. It's always trouble.'

'You do know what you're looking at . . .' She grasped his arm to stop him answering and kept her own voice very low. 'I thought this was fairly straightforward. Now, I'm not so sure. Once I get him on the table, I hope everything comes clear. Apart from that, we could have an unexpected problem. Again, let's get to that tomorrow.'

With a nod, Dan pulled on the latex gloves a tech gave him and went to crouch at the shoulders of the victim. Molly stayed with him which was not like her. Her habit was to stand back, waiting to deflect questions with her characteristic oblique responses.

'Any idea on time of death?' he asked, out of habit but not expecting a definitive answer.

'Longer ago than you'd expect.' Molly surprised him; she was usually even more evasive. 'I can't be definitive until I get him on the table. Rigor is passing, although the cold might account for speeding up the process. But the defensive signs make me think he was very active before he died which could also play a part.' She bent to touch the eyelids. 'Twelve to twenty-four hours ago, I'd say.'

Dan digested that and it didn't help his frustration level. 'Right.' He wouldn't get more out of Molly until she was certain. 'In his thirties, you think?' he asked.

'Probably. Late thirties at a guess.'

The knife was an attention grabber, but not the only remarkable aspect in front of them. 'He must have been working in here,' Dan said. 'Shirtsleeves on a night like this. It's bloody arctic.' He glanced at Bill, who grinned. He appeared as ready for action as ever. Crew-cut sandy hair, clear, light blue eyes, an open face – average height, slim but solidly muscled. For a man who liked his bacon butties, Detective Inspector Bill Lamb was a picture of fitness and acuity.

'Who found him?' Dan asked him.

'A farmer saw lights on and came in to check,' Bill said. 'There shouldn't be anyone here. There's no play on. The place was supposed to be shut down.'

'That answers our question about whether they were doing a play,' LeJuan said.

'And raises a bunch more questions,' Dan added. He moved around to look at the dead man's face. Blood caked his mouth and chin and had hardened in smeared rivulets on his neck. The nose looked swollen and purplish, the lips hugely puffy. A fine-checked blue shirt was fresh except for bloody stains on the rolled-up sleeves and collar.

Dan got down to peer at one of the man's hands. 'A lot of blood on the front of the collar. Down the front of the shirt, too,' he said. 'And blood under the nails and on his knuckles. As you say, Molly, defensive. Did he roll up his sleeves when he was already beaten up? Not likely. But he looks as if he was in a fight – apart from the mostly clean back of the shirt and trousers. Bill, do we know which is his car?'

'The farmer says there weren't any vehicles here when he came over.'

'Damn.' Dan sat back on his heels. He glanced at Bill and LeJuan. 'I didn't want to hear that. Where's his coat? Wallet? What else?'

'None of the above,' Bill Lamb said. 'What you see is what we've got.'

'Right,' Dan muttered. 'The scene didn't strip itself. This is one for CSI – again. It's getting more familiar all the time. Edward Coughlin was wet-through in a sea of churned-up mud and with no coat or wallet.'

'And no shoes,' Bill added.

Dan turned to look at the dead man's feet. 'Ditto. Have we got one killer or two? He must have been carried in here – unless there are signs he was killed in the building. If he was, we'll soon know.'

'The farmer doesn't think the doors could have been left unlocked but there's no sign of forced entry.' Bill studied the knife handle closely, shrugged and stood again.

'So, there's no play in production,' Dan said, exasperated. 'If the lights had been turned off, who knows when the body might have been found. First thing tomorrow I want the names of the group members, including who's responsible for what. We need whoever the leading lights are – that means who calls themselves a director and where the money comes from. Do they have backers – even in a small way? In these amateur things there tend to be a lot of small fingers in the pie. Doesn't matter how low budget the productions are, they cost. Who owns the barn? What are the arrangements between the players and the owners? And above all, who has keys to the place?'

'I'm on it,' said LeJuan.

'Longlegs can help you, and the new woman, Glynis something.'

'Glynis Drake,' said LeJuan.

They gathered silently by the body while techs moved around them. Exhibit bags passed hand-to-hand while photographer and videographer ranged the area. The impression of calm and quiet that attended a death scene was deceptive.

'Are you thinking what I'm thinking?' LeJuan said. He bent over the body again.

Dan stepped closer and murmured, 'Don't talk here,' to LeJuan. Molly had given a small but sharp shake of her head. He got the message.

FIVE

'I really messed up tonight, didn't I?'

This was where she was supposed to argue the point, to disagree. 'It wasn't your finest performance. Or mine.'

Tony braced himself on the mantel with both hands, looked down into the fire. 'What are you thinking now?'

That I want a way back to being us the way we are when we're at our best together. 'I'm a bit nervous. On edge. I want to know what's going on with you – and then I want it all to go away. In other words, I'm just human.'

This used to be a breakfast room. Now it was the sitting room, but they still called it the breakfast room. Alex sat in her favorite spot, on a finely multi-striped chair where she could see through an open doorway into the big, well-used kitchen and large windows on to the back garden beyond. Outside lights shone on evergreen clematis that made a thick border around the panes. Several times a year the leaves vied with luscious flowers that could compete with gardenia for heady scent.

'Wait till the conservatory's built.' He glanced at her over his shoulder, and smiled. 'They say conservatories are like greenhouses. Decide how big they should be, then build them twice as big.'

The change of subject didn't fool Alex. If she didn't need a lifeline herself, she might try throwing one to Tony – if she could find one. He was as agitated as she had ever known him.

'You're still excited about it, aren't you? The conservatory, I mean.'

'Yes.'

'I know how much you miss the one you built at your old place. It was wonderful.'

'I loved it, but I know how to move on.' *Are you really ready to do that?*

She got no response from Tony.

'This house is plain to look at. Very well built but, yes, plain.

The conservatory will be a good start on changing that a bit. I'm glad we put the Velux windows in the roof, too. They make the attic room so light. But I know your devious plan to get me painting again.' She gave a short laugh.

Tony didn't seem to hear her.

Bogie sat at attention beside her, his black button eyes bright and wary. His wiry little gray and black body trembled. 'It's OK, boy,' Alex told him softly. She pulled one of his plaid blankets from his basket to make a nest for him. 'It'll warm up now the fire's going. Come on, Katie. You, too. Lie down with Bogie.'

'They sense it when we aren't quite ourselves,' Tony said. He knelt to feed another log into the grate. Katie's whitening face showed her age now. She still loved every moment with her people and sat close to Tony, nuzzling his shoulder.

How long were they going to make small talk? Her stomach squeezed and she felt a flush of anger. They weren't here to chat by the fire, and it was Tony who had said they must talk through the serious stuff. All the way up into the hills from the Black Dog they had made small talk. It was time to confront their issues. The ordinary, empty chat felt phony – it was phony. A wedge had been driven between them and she could feel it getting wider.

'How about some Irish coffee?' Tony asked. He didn't actually look at her.

This guardedness between them had not just started tonight. Tony might have been avoiding honest conversation lately, but so had she.

'Alex,' he said. 'Irish coffee?'

'Not for me, thanks. But don't let that stop you.'

He stood and held out a hand. 'Come and sit on the couch with me, sweetheart. I need you to listen to me.'

She wanted to say she didn't want to hear whatever he wanted to say, not if it was something about Penny. Alex took hold of his hand and let him pull her up beside him.

'We're both tired,' she told him. 'Shocked, too, I think. The last thing you expected was for me to talk about setting a date. Should we forget that for now – until things are sorted?' Her heart beat hard. She didn't cry easily but she'd like to be alone now – to cry if she wanted to.

'No!' he said, and color rose on his face. 'I am who I am, Alex. Just as you aren't any different today than you have been as long as I've known you, not really. Please don't turn away from me. Is that what you want to do – step back and see if you still want to be with me? Do you think you've made a mistake with me?'

Her every instinct was to hold him and tell him he was everything to her. He *was* everything to her, but she had been betrayed before. She was sure Tony would not hurt her, not deliberately, but he was human and he had also suffered.

'Tell me all about it, Tony,' she said, standing close to him. 'Please don't hide anything from me. Not anymore. I can't stand it if you don't trust me enough to tell me everything and . . . we have to find a way out of whatever's happening.' She looked at the ring on her finger. It looked so right. 'If we can't be honest, what do we really have together?'

'I love you.' He pulled her close and held her head against his chest. 'I was going to ask you to look at something, but I think it would be a mistake. And it wouldn't help. My own fault. I overreacted.'

Whatever happened, she was not about to come off as the whining victim in this.

'I can't bear to do this to you,' Tony said. 'I hate it for both of us. No, I'm not letting it happen. Forget it, sweetheart. I almost didn't mention it at all and it's not important. Please forget I said anything.'

'What do you mean?' Bogie stood between them and rested his muzzle on Alex's knee. His black eyes moved back and forth between them.

'Just put it out of your mind. Please. It's nothing. Just some spiteful nonsense that's unlikely to have anything to do with Penny. She wasn't spiteful – or not generally unless she was pushed.'

'Whatever it is, I want to see it.' Alex put a little distance between them. 'You've got to know I'm not simply going to forget what you've said tonight.'

'Damn.' He scrubbed at his eyes and dropped to sit on the couch. 'Why can't I learn to think for a good long time before I talk about things that could be destructive? We've got so much going for us, we don't have to let this or anything else mess it up for us.'

She made up her mind. Tony was talking himself into keeping her in the dark about what was as much her concern as his. 'The email you talked about. You've got it with you, haven't you? I need to read it. You said this was something we had to confront together and I haven't changed my mind.'

For moments he sat with his lips pressed together, staring into the distance. At last he muttered, 'All right. If you insist. I don't want to say anything else until you've read this email. I want you to form your own opinion and tell me exactly what you think.' He took folded sheets of paper from his pocket and gave them to her. They looked as if they had been refolded more than once.

'Why did you bring it up tonight?' she asked him, hearing – with a kind of horror – how her voice got higher. 'Why not as soon as you got it?'

'Read it, please,' he said. 'Let's see if you get the same feelings I do. I will say this seems malicious, but we'll get over it. We'll handle it.'

Alex remained standing. She went around to the back of the couch and started reading:

This is a shock, isn't it, Tony? I bet I'm the last person you expected to hear from – ever again. You hoped you never would. After all, I'm dead, aren't I?

You must be expecting to get me declared dead any day now. I've been watching the time pass, too. So much for that – unless we can work things out sensibly. No, I don't mean I'll roll over and play dead, not necessarily, but I could stay out of your way now you've got your strange little waif, Alex? Well, I don't know if I can just give you to her, but I can think about it – if everything else is right.

She isn't your type, you know. You always needed a strong woman. That's why you chose me – why we chose each other. Too bad you changed. You lost your ambition, didn't you? You didn't want what I wanted anymore. I was never intended to be the quiet wife – your partner in an unexciting vet clinic, and the junior partner at that.

I haven't been alone, you know. At first I didn't know what I should do after the accident. I won't go into all the details of that, they don't matter anymore, but I was not myself. My memory suffered and didn't completely come back at first. By the time it did, I decided the fairest thing I could do for you was leave you to carry on with the life you were making – back in England. You see, I cared about you – always.

You weren't so thoughtful, Tony. Perhaps you've tried to forget that, but I can't. You had different expectations from mine – for a marriage, I mean. You never understood me. You didn't meet my emotional needs which hurt me. These things should give you pause if you want a smooth transition to freedom. And isn't that what most men want, freedom? If I had ever liked your little mouse, Alex, I might have ignored you and gone straight to her to warn her about you, but I never did like her, so there it is.

Perhaps it would be easier if you walked away from her. How much simpler would it be if I, by a miracle, returned to you in charming Folly-on-Weir and we picked up our marriage again. We could make a huge success of our business. Expand. Open a chain of clinics across the county. No need for the unpleasantness of wrangling about our marriage, or my supposed death then.

Or I could open my own practice. That would make it pricey – with two businesses to fund. It's the start-up funding that's so expensive. But I deserve a fresh start, too. Think about it, Tony.

I'll let you know how to contact me . . . when I'm ready. If I'm ever ready.

Alex refolded the letter slowly, watching Tony's face while he looked away.

'Does it sound like a blackmail attempt to you?' he said.

Alex swallowed past a dry throat. 'I suppose so. Not directly, though.'

'I'd say it was pretty direct. I don't owe her anything.'

Alex felt weak. She locked her knees then remembered that was a bad idea and tried to make herself relax.

'Let me have that.' He held out a hand for the email, took it from her and immediately tossed it into the fire. 'To hell with it. I've already deleted it from my inbox.'

'No. No, Tony. You should keep that. You said we were going to go over it.'

'Whoever sent this is bluffing.'

'What if you want – or need – to show it to someone?' she said. 'For proof or whatever?'

He crossed his arms and backed away to lean against the wall. His expression was intensely disturbed.

'Tony,' Alex said, keeping her voice quiet and as calm as she could manage. 'Tell me what you're thinking. Are you really going to pretend you never got the email?'

'Please just leave it alone, Alex.'

'You told me we needed to talk about that.' She pointed to the blackened curls of paper that sparked and fizzed.

'And now I'm saying forget it. I've got to think.'

'You've been thinking,' she told him quietly. 'For how long, exactly? Three weeks? Four?'

He glanced away. 'Not that long, but it doesn't matter. I'm doing the best I can. And I don't want to talk about this now.'

'Oh, no, you don't,' she said and straightened her back. 'You're not going to intimidate me.'

'You're overreacting.' He shrugged away from the wall. 'I would never do anything to hurt you. You're all that matters to me.'

'Tony, look at me. Do you expect me to forget what I just read?'

'Alex, I expect you to let me make my own decisions. Now just trust me and we'll get through this.'

SIX

The easiest route back to Gambol Green was a loop through the outskirts of Winchcombe, then north on Winchcombe Way. Dan was glad to be on his own for the return drive. LeJuan had hitched a ride with Bill and Sergeant Miller to pick up his own car. It wasn't that Dan didn't enjoy the company of his sergeant, but when you had become basically a loner, sometimes you needed time to yourself to really think things through.

What was on Molly Lewis's mind that had made her so cagey tonight? Dan had been playing with a theory from the moment he got a close look at the victim, but knew better than to open his mouth in front of Molly. Particularly when she made it clear she didn't want him to say anything. Who did she think was both listening and likely to talk out of turn? That had to be what she was afraid of. What could be said that would be a problem? Damned inconvenient and frustrating. He was almost persuaded to call as soon as he had given her time to get home. On the other hand, the stronger temptation was to pull over on the verge and try phoning now. Unprofessional, he supposed, not that he cared too much about following the straight and narrow these days.

He smiled to himself and rolled his window down a couple of inches. Wet, black earth and the piles of rotted leaves that ploughed beneath the wheels of the Lexus sent their own earthy aroma into the car. Dan loved it here. He was completely at home in the Cotswolds. His headlights bored through the darkness, bounced with each dip in the old road. Even the resident animal nightlife had headed for safe hideaways and no bright eyes gleamed out at him.

Edward Coughlin had been single and living alone. With no identification on the body, it had taken more than twenty-four hours to find an identity, and only then because a woman in Chipping Campden – Coughlin's home – noticed her neighbor's grocery delivery at his front door for hours, and his car parked outside all day and late into the next evening. Similarly, the victim at the tithe barn had no wallet, no driver's license or credit cards; nothing to say who he was. And apparently no vehicle in the vicinity that belonged to him. Both dead men had been parted from their shoes. This was serial killing in the making.

That couldn't be anything to do with whatever bee Molly had in her bonnet, could it? When she had stopped him from talking, he had been about to comment on what looked like another staged death scene. Thinking aloud really. Nothing that should not be heard by the team, or he couldn't come up with a reason why.

Moving out of Gloucester was the best thing he'd done for himself in a long time. While he stayed in the house he'd shared with Corinne, the ghosts of their joint life there with Calum found it too easy to walk into his mind whenever it wasn't occupied. Even if he had stopped blaming himself for the near disaster – an ex-felon with a grudge broke in and Dan barely headed off an attack on his family – it had been the catalyst.

Did he feel sorry for himself? Not that, not anymore, but when he was in the mood to reflect, he admitted he wished he had someone to share his life with. There had been Alex – Alex Duggins. For a time after he'd started working cases in the Folly-on-Weir area, he'd hoped she might become the missing piece to fill him up. Finally, he had given up on that idea. She was a good friend and Dan had settled for the compromise.

Admitting to loneliness was supposedly a sign of weakness to some. He wasn't admitting to loneliness, Dan decided, but he was not a man who enjoyed playing the field – those times had passed.

Fleetingly, Siobhan French crossed his mind. She was a partner in the same psychology practice as Leon Wolf, friend to the chief constable and sometime thorn in Dan's side. He and Siobhan had enjoyed dinner together at the Royal Chestnut pub in Gambol Green and they'd met for drinks several times. He liked her and sensed the feeling was mutual, but so far he wasn't sure how much farther either of them was interested in pursuing a relationship.

Dan concentrated on the road, stared through the rain-dashed headlights. Now he had Canal Cottage, and it had already begun feeling like home, thank God. He had better start using what little spare time he had to make some changes before Calum arrived – not that he would be critical. Dan was convinced his boy would fall for the cottage once he had time to get used to new surroundings. He would be freer out here than in Gloucester . . . Would it be easier for him to roam around? Dan rolled his shoulders. Calum had nothing to do with the murders Dan was investigating. They were connected to something entirely removed from anything that could get personal. Had to be. There was no reason to think of protecting Calum any more than usual. And with a lot of hard work and some luck, the case might be solved before Christmas.

By the time he made a left turn on to Winchcombe Way, the rain had dwindled from a cow-smacker to a spitting match. The windscreen wipers squealed sporadically across the glass, doing more harm than good. Darkness and chill outside the car pleased him. This time of year felt very right, comfortably familiar. Within a month Calum would arrive for Christmas and there would be fires in the stone hearth at the cottage. Warmth and the companionship Dan and Calum found together.

As he might have expected, a premonition of disappointment immediately spread its shadow. Time didn't stand still. His boy was growing up, in his mid-teens. He might be changing more than Dan could imagine, perhaps no longer wanting to spend time with his old man. Wasn't fifteen about the time when a teenager found any parent an embarrassment? The crushing of his plans the previous year, and his reaction then, had a way of coming back with nasty clarity. His stomach turned at the thought. It couldn't happen twice in a row, could it? If he had to, he'd go after his boy this time. It wasn't as if Calum had not been as fed up as Dan with the change in plans. No repeat of the gracious loser act for him, then.

The divorce from Corinne had hurt, for a long time, but he had accepted what could not be changed and they both understood the importance of being on good terms – for Calum's sake.

He approached the lines of trees that edged the river, running on both sides to show the Isbourne's slender path for miles. The little bridge he must cross to the part of the village where he lived would always be no more than a single lane, where locals usually observed polite give-and-take in getting across. Headlights told him a vehicle was approaching his direction from the other side and he pulled to the verge.

There were more cottages and houses on this side of the river, some of them newer – the part of Gambol Green built mostly in the 1700s and early 1800s. When he looked at it all, or even thought about it in quiet moments, and from a distance, Dan could scarcely believe his luck in having found and been able to buy Canal Cottage. He would always wonder if the former owner, Mrs Fermer, had sold the place to him – at a supposedly ridiculously low price – to spite her neighbors, who had wanted badly to buy and restore it to the estate they now owned, and to which the cottage had originally belonged. Ham's Platt, Canal Cottage, and Silky's Cottage had been Mrs Fermer's until she opted to sell, first, Ham's Platt, and then, a couple of years later, Canal Cottage to Dan.

Silky's Cottage remained in Mrs Fermer's hands and was rented to Beth Wills, a divorcée, and her two children. Beth ran a second-hand shop in Winchcombe and Dan had wondered how easy it was for her to make a living. He liked her. She and her kids were good neighbors.

Instead of passing him, the approaching vehicle crossed the bridge – too fast, he noted – stopped a few feet in front and the door swung open.

Dan squinted into the headlights the driver had left on. From habit, he kept the window mostly rolled up and waited. Coming immediately to his side and ducking, he saw it was Beth Wills, her curly red hair dark and dripping, plastered to the sides of her face.

'Don't want to frighten you,' she said. 'But I thought I'd better let you know.'

If he had the time, he'd be amused at the warning. 'Hello, Beth. What's up?' He got out, grabbing a torch as he went and turning up his collar against the rain. 'What's happened?'

'I don't have a torch,' she said, sounding annoyed with herself. 'I still forget these things. I wanted to call you, but I've lost the card you gave me. Sorry about that. Listen, it's probably nothing but . . . I got nervous.'

'Where are Shandy and Jack?' he asked of her children.

'Oh, thank you for asking. They're in the van. When I saw

the light moving around outside, I put them in and left. I'm afraid I'm not very brave.'

'You're very smart,' he said, peering around for signs of her mysterious light. 'Just tell me what you think you've seen.'

'I didn't notice anything until the torchlight flashed across our front windows. It really scared me, I can tell you. Luckily, the children just think it's a lark and I'm weird.' Her small laugh cut off. 'Detective Chief Inspector—'

'Dan,' he said. 'We're neighbors. What did you see then? Anything?'

'I saw the torch moving around at the back of Canal Cottage, then it went behind the far side from us and I didn't see it again.' She looked back over her shoulder. 'Someone was there. I don't imagine things. But they may have moved on now – only it doesn't feel nice to think of him creeping around the area in the dark like this.'

'No, it doesn't. Do you have anyone nearby you could go to until I get things checked out?'

'There's just us, really, but we're OK. I should stand by in case you need help.'

It didn't seem a funny reaction anymore, courageous and rather appealing in fact. 'Get back in your car. Stay exactly where you are unless I tell you to move. I'll call for backup and take a look. As you say, they've probably gone. It'll be a tramp or someone who got lost somehow. They might need help.'

'Oh, yes,' she said, and he heard her shoes sucking through the mud as she turned back to her car. 'I was thinking that could be it. I should have called out, shouldn't I?'

'No,' he said, shortly this time. 'Sit tight with the doors locked, please. Just a precaution.'

He left her to follow his instructions, got into his car again and drove across the narrow stone bridge. Canal Cottage was to the left and down a dip. Behind it, the walls and tall trees surrounding Ham's Platt rose black against a gunmetal sky. Silky's Cottage, where the Willses lived, was on the opposite side of the lane from Dan's property, with only its roof and chimney visible without going down a steep flight of steps.

Parking was easiest on a graveled area at the top of the drive down to Canal Cottage. Dan left his car there and got out – with the torch, again. Instantly a soggy animal threw itself at the legs of his trousers, which he registered vaguely would have to go to the cleaners.

'Busy,' he muttered, seeing the white tail wiggle madly back and forth. The dog yipped and leaped around Dan's ankles. 'OK, OK, cool it,' he said, trying to keep his voice down.

He gave up any attempt at a stealthy approach, turning his torch on full instead.

His heart gave a familiar hard thump as adrenalin made its rush. A movement in the covered porch snapped him to alert. He turned the torch off again and waited. A shadow separated itself from deeper shadows and slipped from the porch.

'Police,' Dan announced. 'Show yourself.' And he prayed there was no weapon, either gun or knife. These miscreants liked their blades and used them with vicious accuracy. He might yet regret not calling for backup.

The figure came toward him, running. 'Dad! It's me, Calum.'

SEVEN

He could not, Tony thought, consider what his life would be like without Alex. If he had managed to destroy what they had together, he couldn't even begin to see a way forward for him. He would carry on, throw himself into his work with the practice, but how could he deal with knowing the woman who was his mate in every sense of the word was no longer his?

Very quietly, he let himself into the large, partially finished space in the attic of the house. His plan was for this to become Alex's studio, and for her to paint again, really paint. For too long she had avoided even talking about her art, and he hated the thought that she was wasting her talent. She was too good to waste.

He wondered if she had any idea that he sometimes came up here to think.

What a fool he'd been – hoping he could keep the apparent mess with Penny under wraps and simply clear it away without involving Alex. Tonight, he had left her asleep and come in search of the utter peace at the top of the house. Could he work his way through this resentment he was largely responsible for creating?

According to his solicitor, Barstwick, he could have chosen to get a divorce from Penny on grounds of desertion. Tony hadn't wanted to go through the muckraking of dragging out everything that had been wrong with his first marriage. It would make an ugly litany, and for what purpose when a declaration of death would achieve his ends? His father had come up with a number of reasons for the divorce route – all mostly based on James Harrison's desire to clean any blame from Tony's name. It would continue to be a contentious topic between father and son. Tony wasn't changing his mind.

Set squarely beneath a Velux skylight, a shabby reclining chair was the only furniture in the room. Tony already planned to install more skylights, and to bump out glass half-walls, if Alex gave a thumbs up on the idea. He liked to sit in the old chair at night and push back to watch the shifting patterns in the darkness outside, and a million miles above. When the light was dim like this, the exposed wall studs waiting for plasterboard didn't show. With the chair's footrest raised, bare floorboards disappeared. He had dreamed a lot of dreams in this space.

Back at the Black Dog, he and Alex had stumbled over excuses for ducking out on family, and on Hugh, after so much had been made of the importance of getting together that night. The memory of their worried faces shot him full of guilt. They needed to do a better job of explaining, but giving them the full story of the Penny debacle was out. His dad would flip, and Lily was likely to join forces with him.

In the bedroom, sleep had evaded him while he tried to keep very still beside Alex. She was just as still, and he'd wondered if they were both awake and on watch, but when he slipped from the covers she hadn't moved or spoken, and he decided she was in an exhausted sleep.

His fault. And tonight of all nights, when everything should have been perfect. He'd waited several weeks, why not another night? She had planned to surprise him. But if Penny had really written that email, she was trying holding him hostage. Threatening to turn his world upside down, to ruin his relationship with Alex – and giving him no way to try and resolve their issues, at least not so far. Penny liked to have the upper hand. If she was still out there, she would contact him again, he was sure of it. What did she want, really want? He couldn't believe she meant what she'd written about continuing their marriage. That could never happen. Had she wanted him to forever regret that his marriage to her hadn't worked and decide to remain alone? Was the email really from Penny?

His mind moved rapidly from conviction to question, and back again. There was also a good possibility Penny would have lost interest after the first nasty salvo. She could have turned away again with no intention of following through. He had come to know she was like that, given to stirring up dissent, then behaving as if she had not meant anything by it, and eventually flipping the whole thing around to being his fault. In her ideal scenario, he would become the one guilty of initiating and pursuing the row.

Did it have to matter whether she was alive or dead?

He didn't wish her dead, just far away from him. If she was alive, that was what she'd chosen for the last eight years anyway – not to be with him – so why change anything?

A sheen passed over the bubble skylight and became still, shimmering over the glass.

Tony slowly kicked the footrest backwards into place but kept staring upward at the light. He wasn't sure of the time, but it had to be after three in the morning.

He strained to hear.

Nothing.

But the light didn't move away.

Silence felt stretched, an empty space filled with something that clamored at its edges. No sense at all. Damn it, he should get up and put on lights. Make noise. Go where he could see the grounds in front of the house. He pushed himself upright.

A sound reached him. From the driveway, he was sure of it. Wheels turning over soaked leaves, but no engine.

Barking sounded from downstairs. The dogs would have woken Alex.

Tony left the attic and scrambled down the bare flight of stairs to the landing between bedrooms – and walked into Alex. He put his fingers over her lips and whispered in her ear, 'Nothing to worry about. I think someone got lost looking for an address. Stay up here with the dogs.'

By the time he'd started down the next flight, he heard her behind him and glanced back. He could make out that she held a dog collar in each hand and was right behind him. Tony actually smiled – of course she was right behind him.

In the front hall, he eased Alex and the dogs against the wall. 'Please stay here. If necessary, call the police. I don't think it'll be necessary.'

She nodded.

The only way to play this was by confronting. Tony threw open the door and stepped out on to the freezing top step. Damn it, bare feet could hurt. He went forward and down the steps – and stood immobile.

The front driveway sloped up to the road where headlights shone, left to right, straight across the entrance. The vehicle was hidden by a wall.

Silhouetted in the glow was the shape of a man; at least, Tony thought it was a man. And whoever it was held something in front of him and made no attempt to hide.

'Hey there,' Tony called. 'Are you lost? Who are you looking for?'

No response.

Steadily the person's arms raised – very steadily. Did he have a gun? Tony's breathing shortened. He wanted to tell Alex to get away, leave by the back of the house, find a safe place to make a phone call. He was trapped, certain his every move was visible.

A yip, then a burst of barks, and Bogie shot past Tony, who gritted his teeth, waiting for gunfire. 'Come, Bogie,' he yelled, but the little dog had one target in mind, and it stood at the entrance to *his* house.

The figure disappeared to the far side of the wall and an engine burst to life. By the time Tony reached the open gates, all he could make out were the side lights on a vehicle about to disappear downhill.

'My god, Tony, what was that?' Still clinging to Katie's collar, Alex leaned outside. '*Who* was that? Could you tell?' She looked at his bare feet but said nothing about them.

With Bogie in his arms, Tony trudged through the front door and stood with a shoulder resting on the wall. 'First question. To call the police or not to call the police?'

'I don't know. I heard what you said to him. He could have been lost but if he was, why not call back to you? Why . . . no, he was trying to frighten us. That or he was watching and hoping not to get caught. Planning to break in. Or one of those peeping Toms.' Her heart thundered. She put her arms around Tony and Bogie jumped down, ran back up the stairs. 'He's cold, poor boy. And so are you.'

'We're not calling the police,' Tony said. 'We'll only end up looking as if we get scared over nothing – which we don't. I just wish I knew what he was doing out there.'

'He had something in his hands,' Alex said. 'I was afraid it was a gun.'

'So was I. If it was, he would have fired, wouldn't he?' He narrowed his eyes and she could tell he was turning over possibilities, weighing probabilities. 'Guns don't have to mean someone wants to use them. Not if they're for protection. Let's think about this, at least until morning. I think whoever it was got lost, like we said. Then they were too embarrassed to say anything after they'd woken us up.'

'Let's get a hot drink,' Alex said. She felt shaky and chilled. 'He could have been holding a camera. Trying to get pictures of us to prove something.'

Tony went with her but didn't reply. What she stopped herself from saying was that she feared a link between this episode and the Penny email.

EIGHT

Calum had told his dad that his mum thought he was spending the weekend at a friend's house. She had believed him, so calling her could have waited, couldn't it? Dad didn't have to phone Ireland in the middle of the night and wake everyone up. Mum wasn't good at being disturbed when she was asleep, but Dad hadn't listened to Calum trying to persuade him to put it off till tomorrow.

He sat at the bottom of the stairs leading up from the sitting room to two bedrooms on the upper floor. His dad was in the conservatory, speaking to Mum on the phone in a low voice so all Calum could catch was the odd word.

Until the packing boxes in the second bedroom were unloaded and the stuff put away – if Calum was there long enough (Dad had told him that like a threat) – he'd sleep in the sitting room. The lumpy old pull-out bed from the Gloucester house had been opened up; to air it out, Dad said.

It didn't matter how ticked off his parents were, Calum was glad to be here. And he was glad to be dry and more or less warm again. A fire in the stone fireplace had caught easily and was already curling flames up the chimney. After a bath, he had rubbed himself down with a big, warm towel and climbed into a worn pair of pajamas his dad produced from somewhere. The legs and arms were too long, but rolled up they would do.

Dad might be mad, but he'd given Calum a bear hug even before he'd opened the front door and hurried him inside. Please, please, please let this work out without him being sent back to Dublin. Surely Dad wouldn't want him to make the big move that Mum and her husband were planning.

This cottage was brilliant. All crooked walls and sloping ceilings; lots of exposed stone. Even without an opportunity to really explore the place, Calum felt as if he was meant to be here. If he could just get some sleep first, he wanted to see exactly what was outside, and the village he'd walked through to get here.

Gambol Green. Always a big-town kid, he'd never thought about what it would be like to live in a village. Before Dublin, he would probably have kicked up at moving to some pokey little country place, but not anymore. And that didn't mean Dublin wasn't a great city, but the Cotswolds were his home.

The rumbly voice droned on. At least it wasn't shouting – yet. He'd eaten too much cold pizza too fast and felt a bit sick. What he'd done, all the planning and finally running off into a foggy morning to catch a bus to the boat, to a train and more buses, was too fresh not to make his skin tingle. Margaret was the only one he'd talked to about his plans. He liked her a lot and they intended to keep in touch and get together when they could, although they were old enough to know that wasn't going to happen often. But they were best friends and they'd kind of promised they intended to find ways.

Calum was fifteen and Margaret was sixteen. She'd teased him about the dangers of getting tangled up with an older woman. There was only six months between them. He smiled at that. He'd like to tell her that he thought she was perfect for him because he needed someone older and more sensible to keep him in line, but he hadn't decided how to do that yet. You could jinx something by pushing too far, too fast. He liked Margaret, he really did, and he thought she liked him just as much, but they were both still kids, so it was pointless getting too sappy.

She had straight, dark blonde hair to her shoulders and bright brown eyes. Almost as tall as him, and a bit thin, Margaret moved as if she had an extra engine – very fast. If she wasn't running, she was trotting, or at least walking double time.

Calum smiled tightly. He wouldn't tell her so, but he already missed her. He'd wished she had been on that ferry boat with him and bound for England.

His parents had been talking a long time which probably wasn't good. Unless it *was* good. He rubbed dry palms together.

The voice went silent.

'You could have told me, Corinne!' Dad wasn't quiet this time and Calum jumped. 'I'm not losing my temper, but I'd like to. I need time to think, and I suggest you do, too . . . no, I haven't said this is your fault, but you can think about that possibility if you want to. I'll call back tomorrow. Good night.'

Calum held his breath.

'OK, my boy,' Dad said, coming into the sitting room. 'We've got a pickle to work out but at least your mum and I are on the same page. We want what's best for you, but we can't make hasty decisions.'

'I suppose not.' Calum shivered. 'You didn't sound as if you were on the same page. Not at the end.'

His dad put an arm around his shoulders and urged him from the stairs. 'Sit by the fire. Would you like some cocoa? You're probably really chilled.'

In other words, anger subject closed. 'No thanks,' Calum said to the cocoa offer, but he sat in a familiar green wing chair and held his hands out to the fire. 'I'm sorry I've made trouble for you. I had to get away before all their plans were made and everyone thought I would go along with them. I won't, Dad. I'm not going to California with them.'

His dad sighed. 'You know I don't want you to go, either.'

Calum's heart leaped. That was one of the absolutely best things about his dad, he got straight to the point. 'So even though I probably made you mad, you'll still back me up, Dad?'

'Yeah, I'll be backing you up. But this isn't going to be easy. Your stepdad has this great opportunity in California and your mum seems to think we could work things out so nothing has to change with the stipulated agreements.' He sat down opposite Calum. 'Nothing but about six or so thousand miles.'

And Dad didn't look happy. Calum wished he didn't feel so glad about that; no, he didn't. Of course he was glad. He had promised himself he wouldn't come off as a pushy, unreasonable kid who just wanted his own way. He did want his own way, but wasn't it reasonable not to be happy about being moved far away from everything he knew? And he hadn't been with his father enough in the past year – everything had turned into a muddle and he'd had to do whatever his stepdad decided was best for his family, including Calum. He felt the burn of anger that was getting more frequent. Who gave a stranger the right to order him around? He knew the answer. He loved his mum a lot, but she put her new husband first and wanted Calum to do the same. It wasn't going to happen.

'You're quiet, son. What's on your mind?'

'Can I stay here with you, Dad?'

'For the time being. Your mum and I have to work all that out.'

'I'm not going, you know.'

His dad leaned forward in his chair and dropped his laced fingers between his knees. 'What does that mean . . . exactly?'

'I'm not going to California.'

'Let's take this one step at a time. Your mother's agreed to letting you stay with me through Christmas, and—'

'That's big of her.' He knew he was talking louder, but he was getting mad. 'I'm supposed to be here for Christmas. Last year they messed up everything you and I had arranged, and dragged me off to that Spanish holiday place. I hated it. I didn't want to be there. Now I'm supposed to be grateful I can be here for Christmas?'

'You're tired.' Dad looked tired, too. 'Trust me to work out the best solution for everyone. I won't push you into things you don't want but I do expect you to be reasonable. And I'm no more happy than your mum is with this stunt you've just pulled.' He stopped talking and stared into the fire.

After a while, Calum got too antsy to keep quiet. 'Why didn't you talk to me about California before now? I thought you would call me and see how I felt.'

That got him a long look from his father. 'I hadn't intended to say this, but I suppose I have to. The first I heard about the move was when I just talked to your mum. Now wait.' He held up a hand to stop Calum from interrupting. 'I don't blame you if that makes you angry, but look at it from your mother's point of view. She's been trying to work all this through without upsetting anyone and it's not easy.'

'I don't care. She should have told you. She should have *asked* you – I'm not just her son, someone who has to go along with whatever and not have opinions.'

'No, you're not. How would you like to go to school here for the rest of the year?'

'Yes! Yes, Dad, that's what I want, to go to school here and live with you.'

'Hold your horses. It won't be that straightforward. First, your mum and I would have to work things out. And I'd have to get you into a school and work out transportation. Remember the kind of hours I work. I would have to trust you to make wise decisions when you're here on your own, and you'd have to be more responsible for yourself than most fifteen-year-olds.'

'I am responsible. You know I am. I can get anywhere on a bike, too. And I could do the grocery shopping and look after the cottage. It would be easier for you because I'd be a big help.'

Dad bit his lip thoughtfully. 'Right. Don't jump ahead, please. Your mother will want to arrange reciprocal visitation and I will honor that.'

'How would that work if she's not in Dublin?'

'You'd split your time between here and California.'

Calum turned icy, then heat swelled into his face. 'I bloody won't.'

'Calum!'

'Well, I won't. And if anyone tries to make me, I'll run away again. This time, I'll run and I'll get lost until I'm old enough to make my own decisions.'

NINE

'You look like hell,' LeJuan said. The words were out of his mouth before he could stop them, but if his boss said he had not been to bed all night, he wouldn't be surprised.

'Is Molly here?' Dan said with a sharp stare that quickly flicked away.

'Well, more than an hour ago, boss – maybe two.' He delivered the last in a mutter. The police pathologist had arrived before seven. 'I thought I should wait for you before going in.'

'Why? Because you thought going in alone would make it look like you were Johnny-on-the-spot and I didn't give a shit? Don't be daft, man. Why should I care? Hop to it.'

So much for easing into things. 'You've got it.' He followed Dan through swinging doors into the morgue.

It wasn't that his boss looked rumpled, just drained, pale faced, and mad as hell. LeJuan thought – and not for the first time by a long shot – that Dan O'Reilly needed more in his life than his work and worrying about his son. A woman would be a good start, and the sooner he stopped wishing Alex Duggins would suddenly forget her sidekick, Tony Harrison, and realize she really wanted Dan O'Reilly instead, the better. *Oh, please let it be, God – for my sake. I'm a good man, peaceable, and if my boss finds something or someone to sweeten him up, I'll atone for past wrongdoings. At least I'll try.*

Talking to himself, albeit mostly silently, was a lifelong habit, but was he indulging far more often lately?

'Chop-chop,' O'Reilly snapped over his shoulder, as if he'd been the one standing in a very cold anteroom for almost two hours. Once you were inside the actual waxworks, the blasted morgue didn't even run to a coffee machine.

'Right behind you,' he mumbled, wrestling his way into a gown that was too tight across the shoulders, and managing to tie a knot with the tabs behind his neck. He got the mask on as he followed O'Reilly into the room where Molly Lewis was Boss-of-All.

Without seeing the expression on Dan's face, LeJuan knew how he would feel when he saw that Dr Leon Wolf, psychologist, was present. Present but about to leave with a steely glint in his protuberant gray eyes. There was nothing mentioned openly between them, but to say the two men didn't care for one another would be a vast understatement. Wolf appeared to have a malevolent distrust of most police, usually fairly well hidden under a supercilious sneer. Dan couldn't stand the man, loathed him in fact, and considered his presence anywhere near a case an intrusion bordering on breach of ethical standards.

O'Reilly and Wolf didn't respect one another . . . At all.

White light on white everything that wasn't stainless steel, assaulted senses that hadn't had enough coffee yet.

'O'Reilly,' Wolf said in his deceptively quiet voice. 'Late to the party, aren't you? I shouldn't bother – it's all over, or that's what I'm led to believe. Looks as if you've got your second staged killing. That is if the Coughlin fiasco was the first in the string.'

LeJuan puffed up his cheeks and waited for his boss's response. Dan walked past the other man without a word and stood at the foot of the table where the victim was being patched and covered.

'Um, O'Reilly.' Wolf had turned back and Dan looked over his shoulder. 'A word?' Wolf said, and LeJuan could swear he was going an odd shade of red.

'What can I do for you?' Dan asked, returning to where the psychologist had halted his exit.

Wolf closed in on Dan and LeJuan, putting the three of them in a group that allowed for privacy, or muted conversation anyway. 'I know I can trust Sergeant Harding,' Wolf said, giving LeJuan a cool nod. He crossed his arms and looked at his feet. 'This isn't easy. I could be putting myself at a disadvantage.' His already soft voice sank close to a whisper.

Dan had narrowed his eyes. The mask camouflaged his complete expression.

'I know we haven't exactly had a warm relationship,' Wolf said. 'But it's the work that counts, not personal feelings.'

'Right you are,' Dan said, glancing toward LeJuan, but that

glance was inclusive rather than suggesting LeJuan should absent himself.

Wolf spread one hand, palm up. 'Could we get together for a chat? Say late this afternoon? Gambol Green can be on my way home if you feel like a pint at the Royal Chestnut. You live nearby now, don't you?'

'I've got something else on,' Dan said. 'But if we can keep it short, I should be there around five.' He didn't answer the question about where he lived these days.

Wolf nodded and walked away. As soon as the door swung shut behind him, Dan returned to the table and said, 'Good morning, Molly. Morning, Werner.'

'Mm,' was all Molly responded. She continued examining the victim's head.

Werner gave a quick lift of expressive eyebrows, flicked aside a white cloth covering a small tray, and picked up a pack of cigarettes. He pulled the mask beneath his chin and lit up, squinting toward the ceiling through his smoke. Werner was a law unto himself in Molly's domain . . .

'Sorry I'm so late,' Dan said. 'I've got an unexpected newcomer at my place and I couldn't leave as early as I'd have liked. Can you give me a rundown here, please?'

'Who's the newcomer?' Molly asked with characteristic baldness. 'Is she good looking?'

'Of course, she is.' Werner gave a downturned little smile.

Dan's expression didn't change. 'My son, Calum, arrived. He decided to duck out on his home, and my ex-wife, in Dublin, and make his way here by some God-awful convoluted route. Buses, ferries and trains – and more buses. He got here last night. Soaked to the skin and starving. He had made sure his mother wouldn't even know he was missing, the little toad.' He paused and scrubbed at his jaw through the facemask, rubbing at the site of an old knife wound. 'He's a good boy. Fifteen and muddled, although he thinks he knows exactly what he wants. But we'll work it out. What do we have here?'

'Werner, can I leave you to it?' Molly asked, leading the way to wash up without waiting for, or apparently expecting, any answer.

When the three of them were crammed into her office, she

made sure the door was shut before sitting behind her tidy desk. Dangerously high piles of files were stacked there, but with military precision.

'You were going to say something last night when you first saw the victim,' Molly said. 'What was it?'

Dan tapped his bottom lip. 'The obvious was what looked to be another carefully arranged death scene – like Coughlin. But there wasn't any blood to speak of where the knife went in – that's what I was really looking at.'

Molly nodded agreement. 'We all know how dangerous it is for too much detail of a killing to get out – especially anything unusual that points to a specific killer repeating his pattern. Unless you want to invite copycats. That's why I wanted to have this conversation in private.'

LeJuan leaned against the wall and crossed his arms. He knew what was coming. Little was said about suspicions of internal information leaks in the past year, but he and Dan were not the only detectives puzzled – and angry – at evidence of a mole. What they didn't have was motive for any deliberate betrayal, other than kickbacks from the media presumably. Although there was plenty of unfounded speculation about the Coughlin case, so far there had been no revelations of the most sensitive specifics, which only added to the mystery, but if they were facing a second entry by the same killer, the likelihood that it would happen grew.

'What are your thoughts about this victim?' Dan asked. 'Similarities to Edward Coughlin?'

Molly brought up a screen on her computer and turned it for them to see an X-ray. 'The blow Coughlin sustained appeared to account for both the massive injury to the occipital bone' – she indicated the lower back of the cranium – 'and the crushed $c1$ and $c2$. The vertebrae here. Quite some follow-through.'

LeJuan moved closer to see. 'Are you saying now that the whack he took to the head might not have damaged his spine?'

'An injury like that to the spine – at that point – would have killed him anyway, wouldn't it?' Dan added.

'I'm not necessarily saying that, LeJuan. It was assumed, reasonably, that the blow with the bat, or whatever, accounted for both the spinal injury and the crushed occipital bone, but in light of what I've seen today, I'm reassessing. Reassessing, not definitely changing my mind.

'As to your point, Dan, that kind of spinal injury is just about always fatal – most often almost instantly. If the subject does survive, he probably faces paralysis, if he survives long enough to find out.'

'Bat, or whatever?' LeJuan said. 'You don't think the cricket bat from the scene caused the damage?'

She straightened her screen. 'I'm leaving all options on the table. But a missing chunk of tissue and hair wasn't on that bat and it didn't turn up at the scene.'

'Cheery,' Dan said. He leaned back in his chair. There hadn't been much improvement in his air of weariness. 'And so definitive. But you've got more on your mind, Molly.'

'There was virtually no blood – very little, anyway – from the current subject's knife wound. You saw that, didn't you, Dan?'

'I did.'

'Would you both understand if I suggested it could be to our advantage to keep some . . . *possibilities* between ourselves, at least until we're more sure of our findings?'

Dan met LeJuan's glance and said, 'Of course.'

They would have to spell this out more clearly for him, LeJuan thought. 'Yeah.'

'Was he already dead when he was stabbed?' Dan asked.

Of course, now he understood.

'I'm almost sure he was,' Molly said. She drummed fingers on the desktop and looked sideways, thinking. 'Why would anyone bother doing that?'

'Beats me,' Dan said.

'Because he's a mean son-of-a-bitch?' LeJuan suggested.

Neither of them laughed.

Molly shrugged. 'I don't believe the knife we removed today was the one that made the initial entry wound.'

'And a similar scenario goes for our "bat" murder weapon?' Dan made air quotes.

'You've got it,' Molly responded. 'Our killer could be collecting actual weapons used during the attacks – a cricket bat and a knife so far – as trophies, and leaving place-holders as window dressing.'

TEN

'Why aren't I praying this won't turn out to be our man?' LeJuan asked, slouched into his usual relaxed driving posture for the trip from Gloucester to the Winchcombe area. His light touch on the wheel was deceptive; the advertised drive time for the trip was half an hour, but LeJuan's foot was anything but light. If they didn't get there in twenty minutes or less, you could presume there had been a surprise sheep crossing or slow-moving farm machinery involved.

'You're human,' Dan told him. 'And you're a copper. Don't be too hard on yourself. Someone who should be alive is dead. Usually that means heartache for some. We don't get to choose who – in either case.'

'I get a rush when we're on a case,' LeJuan said. 'From when the first call comes in. Putting all the pieces together, closing in, even false starts and dead-ends – some of it can drive me crazy, but I enjoy the process.'

'That has to be true for all of us if we're honest,' Dan said. 'We're no use if we get lost in mourning the dead and aching for their nearest and dearest. Sink into that hole and you'll need another line of work. That doesn't mean we shouldn't feel anything for a victim – and some cases are harder to keep emotional distance from than others.' He didn't say what they both knew; it was the dead children who affected them most.

They were actually heading for an address on the outskirts of Bishop's Cleeve, a large village south of Winchcombe. The weather was clear and cold, with a bedazzling intensity to the light. Dan was glad to be out in the wintry landscape, separated from the station bustling with wooden-tops and the ever-present interfering bosses. He and LeJuan had been on their way to call a squad meeting when the desk officer hailed them to pass on a tip.

'This is probably going to be a husband who's been on a

bender. Got too plastered to get home for a couple of nights,' Dan said. 'Not our boy at all.'

'Yeah. It creeps me out, though, asking already frightened people to look at post-mortem photos.'

Dan nodded agreement. 'Werner's pretty good at making them passable. As passable as they can be, that is.'

'I don't understand him,' LeJuan said.

'The victim or Werner?'

When LeJuan threw him a confused look, Dan added, 'He can do anything and everything. And he does it all so well. Some of his crime scene shots are better than those taken by the guys who do that and nothing else for a living. I'm surprised we haven't lost him to bigger things before now.'

'Nah, not likely,' LeJuan said with another sideways glance. 'I'd be surprised if he went anywhere without Molly Lewis.'

'Right. They're a difficult pair to figure out,' Dan said. 'Sometimes she seems so angry, but rarely at him, not really.'

'And he's protective of her.' LeJuan turned on the wipers, streaking the start of a fresh rainfall across the windscreen. 'That wobbly balance of hers sometimes? What do you make of that?'

'I don't know, except I don't buy it that Molly's a lush. No evidence of that. Anyway, I haven't noticed it lately. That could be a good sign. This is that back lane we need, I think.' He nodded at the satnav. 'These half-timbered buildings are something. I'd forgotten about Bishop's Cleeve. Good-looking place. The next left turn coming up should be us.'

'I've got it now,' LeJuan said, straightening up. 'Meadow Close.'

Detached Cotswold gold stone houses, built in the last couple of decades, Dan thought, stood in spacious gardens on either side of a road that curved out of sight. Separated by tall hedges and trees, the properties had the aura of well-heeled comfort, peace, settled lifestyles. But Dan didn't allow himself to make comments like that aloud, not when they might be about to fracture some lives behind the calm façade of one of these houses. Each one was individual in style: a turret here, a conservatory there, gables, terraces, and all backed by woods as far as Dan could see.

The house they were looking for was at the nearest end of Meadow Close, next to an unimproved expanse mostly covered by trees. 'This is it,' LeJuan said. He turned in at the driveway and parked. 'Let's do this.'

For all his unconcerned air, LeJuan cared about people. He would go the extra mile to be supportive. The prospect of delivering bad news ate him up every time. At this moment he wore his professionally nonchalant mask, but Dan saw beyond that.

The photograph was in a manila envelope. Dan tucked this under his arm, got out of the car and walked with LeJuan to a double front door with large, etched-glass panels. Visible in a hallway beyond, creamy tiles shone in the light from a chandelier suspended from an upper floor. He rang the bell and they gave each other a stare. Neither of them expected to enjoy this.

Seconds passed. No sound came from inside the house.

This time, LeJuan pressed the button. Again, rich chimes reverberated inside.

There wasn't a car parked in the driveway, and there was no way to know what was in the garage without opening a door.

'Are they expecting us?' LeJuan said.

'The desk officer said so. Let's check the back.'

They separated and started walking around the building. Dan saw who they were looking for before she saw him. Her back to the house, a woman sat in a lone green lawn chair, smoking, and staring over a winter-pale lawn. She balanced what looked like a glass of red wine on one chair arm.

LeJuan appeared at the far corner of the house and stood still.

'Excuse me, madam,' Dan said, in what he hoped was a pleasant voice.

She started, and whatever was in the glass splashed over the front of her puffy silver coat.

Dan's eyes met LeJuan's for an instant and they both started forward.

'Sorry,' Dan said. 'We rang the bell a couple of times.' He took out his warrant card.

'You shocked me,' the woman said, although not in an accusatory tone. She faced them as she stood up, swiping at her coat. 'You're the police, aren't you?'

'Yes,' Dan said. 'Mrs Seaton, is it?'

'I'm Kelly Seaton. I can't find my husband.' Delivered with a helpless shrug, the statement sank to nothingness and she looked from Dan to LeJuan and back again. 'He isn't anywhere.'

When people least expected, their words could sum up the truth with painful simplicity.

This time Dan didn't let himself glance at LeJuan. 'Detective Chief Inspector Dan O'Reilly,' he said, raising his card. 'And my partner is Detective Sergeant LeJuan Harding.' LeJuan reached the red-brick patio and joined Dan. He had already slid out his identification.

'Is there any news?' she said. She looked Chinese. Glossy black hair pulled into a loose knot at her nape. Equally dark eyes that were deeply troubled. Perfect skin and small features. Dan didn't think she wore any makeup. She didn't need it. Kelly Seaton was lovely, taller than he would have expected, and slender inside her padded coat.'

'The description you gave on the phone was clear, Mrs Seaton.'

'Kelly, please. You stop really thinking about what people look like, don't you? When you've known them a long time? I had to really think when I was answering questions about Richard. Isn't that silly?'

'Not at all,' Dan said. Was she already showing signs of shock, even though she had reason to hope her husband was still alive?

'Everyone calls him Ricky,' Kelly Seaton said. 'Except for me. He's Richard to me. I've been thinking in circles. He doesn't have a lot of friends. Not any really, except casual ones . . .'

She paused, frowning at him. 'It's not because he isn't nice,' she said, her voice lowered and scratchy. 'I don't want you to think that. He's quiet – Richard is quiet. Except when he's on a stage.'

Dan made sure his expression did not change at that.

Pushing a stray piece of hair from her eyes she added, 'He would help anyone. I suppose you'd say he's naturally reserved but really kind.' Her hand was white-knuckled and shaky on the all-but-empty glass.

'I phoned his office, but he still wasn't there. He wasn't there yesterday, either, they said. He leaves before I get up in the morning, so I didn't know he wasn't there – in his office. I didn't look in his study here. But I just thought he was getting home late last night. He does that sometimes. I was asleep before he came . . . before . . . when he came home yesterday. Only he didn't, did he? He's never off work but they . . . at his office . . . they thought he must be sick for a couple of days but had forgotten to let them know. That was hours ago when I phoned, and they said they'd call if he came in or contacted them. They haven't called. Lately he's stopped for a drink with the father of an old friend – just a couple of times. He says the man's lonely . . .' Her voice faded away and she turned pink along her cheekbones. 'I was thinking of checking at the pub a bit later. To see if Richard's there.'

'Have you tried Mr Seaton's mobile?' LeJuan asked.

The woman started to shed silent tears. 'It's in his study,' she managed to whisper. 'I called it today and heard it ringing in there.'

LeJuan glanced at Dan who nodded for him to continue. 'So you went into his study, then? And he wasn't there?' The question sounded ridiculous but she was so fractured they had to take this in baby steps.

'Richard keeps the room locked. Not to keep me out but because he's got things in there that are very important to him. Keeping them safe. He's told me I can go in if I want to.'

'But you weren't able to do that, Kelly? Because you didn't have a key.' Dan this time.

'There's a spare key,' she said, her voice hollow. 'I opened the door a couple of hours ago.'

No need to ask if her husband had been on the other side of that door. 'The man he sometimes has a drink with, this father of a friend? Who would that be?'

She rubbed the space between her eyebrows. 'I've never met him. Or the friend. It's awkward, you see. Richard doesn't believe in talking about other people's business.'

'That's a good thing,' Dan said. 'But under the circumstances . . .'

'Harry, that's the friend. I don't really know what he did, but he's in prison. Richard says it wasn't anything serious.'

'And the last name?' LeJuan was taking notes.

Kelly looked miserable. 'Stroud, I think. Harry Stroud, and his father is Major Stroud. I don't think I ever heard his first name.'

LeJuan looked up. What were the chances? He and Dan had both been involved in the Harry Stroud case.

Not in prison for anything serious, Dan thought. *Only serious enough to land Harry behind bars for fraud and money laundering.*

'When did you last see your husband for sure, Mrs Seaton?' Always an awkward line of questioning in similar circumstances. Dan gave her an encouraging smile.

'I don't sleep well, not without pills. The pills let me sleep for five or six hours. Nine, that's when I think I went to bed the night before last.'

'So, is that when you last saw your husband?'

'I – I suppose it must have been.'

'So, he wasn't in bed when you woke up at, say two or three or so yesterday morning?'

Her dark eyes rested on his face for so long Dan found it difficult not to look away. 'Mrs Seaton?'

'No.'

'Forgive me if this is intrusive, but do you sleep in the same bedroom?'

Her throat jerked. 'Often, we do. Richard is restless, too. He walks around in the night. Sometimes he's up most of the night, watching the television in his study.'

'He could have gone somewhere other than his study yesterday morning, perhaps? Or do you keep one another informed of all your movements?'

'No.' The tissue she took from her pocket was crumpled into a ball. 'I didn't call the police yesterday, even though I'd searched the house and couldn't find him – and his car is parked outside – around the corner in the front.' She waved a hand vaguely and set her glass on the arm of the lawn chair. 'How could he go somewhere without his car?'

Dan made a noncommittal sound.

'He's . . . well, he didn't come back overnight once before. I didn't want to embarrass him by raising the alarm for nothing this time – even though I was so upset and worried. I took my pills last night, the same as usual, but when I got up Richard still wasn't back and I was scared for him. I waited until he would have been in his office for a while and phoned. Someone else answered and that's who I talked to. Like I said, there was no point in trying his mobile because it's in his study.'

'I think we'd better take that mobile with us,' Dan told her. 'And we'd like to look at his study. You'll be all right with that?'

'Yes! You know something about what's happened to Richard, don't you? That's why you're asking these questions.' Her eyes were wet.

'Is there someone you'd like to have with you?' Dan asked. He could feel her panic increasing. 'All these questions can be so hard.'

'No, I don't have anyone.'

'No family or friends?'

She shook her head. Emphatic. 'I told you, no.'

Hating to do this, Dan slid the photograph from the envelope. 'We'd like you to take a look at this. You don't have to dwell on it but just say if you know who this is.'

LeJuan moved quietly in beside her, took the photo and held it while she hesitantly touched the image. Without a word, she stroked the closed eyes, the nose that even Werner had not been able to normalize, and the swollen mouth.

When she swayed, LeJuan wrapped an arm around her shoulders and she buckled against him. Whatever she muttered was undecipherable.

'Who can we call?' LeJuan asked. 'We can arrange for someone from Family Liaison to be with you if necessary.'

Kelly Seaton shook her head again and reached for the photo. 'How did this happen? Where is he? He's dead, isn't he?'

'I'm afraid so,' Dan told her. 'He was found last night and we're sure he didn't take his own life.'

'Was he crossing the road?' Tears streamed now. 'Did a car hit him?'

'Kelly,' Dan said, coming closer. 'It appears he was murdered.'

At first there wasn't a sound. The woman raised her face and stared into the distance, only Dan realized she was not seeing anything. She began to shake, to shudder really, one hand clinging to LeJuan's sleeve and the other spread over her face.

'Kelly,' LeJuan said. 'Let's get you inside, into the warm. It's freezing out here.'

A noise, very faint at first, came from her. A soft keening that made an almost animal sound in her throat. It grew louder. She drew her lips back from her teeth and sobbed, bent forward, and let the sound grow into a terrible cry.

Dan stood at her other side from LeJuan and braced her. Her attempts to shut the bursts of despair away were desperate, and useless.

'Sit down, Kelly,' Dan said. 'When you're ready we'll get you some tea and see about having your doctor come by.' She allowed them to guide her into the lawn chair. She cried louder, bent forward to bury her face in her knees.

LeJuan produced his phone. 'I'll call for Family Liaison—'

'Not yet,' Dan said before LeJuan could finish. This was harrowing, but it was in these early phases that useful details sometimes slipped in. Given the progress they had not made on Coughlin's death so far, they needed to take any help they could get.

'What the hell's going on here? Get away from her.'

Pushing a bicycle, a slim, blond man had come from the side of the building they weren't watching at that moment. Decked out in black Lycra, he dropped the bike on its side and ran toward Kelly, ripping off his helmet as he went.

'Boss,' LeJuan said, warning, and braced himself.

The man glared at them both and went directly to bend over Kelly.

'What are you doing here, Gordon?' Kelly said. 'You know we can't—'

Gordon, whoever he was, stroked her hair. 'I tried to call you several times . . . about the other thing. I got worried.' He turned to Dan and LeJuan. 'Who are you? Why are you here?'

'Police,' Dan said, and introduced them both. 'I'm afraid something very difficult has happened. We came to inform Kelly. And you are . . .?' He let the query trail off.

'An old friend.'

'What's your last name, Gordon?' LeJuan asked, extremely polite.

'Dulles,' the man said, and he clearly wasn't happy about

talking to them. 'I tried to call Kelly or Ricky several times. They aren't the kind of people who don't answer a phone.'

Dan watched Gordon Dulles's expression. He looked unwaveringly at Kelly, and Dan could have sworn he was trying to convey a silent message.

'What's going on?' Dulles said. He straightened, keeping a hand on Kelly's shoulder, and looked from LeJuan to Dan.

'Kelly,' Dan said. 'Would you be OK with us sharing the news with Gordon? Would that be a help, perhaps?'

She nodded miserably. 'He's my friend. Richard's, too.' *Yet she'd been adamant they had no friends.* 'Richard is dead,' she finished softly, and slumped over in the chair again.

Gordon frowned. He stared at Dan. 'An accident?'

'No,' Dan said. 'Kelly, do you have an address for Major Stroud?'

'No. I told you it was Richard who knew him, not me.'

'Perhaps there are people at the pub who know both of them,' LeJuan said. They both knew how to reach the major, but were in unspoken agreement not to close off any potential information from Kelly. Every answer to a simple question had the potential to produce more information than the witness intended to give. 'What sort of time did your husband usually meet him?'

'He didn't meet him often.' Kelly's voice scaled upward. 'I told you that, too. You keep asking the same things. I think Richard went one or two times on the way home from work. About seven or eight, that would be. It's not far from here. Or he went out later, I believe, and that could have been to meet Major Stroud, too.'

Dan said, 'So Richard and Major Stroud are good friends? It sounds that way.'

'Well, it shouldn't,' Kelly said, getting angry, he thought, although he had no idea why.

This was not going to be easy. Nothing suggested that either Kelly or Dulles would go out of their way to be useful – which might be useful on its own. 'Where did they meet?' Dan asked. 'What's your closest pub?' He expected her to say the Corner Cupboard or one of the other Winchcombe pubs.'

'They met in Folly,' Kelly said. 'At the Black Dog.'

Dan digested that. Once more to the Black Dog . . . and Folly. 'The timing for this may seem difficult,' he told her. 'It is difficult, but there has to be a physical identification of the victim. Do you feel able to do that, or is there another relative who—'

'I'll do it.' She cut him off sharply. 'I owe Richard that.'

ELEVEN

The colored lights sparkled along the rooflines. In the frosty early evening, mist curled from the thatch to wisp away against a leaden sky. Alex turned off her Range Rover and sat still in the car park behind the Black Dog. This had always been her favorite season . . . but not this year, not at this moment, in these hours of turmoil.

She glanced to the side of the building, at lighted window reflections that stretched across the shaded ground, bright squares framing the shadows of customers in the saloon bar. Going inside, smiling at them, chatting, felt impossible. Should she take off the ring? There were bound to be questions, the ones she didn't want to answer, not yet – if ever.

Tony would notice and come to accurate conclusions. She couldn't do that to him.

Alex rubbed her hands together hard. The decision to stand with Tony, to carry on as if there was no question of their plans going completely pear shaped, had felt right. It probably was right; if it wasn't utterly wrong and bound to end when it all exploded in their faces. As she had so many times today, she turned the ring on her finger.

'Come on, Bogie.' He pushed his warm little body close to her side, reached up and licked her chin. 'Let's do this. We're tough.'

The dog jumped past her before she could get out herself, but he knew the routine and promptly sat on the gravel to wait for her. She gathered as many boxes of new Christmas lights as she could from the back seat. They were replacing all the inside strands this year. With the weather taking its toll, the outside ones – up all year – had to be changed more often.

After only a couple of steps toward the kitchen door at the back of the pub, Alex hesitated. A sound reached her, like wheels rolling on the gravel, but she couldn't hear an engine or see headlights moving. Trundling? Was that it? Someone pushing a cart . . . in the gathering darkness and without so much as a torch?

She got a sudden memory from last night. The figure by the gates. In the dark and with no torch. With something in his hand that could have been a gun or a knife. *Or, more likely, a torch they chose not to turn on.* Reason had a way of stepping in eventually.

Alex estimated how quickly she could get to the kitchen door. *So much for reason.* 'Come, Bogie,' she said in a hoarse whisper. 'Now!' He had decided to trot away, snuffling the ground as he went.

Holding her breath, Alex took a careful step forward. She had picked up too many boxes and they started to list in her arms. Juggling, lifting a knee to rest the bottom of the pile, she tried to clamp it all together with an arm across the top.

The whole lot hit the deck and slithered away in several directions. 'Rats!' Leaving the fairy lights where they were, Alex set off at a trot for the back door and met Bogie on his bouncing way back to her. 'Heel, boy. If you remember how.'

'Alex, are you all right?' A thin, breathless voice reached her. 'It's Mary and Harriet. Our blessed torch battery's gone dead.'

She sighed with relief. One of these days, perhaps when nasty surprises stopped coming – if they ever did – the worst possibilities might not be her first assumptions.

'Stay where you are, ladies. I've got a torch in my pocket.' And since her boxes were scattered on the gravel, she had two free hands.

Harriet and Mary Burke waited for her on the side path to the bar door. Mary pushed her walker, with her tiny Maltese, Lillie Belle, blanketed inside its little basket. Harriet pulled the tartan-covered shopping cart containing, as Alex knew, Max, their one-eyed ginger tabby cat. They maintained that Max could not be left at home with First-cat Oliver, because the two did not get along.

Bogie had slid to a stop only to take off again to meet the little convoy. He snuffled at Lillie Belle, who promptly buried her nose in the blanket.

'We saw you turn in,' Mary said. 'We're hoping we can have a chat about a problem we've got.' She sounded irritable. The sisters owned Leaves of Comfort, a tea shop a short distance from the Black Dog, on Pond Street. They lived in the upstairs flat.

'I don't have a problem,' Harriet commented, mildly, although Alex thought she heard and sensed a disagreement.

'It's cold, ladies. Let's get you inside.' And she had better rescue her fairy lights before someone else arrived and drove over them. 'Settle in by the fire. I'll catch up with you shortly. Keep up, Bogie.' She aimed the torchlight ahead of them on the path.

It took two trips to carry her slightly battered boxes into the bar and pile them on a chair. The warmth felt wonderful and it didn't all come from the fireplace. The bar was hopping, crowded with customers, which surprised Alex on a weeknight.

Hugh worked the bar with Liz Hadley. The two of them moved smoothly around one another, sliding glasses across the counter in quick succession. Since her Broadway dress shop had closed, Liz worked almost full-time at the Dog. Scoot Gammage did table-clearing duty. He and his brother Kyle were still Doc James's wards while their dad was in prison. Scoot delivered meals to the up-room (an area one step up from the main bar room), where people ate dinner when they didn't want to be in the more formal restaurant. And his clear voice also rang out to announce hot snacks ready for customers in the rest of the bar. He was a hard-working teenager who had lived a tougher life than most.

Alex was grateful for the noise and activity. It diverted attention from her. With a wave to the staff, she threaded a rapid path until she could slide into a chair at the Burke sisters' fireside table.

'Wow,' she said. 'I didn't realize I was tired until I saw how busy it is tonight.' She smiled from one to the other.

'Coming out of the cold into the warm can do that, too,' Harriet said. 'Make you feel tired, I mean.'

Mary concentrated on the darts team, warming up for a match with a team from Knights-in-the-Bottom, a Cheltenham pub.

'She's designated reserve tonight,' Harriet said in a lowered voice, her bright eyes meaningful. 'They can't believe she can still stand with her walker and actually hit the board. Makes her furious, that.'

'As it should,' Alex said, and meant it. Mary had been the mainstay of more than one darts team, but with her arthritis and failing eyesight, most other players couldn't seem to trust that her accuracy wouldn't fail her.

'She handles it well, especially if they have to call on her and she saves their bacon.'

Alex grinned. 'So, what's up?'

'It's silly.'

'It is not silly, Harriet.' Mary hadn't been missing the conversation. 'That's like calling me silly, which I truly resent, my dear. You know better.' A black and silver Spanish comb, one from a considerable collection, sparkled above her wispy white chignon. Fortunately, she never wore a mantilla. Her pallid blue eyes filled the thick round lenses of her glasses.

'Will you explain, or shall I?' Harriet asked.

'Go ahead. We might as well start with your rosy view.'

'Hardly rosy.' From a back pocket on the shopping cart, she drew out a package which she unwrapped to display a small oil painting. 'This is an idea. Nothing more yet. But it could grow into something and it costs us nothing if it doesn't work.'

'Except the reputation we've built over the years for specialization,' Mary said tartly. 'And our self-respect.'

'Take a look at this.' Ignoring Mary, Harriet slid the picture in front of Alex. 'I know what I like, but you have expertise. Tell us what you think, as an artist.'

She hadn't painted in months and didn't feel much like an artist at the moment, but she did appreciate pleasing works. 'It's our folly,' she said, smiling. 'The Tooth,' as all the locals called Tinsley Tower, jagged because of masonry falls, but still visible on its hilltop for miles around. Word had it that this was where Folly-on-Weir got its name.

'We brought that one because we thought most people would recognize it immediately.'

Mary hunched her shoulders. 'Tourist bric-a-brac.'

'I want to see this in good light,' Alex said. '*Plein air*. We see so many artists at work in the outdoors – especially in the Cotswolds – but this is really good.'

'*En plein air*,' Mary said in a flat voice. 'For people who paint outside because they don't have studios.'

Fortunately, Alex managed not to giggle. This wasn't the time to pontificate on the values of painting in natural light and being outside while you worked – at least until light failed. 'You've got a bee in your bonnet about this,' she said. 'Tell me about the problem you have with it. And why. If you want to, that is.'

'Harriet wants to expand the business,' Mary said, in the same curt manner. 'Take on some new, *modern* stock. Our profit margin has been getting thinner—'

'Or non-existent,' Harriet put in. 'It's threatening to go backwards. We need fresh ideas. Not everyone wants another teapot or an embroidered doily, and this time of the year we don't get enough of the tourists you're sneering at, Mary. That means we're not doing as many teas. For the very first time, we've had to significantly cut our order from George's Bakery, and I don't like doing that to them, I can tell you.'

'But why turn to new people, like this?' Mary swept a dismissive hand at the painting. 'He doesn't live around here. We don't know him. We've always known all the people we deal with. How are they going to feel if we start carrying incomers' work?'

'The artist is Henry Childs and he lives in Gambol Green – twenty minutes from Folly,' Harriet said, clearly exasperated. 'He and his wife, Judith, have a small shop. She sells new and used books, so we shan't be cross-pollinating with her since we already have our own book business, but we've never had anyone come to us with paintings. And instead of making pennies on items sold – and I love the things we have always sold, and will always sell, I hope – the idea is to deal in things that are likely to turn over more rapidly. And with a higher price point, but with local appeal. We'd get forty per cent of any painting we sell. They're not a fortune – not as much as they're worth, I think – but it could be a start in the right direction.

'There's a local art sale in Upper Slaughter from time to time. Near the gift shop and the tea garden. I've seen people buy small paintings in groups. Two, and as many as six. I've considered them myself. We've got loads of talent around here.'

Alex cleared her throat. 'I do like the painting,' she said, not sure she should be getting involved. 'I think people would buy small works like this of Cotswold sights. A really nice selling argument would be that they're easy to pop in a suitcase or a bag to take home.' What she didn't say was that it sounded as if they might need more than the commission from the sale of a couple of paintings to change their financial outlook. 'It's also appealing if they come already framed so they really do make a lovely little gift.'

'They're all framed,' Mary said, crossing her arms over her pink twinset. 'There's plenty more where that one came from. We've got a big boxful at home. And apparently, *we've* already more or less agreed to the venture. I know they're small works, but where are we going to hang them, that's what I want to know? If we stick them between the *teapots and embroidered doilies* they will hardly stand out, will they?' She shot Harriet a quelling look.

'For a start you can put a few in here,' Alex said, and instantly had a feeling she had spoken too quickly. But they could put some in the Black Dog under the wall sconces where they would probably look lovely. 'I do believe they would fit in here.' *In for a penny . . .*

'Alex!' Harriet beamed. 'That's lovely of you. And, of course, we'd split the commission on any sales.'

Mary became absorbed in stroking Lillie Belle on her lap, but her powdered face turned quite rosy.

'No,' Alex said. 'They would add something here, but the commission would all go to you. I like the idea. I'll come over and see more of them. I'll go ahead and hang this one, if you like. Give me a few of your cards to pin up. And put prices on them.'

'Hmm.' Mary didn't look up.

'After all. What do we lose by giving it a try, ladies? We're doing well with Carrie Peale's Black Dog mugs.'

'Carrie lives in Folly,' Mary said. 'Her pottery's here.'

Not meeting Mary's eyes, Harriet said, 'Thank you, Alex,' and patted her hand. 'I would never have thought of that. I'm hoping we can come up with other ideas, but this will be a start. I'm hoping they go as Christmas presents. Oh, I do hope we get a pre-Christmas rush.'

'Other ideas?' Mary said grimly, but she managed a smile for

Alex. 'You're a good friend, my girl. Don't worry too much about us. We'll make it through.'

Alex smiled back and looked around. 'Why so busy, I wonder. Even some of the Gentlemen Bikers' Club is in. We don't see them so much in the winter.' The people in question wore expensive black leathers and inevitably seemed to find anything said hilariously funny. However, they were good customers and well-behaved most of the time.

'There's talk about that Phoenix Players' tithe barn,' Mary said, inclining her head to the darts players. 'They're saying the police were called. I'm not even sure where it is.'

'Not far at all – fairly close to Underhill,' Alex said. 'The old Playing Fields. I saw a play there once. I keep intending to go back.'

'Something's happened there. That's what they're saying, anyway. Police activity coming and going . . .' Mary broke off to listen more closely.

Tony had mentioned something like that after he arrived last night.

'Probably vandalism,' Harriet said. 'Or fly tipping. They seem to get worse all the time. Throwing their rubbish on other people's property.'

'I'd better move those boxes of lights I put on a chair. Someone's going to need it.' She stopped talking and straightened. Voice volume in the room quieted a few notches, then fell to a hum.

Dan O'Reilly had walked in, followed by LeJuan Harding, and no detecting skills were needed to decide they were looking for someone.

TWELVE

Tony closed the front door of his cottage veterinary clinic and returned to the office, where crates for post-surgery patients lined two walls. This evening was quiet, the crates empty.

He looked through the diamond panes of the front window in time to see Bill Lamb shut the passenger door of his car on Radhika, Tony's assistant. Love was a wonderful thing when it was real, and those two proved it.

Tony squeezed behind the desk – the room was cramped – and slid into the wooden swivel chair. Radhika had been with him for a couple of years, which seemed to have passed so rapidly. She had transformed his practice from a haphazardly kept, or mostly totally disorganized wreck, into something that ran smoothly and made his professional life easy.

No matter the bumps, his own life was pretty terrific, Tony thought, grinning to himself. Alex was on his side all the way and he knew how he was going move them ahead.

In a manner he admitted to himself was a bit twisted, he was ecstatic to have got the news from his solicitor that the declaration of Penny's death had just come through. The timing was bizarre. Had she somehow known this was about to happen and decided to take one last swipe at him? Why would she do that? What did she really want? And if she *was* alive, why would she have waited over eight years to contact him – if she was ever going to want to.

His solicitor would be handing over the certification from Australia. The law was, according to Barstwick, that once the person was certified dead, any subsequent new marriage stood. God, it was a mind bender and he, Tony, only wanted to be free of the uncertainty. If Penny was alive, he wished her well – 'far away from here', as the Fiddler on the Roof's blessing for the czar went.

Now he was truly falling into the realm of fanciful. Tonight, he would go to the Dog to break the news to Alex about the death declaration and persuade her to leave early. They had been through so much and were so much better when they were together.

The bell rang for the patient door at the back of the cottage. Surgery hours were long over, but when had he ever turned an animal away? Hurriedly, he skirted the desk once more and walked through the passageway – past the one examination room, the waiting room and the kitchen – to open up.

'I'm sorry. I'm not sure what your hours are but I came anyway just in case you were here.' A man held his coat over what was obviously an animal and looked hopefully at Tony. 'Is it too late?' He'd pulled his car all the way to the steps and left the engine running.

'I'm really sorry to come without warning like this but I'm worried out of my mind. Is the doctor still here?'

The anxiety in the rushed voice did to Tony what it always did. 'That would be me. You lucked out. Come on in. What do we have?'

Breaking into a nervous smile, he came in, moving the collar of his waxed coat aside to show a Siamese cat nestled there, blue eyes staring piercingly. The cat jerked a couple of times and Tony frowned. 'Follow me. How long – he or she?'

'She. Beatrix. She was almost Betty-Lou – like an American girl – but a friend persuaded me that it was too cute, and she's gorgeous but not cute. This is my fault. She hasn't been eating and she always eats – enough for several cats. You wouldn't think so. She's a long, skinny drink of water. But so healthy. She's always been so healthy. And active . . . goodness, is she active. Oh, damn it, I should have taken her to someone yesterday. I've never taken her to a vet before. I know you'll say that's wrong, but I rescued her and she's been doing so well I thought it was better to let her settle. You know, not put her through any extra stress. She needs to be spayed but she never goes outside. I would never breed her – she's far too delicate. Oh, I should tell you, I've only lived in Naunton – just a couple of miles up the road from here, but you know that – I've only lived there a few months. A nice woman at my pet shop in Cheltenham gave me your name. I prefer to get Beatrix's food from the same place I always have done. It's easy enough since I work in Cheltenham. I trust the people in the shop. It could be worms, couldn't it?'

At last, he paused for breath, and Tony gave him a reassuring smile. Above average height and broad shouldered, with short straight brown hair and dark eyes, a pleasant if unremarkable face. Probably in his mid- to late thirties. Perhaps the eyes were interesting; they certainly had a way of being sharply appraising.

'Worms?' he repeated tentatively.

'We'll figure it out,' Tony said with a slight smile to himself. The cat was 'always so healthy', but 'far too delicate to breed?' The man looked fit and healthy himself from what he could see, but the insecurities of the animal-loving, over-protective owner came through. 'Let's go in here.'

The examining room was small but more than adequate. Beatrix's owner pushed the door shut behind him with a foot and produced a long, lean Siamese Seal Point with ears from the lineage of Yoda. She wore a green safety halter of which Tony approved. 'She eats fresh cooked chicken, peas and rice. Twice a day. I only use the tinned food when I leave her to go to work. She has a tiny bit of high-quality ice-cream for a special treat, which she absolutely loves. Only thing she begs for. I get it from that local dairy. Very fresh and creamy. She did eat about a teaspoonful of chicken last night but nothing today. And she refused to swim this afternoon.' Holding the cat on the examination table with one hand and the lead of the halter with the other, the man looked up. 'She swims in the bath every day. Loves it. If you're going to have Siamese cats, you must stimulate them, or they get depressed. But you know that.'

'She looks alert,' Tony said. Far be it from him to criticize a zealous owner who might just be hyper-anxious. 'May I?' He put his hands on the cat and stroked gently.

Her eyes were Elizabeth Taylor amethyst blue; they regarded him seriously but without anxiety or animosity. Those ears were something else. More horizontal than upright, and huge. The body was the color of vanilla cream, the face, legs and long, slender tail, warm dark brown.

Tony palpated Beatrix, smiling inwardly about her obvious pleasure at human touch. When she tilted her head sideways and purred, he scratched under her chin and picked her up. 'Have you left her for any unexpected periods lately?'

'Oh, no. I know better than that.'

'I know you do,' Tony said. He nodded and met the owner's dark eyes – and frowned.

The man frowned back.

'Do I know you?' Tony said, and laughed, slightly self-conscious. 'Don't tell me. Are you . . . sheesh. I feel as if I should know you.'

'Me, too.' He stroked his cat, inclining his head to one side and staring at Tony.

'Oh, my, word.' Tony snapped his fingers. '*Malcolm!* Right? Wrong? St Edward's? Would have been my last two years before uni.'

'Right. You remembered.' He had a good smile, good teeth. 'But I'm John, John Ross. I think you're mixing me up with Malcolm Loder. And you're Tony Harrison, of course. Should have rung a bell. Day boy. Unfortunately, I boarded. Never liked it. Hated it, in fact.'

'You didn't live in Naunton back then,' Tony said. 'Or did you? I only went to St Edward's for my last couple of senior school years.' He hadn't known John Ross well.

'No. We lived in Lacock. My parents have both passed on and I always liked the Naunton area, so here I am. Convenient for Cheltenham, too.'

The cat had poked her nose into the neck of Tony's jumper and seemed to be relaxing. 'Lovely cat,' he said. 'Perhaps we should do some blood work. Just to make sure.'

John tensed. 'You think there's something really wrong with her?'

'I think there's probably nothing wrong with her, but we might make sure. If I had to guess, I'd say she's in a snit about something, although it's not showing at the moment, is it?'

John let out a relieved breath and nodded. 'She's a bit of a princess . . . I'm surprised you remembered me. It must be going on twenty years.'

'Close to that. Shall I draw blood?'

'Yes. Do it.'

Tony put the cat back on the table. He turned to a tray and tucked a syringe into the pocket of his clinic coat. 'Don't want her associating me with needles. Malcolm was your friend, wasn't he?'

'Yes.'

'Very shy boy, I seem to recall, but nice. Of course he was nice, he was your friend. I mean you wouldn't have liked him so much if he wasn't nice.' Tony chuckled as he drew the cat's blood. 'There. Good girl. Really good girl.'

'Malcolm was the best,' John said, stroking the cat absently. 'My St Edward's days would have been pretty grim without him. You weren't so rambunctious yourself.'

'Not really,' said Tony. 'I didn't want to move schools but my father thought it a good idea at that point.'

'All the big boys liked you, though. You were popular.'

Tony offered Beatrix a treat which she sniffed then ignored. 'What does that mean? The big boys?'

'You know,' John said. 'The ones who were top of everything that was worth the effort. Chess Club. Debating Society and so on. The doers and winners.'

'If you say so. I played a lot of tennis but that was about it for extra-curriculars. If I'd been longer at the school, I might have got more involved, I suppose.'

'You were captain of the tennis team,' John said, in hushed tones.

'My only claim to athletic fame,' Tony responded.

'My father *loved* me going there,' John said. 'But I know what you mean. I didn't like it, either.'

Tony wanted to finish seeing this probably healthy cat and get to the Black Dog. He needed a polite exit 'Let me have your phone number and we'll give you a call with the blood results.'

'I'll do that.' He started going through his pockets. 'Never a pen when you need one. I need to pay you, too.'

'We'll bill you. If you see Malcolm, give him my best, will you?'

John stopped looking for a pen and stared at Tony. 'Malcolm died earlier this year.'

'Oh, I'm sorry. I didn't know him well . . . I already said that, didn't I? What did he die of, if you don't mind my asking? He was too young, darn it.'

'He committed suicide.'

THIRTEEN

A lex put on a smile she didn't feel and headed for the bar. The arrival of a pair of detectives didn't usually mean they had dropped in for a pint of the best.

The noise level was rapidly returning to a normal pitch for the crowd size. Loud. She said, 'Good evening,' to LeJuan, who faced her. Dan turned and both men nodded. No return smiles tonight.

'Just a few words,' Dan said, leaning closer. 'Can we move to the end of the bar?' He indicated the corner where Carrie Peale's deep blue coffee mugs, adorned with a handsome black dog, were displayed on the counter.

'Of course,' she said, just as another cheerfully loud party arrived. 'Do you mind if I clear that chair?' Without waiting for an answer, Alex swept up the fairy lights – all of them – and this time she balanced them more carefully.

Despite her owlish raising of her brows and widening of her eyes, signifying she would rather he not do so, Hugh relieved her of the boxes and strode back toward the kitchens. So much for snatching a couple of extra minutes to collect herself. She was so used to the hubbub, yet this evening it had started to irritate her – everything had started to irritate her.

Liz Hadley caught her eye and beckoned. 'The major's in a funny mood again,' she said in Alex's ear. Tall, slim and elegantly dark, tonight Liz wore a smashing emerald green dress. 'Was he in at lunchtime? I wasn't here.'

Alex glanced around but didn't see Stroud. 'I don't think so. What do you mean by a funny mood? Funnier than usual?'

'Probably not – just even more morose, but he's commandeered the table nearest the snug, you know the one. Comes up for another drink and goes back. He's telling people they can't sit there. Saving the other seats for someone else, he says. He's been there for ages and I wondered if he might have been drinking all the way since lunchtime. He never sits down, or not that I can remember. I bet there're dents in the floorboards where he normally stands.'

'I'll have a word with him when I can. This is the second night in a row he's been difficult. Thanks for the heads-up, Liz.'

'I know it's none of my business, but do you have any idea why our detective friends are here? People are talking about a serial killer in the area.' She wasn't usually one to gossip. 'Makes you a bit nervous to be out and about on your own at night,' she added.

'Let's not get ahead of ourselves,' Alex said. 'I'll know more after I speak with them.' *And if they do reveal anything, no doubt there will be a caveat to keep my own counsel.*

There was definitely something she didn't like about the atmosphere that Dan and LeJuan had brought with them, even if they were now grinning at her from the appointed corner.

'How are you?' Dan asked when she reached them. 'You're doing a roaring business.'

'I was thinking the same thing,' she said. 'Unusual for a week-night, although we have a darts match on, and things do pick up in winter-time anyway, especially when we get toward Christmas. Don't forget your raffle tickets for a fabulous hamper. All proceeds to benefit remodeling the Parish Hall.'

'Our home away from home,' said LeJuan, his expression wry. He and Dan glanced at each other.

Alex had momentarily forgotten that the hall had been pressed into service as a police incident room on several previous occasions.

'We won't forget the tickets,' Dan said. 'We're very fond of the Folly Parish Hall, aren't we, LeJuan?'

'Absolutely, boss.'

'Alex, we'd like to ask a question or two, if that's all right with you,' Dan said – moving right along.

'By all means.' She put her back toward the room. 'Can I get you a drink first?'

'No, thank you,' Dan said. 'We'd like you to take a look at this picture and tell us if you think you've ever seen the man here at the Black Dog.'

That question gave her a déjà vu feeling she didn't like one bit. 'OK.' She feared the worst – a post-mortem photo. Pictures of the dead by unnatural causes were not her favorites.

'Take a look at this.' LeJuan took out the photograph and Alex let out a relieved breath. A man and a woman leaning on a green MGB with the top down. 'I doubt if the woman would be familiar, but this is the best we have of the man.'

A nice-looking couple, Alex thought, looking at them carefully. Both dark haired, the woman Asian; Alex concentrated on the man. 'He's familiar,' she said. 'Or I think there's something familiar about him.'

'You've seen him in here?' Dan asked.

'I could have, but not necessarily. Sorry to be vague. I'm good at faces, I think, but it depends on whether I'm engaged when I see them.'

The men waited without prompting her.

'Yes, I'm not sure where but I do think I've seen him. And that could have been here.'

They both nodded. 'Fair enough,' Dan said. 'Get in touch with me if something more comes to mind. Is Major Stroud in tonight?'

On cue, the major approached the bar. He didn't make eye contact with Alex which was unusual. Perhaps Liz had been right in thinking he wasn't himself again. 'Here's the very man,' she said, and tapped Stroud's shoulder as he passed. 'Good evening, Major Stroud. I almost missed you sitting over there.'

'Is it a problem if I sit there?' Nasty, but not drunk.

'Of course not. Always good to see you. How is Mrs Stroud? And Batman?' She recalled the Strouds' lovely old golden retriever.

'Venetia is well, thank you. I don't imagine you've met the current Batman – Batman III, actually. He replaced the dog you met some time ago. Now, if you'll excuse me . . .'

'Major Stroud,' Dan said. 'We hoped we'd see you. Could you take a look at a photograph for us? Do you know this man?'

After staring at the photo for an uncomfortably long time, the major said, 'Why are you asking me?'

Dan's fingers went to a pale scar along his jaw. He rubbed absentmindedly. 'Is there a reason why you don't want to answer the question, sir?'

'I could have seen him. Not a very good photo, is it?'

'Where did you see him?' LeJuan asked.

'I didn't say I was certain I have, but I'll think about it. Now, if you don't mind . . .'

Stroud was definitely not in a responsive mood. He walked around them to the bar.

'Charming,' LeJuan said. 'Too bad he's going to have to answer sooner or later.'

'We've got company, damn it,' Dan said, and added, 'sorry about that, Alex.'

She glanced around in time for a light-haired man to arrive beside them.

'Leon,' Dan said. 'Did you get my message? I suppose you must have, or you wouldn't be here.' An unconvincing chuckle. 'Evidently the constable told you where we were going. Sorry to miss our meeting, but here you are, anyway.' Another chuckle.

'Hello, Dan – LeJuan. And Ms Duggins. I'm glad we meet again.'

Alex gathered herself. 'Yes, er—'

'Wolf. Leon.' His gray eyes showed the whites all around the iris. The light hair was slicked straight back. Without waiting for her to respond, he stared intently at Dan. 'I was actually at the Royal Chestnut in Gambol Green by the time your man caught up with me. It doesn't matter at all. I'd seen the place from the outside but never gone in before. I shall have to go back. Anyway, this is closer to where I live – on my way, actually – so I thought I'd see if I could find you. If you're up for it, we could have that pint here when you're ready.'

'No problem.' Dan didn't quite sound as if it would be no problem. This was the haughty psychologist Alex had met briefly once before. He had been with Dan then and she recalled a hint of tension between the men on that occasion.

'Why didn't you ask her about the picture?' It was Major Stroud, planting himself near Dan and jabbing a blunt finger toward Alex. 'She never forgets a customer, do you, my girl?'

She reined in the temptation to tell him she was not his girl. He could be wretchedly annoying.

'Are you off duty?' Wolf asked Dan and LeJuan. 'Let me buy you both a drink. You, too, Ms Duggins.'

'Alex,' she said reflexively, and he smiled, which made him almost approachable.

A gust of laughter swept through the room, accompanied by the sound of the door slamming. Alex caught sight of Tony, and a man much the same height. Tony was smiling and appeared relaxed. The second man had a sinuous Siamese cat draped around the neck of his waxed coat like a collar. With one hand he loosely held the end of a lead to the cat's green harness.

'I'd better get to work,' Alex said, edging away.

'Nonsense,' the major said. 'Your boy will find you soon enough. Is he with that cat fellow? Damnably odd, if you ask me.'

Before Alex could protest, Tony saw her and grinned. He said something to his companion and they both joined the swelling group around Alex. 'Hey, sweetheart.' Tony kissed her cheek. 'This is John Ross. His friend is Beatrix and John tells me she's a people and dog person, so she plays well with others.'

The cat kept her eyes firmly shut.

Sketchy introductions barely made it over the ruckus. Alex wished the detectives would take their photograph and leave so that she could get to safety behind the bar.

John Ross leaned toward her and said, 'Nice to meet you,' into her ear. 'This is unbelievable. I needed to get Beatrix looked at and there was Tony. We were at St Edward's together for a couple of years.' The cat opened her blue eyes to regard Alex.

Alex smiled and nodded at John.

Cheers went up around the dartboard. Since Mary Burke was at the oche and smiling graciously, Alex assumed their secret weapon had pulled out another win for the Black Dog.

'People!' Leon raised his voice, and his phone, and backed away. 'I'll have to take this outside. If I don't come back, you'll know I've been called out.'

No one commented to the retreating Wolf, who made a very swift exit.

'Tony,' Dan said. 'Take a look at this, will you? We think the man may have been in here quite recently.'

Once more the photo was produced, and it was John Ross who took and held it where he and Tony could both look.

John said, 'This is my first time in the Black Dog but it won't
be my last.' He smiled at Alex.

'I don't know his name, but he was at St Edward's, wasn't
he?' Tony said. 'Year ahead of us. How strange is that, John?
You and me meeting tonight, now this?'

'Really weird. Looks like Ricky Seaton all grown up.'

Tony wanted to concentrate on Alex, and he was grateful when
John Ross left. The man was nice enough, good company even,
but he talked a lot and gave the impression he craved being liked.
Or Tony was just in a mood, for which he didn't think he could
be blamed.

'I wonder what Kev Winslet's talking to Dan about,' Alex said.
'I'm not getting the impression it's as boring as you'd expect.
Dan's hanging on every word.'

Kev was gamekeeper at the Derwinter Estate, a significant
holding stretching across many acres outside the village. He and
Major Stroud were most often found standing almost toe-to-toe
a few feet from the bar.

'I thought Dan and LeJuan would be gone by now, too,' Tony
said. LeJuan and Hugh talked across the bar, Hugh frowning and
with his arms crossed.

Tony stroked the back of Alex's neck, 'When can we have
some time to ourselves? Now?'

She smiled at him. 'I need to hang around for a bit. Hope
you'll stay with me.'

'Only for you.' He squeezed her hand, felt his ring on her
finger and took a deep breath. They had enough history together;
it was time to start on the now. A waving hand caught his eye.
'I think Harriet's trying to get our attention.'

Still holding hands, they joined the sisters. Alex bent to listen
to Harriet and Tony couldn't hear what they were saying.

Katie hauled herself from a spot in front of the fire with Bogie
and ambled around to lean against his legs. A change in arthritis
meds was helping her move much better.

Alex straightened. 'Harriet's almost sure she's seen that man
in the picture, but she doesn't want to talk to the police unless
she's sure. I know how she feels. We've all walked into more
than our share of . . . well, we have, haven't we?'

'Look,' Harriet said, standing up between them. 'I think it might be best to wait, just see if everything clears up quickly. Without us saying anything. And I'm not sure anyway.'

'If I had your eyes, I'd be sure,' Mary said loudly.

Harriet sent her sister a withering glance. 'Do you know what I mean?' she asked Tony and Alex. 'You make a mistake, and you can come close to causing a disaster – and get yourself on a sticky wicket. We've been there before.'

Alex nodded agreement, but Tony didn't believe in holding back from cooperating with the police. 'When do you think you saw him, Harriet?'

'I can't remember exactly. In the past few weeks. In here.' She leaned in closer. 'I think he was talking to Major Stroud. Lillie Belle had a tummy ache. She was a bit fussy. I mentioned it to you, Tony. Do you remember?'

He remembered wondering how one became adept at diagnosing that a dog's stomach ached just from looking into her bright eyes. 'Yes.' For a moment he looked toward a darkened window. 'Only two or three weeks ago, you think? She got better without having to come to the clinic?'

'She had a scratch on her nose, and she was cross,' Mary put in, inspecting the little Maltese's face. 'It healed up quickly. *And* we know who did it to her, don't we? Oliver can be a sly fellow.'

'You do know that Max is Mary's favorite, don't you?' Harriet said with a meaningful expression. 'What did the major say about the photograph? I saw him look at it.'

'I'm not sure.' He met Alex's eyes and she flicked up an eyebrow. After the last debacle that had involved them – and half the village – with the police, they had vowed to tread very carefully if more intrigue came their way.

'I felt I had to speak up – to you anyway,' Harriet said. 'If this is something to do with a second killing by whoever murdered that poor man at the cricket club, they'll want any information they can get. But if Major Stroud really did know that man, he'd have said so, wouldn't he?'

'You might think so,' Tony told her. 'Of course, we don't know how old the picture is. The car – the MGB – it's classic, so that doesn't help put a date on the shot.'

A tap on his back got Tony's attention. The major himself stood there, his heavy eyebrows drawn down. 'Good evening, all,' he said, as if they had not already gone through the 'pleasantries'. 'Tony, if Harriet would excuse us, may I borrow you and Alex for a few moments? I'm sitting over here.' He walked away without waiting for an answer.

With an arch look, Harriet resumed her seat while Alex and Tony followed Major Stroud to the table closest to the snug.

'Look,' Stroud said when they were seated. 'I believe in clearing the air. It's just that I don't care too much for your copper friends. Don't trust 'em, don't you know? All they want is someone they can pin blame on so they can dust their hands of whatever case is getting them off their posteriors and out of the pub.'

'Or *into* a pub?' Tony said mildly

If Stroud got the point, it didn't show. 'They have no qualms about stitching someone up. That's what they call it when they find a way to blame you for something you didn't do. But you already knew that.'

After several empty moments Alex said, 'I'm not saying that doesn't happen, but I think it's rare.'

'Well, I know there are people in jail who don't belong there.' He sniffed and drew the corners of his mouth – and his steely gray mustache – toward his chin. 'Enough of that. We all know the injustice that was done. Sorry if I was a bit pointed with you, Alex. Not deserved. No. Anyway, I might know the chap in that photo.'

Alex set her mouth in a tight line.

'Why should I have to tell the police anything?' Stroud nodded significantly in the direction of the detectives. 'I've tried to do my bit on more than one occasion and look what it's brought me.'

Clearly, he and Alex had only been singled out to take incoming from the major, Tony thought.

'This is between you and me,' Stroud said, tapping the side of his nose. 'Haven't decided if it's going any further yet, if you get my drift.'

Tony and Alex mumbled assent.

'Everyone knows you're as thick as thieves with the law.'

This time they did not respond. Stroud was not the only local who trotted out the same old saw.

'Look here,' Stroud said with a pugnacious jut of his jaw. 'This is the way of it. I'll sketch it out for you, and you can help me make up my mind what to do.

'If the fella in the photo is who I think he is, he's a pauper married to a woman who is as rich as Croesus, but he's too terrified of her to lay down the law. Tell her what's what. Most of the time he's quiet as a church mouse, downright boring, but he's full of a lot of braggadocio about his silly theater company, and his so-called acting career, and not a thing to show for any of it.'

'An old friend, is he?' Tony asked. Stroud and Seaton seemed an unlikely pairing.

Stroud cleared his throat. 'If you must know, he's a longtime friend of my son Harry's. We knew him as a boy – not that well, of course.'

'Mrs Stroud loves the arts, doesn't she?' Alex asked mildly.

Tony could, and would have liked to regardless, kiss her for breaking up this difficult man's flow.

Not for long. 'Venetia – that's Mrs Major Stroud, of course – she loves them a deal too much,' Stroud put in explosively. 'I made the mistake of mentioning how Seaton was sniffing around for donations. I was hoping she'd see it for what it is, a scam, but oh, no. She's never failed to get the glint of reflected glory in her eye just thinking about plonking our name on a theater program. *Generous contributors!* Load of manure. Doesn't consider the number of people who read those credits just to look for fools with too much money who might be good for another milking.'

'That's where I've seen him,' Alex said. 'At least, I think it is. He was in a play at that Phoenix Players' tithe barn – I think. I enjoyed it. A play about anger, or with anger in the title. Anyway, it was different.'

'Speaking of anger,' Stroud said, 'the man has enemies. Just ask someone from the Rum Hole.'

FOURTEEN

The Royal Chestnut, in the village of Gambol Green, was no more than half an hour from the Black Dog – maybe less – but that was far enough to be fairly sure they wouldn't run into anyone from Folly. Not that it really mattered, except that a comfortable place to talk about the evening's developments, without watching out for interested ears, had seemed like a good idea. It still did.

'What made you think of coming here?' Alex asked Tony.

He frowned thoughtfully. 'I wouldn't have done, if that Leon Wolf fellow hadn't mentioned it. Pleasant place, cheerful. And we wanted to get away, didn't we?'

'I had to get away,' Alex said. 'But I do feel a bit guilty about leaving early when it was so busy.' She led the way into a long, low ceilinged, and blessedly warm, saloon.

The pub wasn't bustling, but a small crowd bantered cheerfully around the bar. On either side of an Inglenook fireplace, more customers sat at tables along an exposed stone wall where ancient, rusted farm implements rested on ledges.

'You really feel guilty?' Tony said mildly. 'I'm not so sure that's what you're feeling . . . how about "uptight" because tonight we got reeled in again by three experts. Harriet, Mary and Stroud. I don't know if they look on us as substitute confessors or intermediaries between them and the police.'

'I don't like either of those choices,' Alex said. She loved the Black Dog being a haven for so many villagers, but the last brush with the law – also caused by a conscience tussle over keeping confidences – had turned nasty, and she had been relieved to enjoy relative calm since then. 'I think there's a little lounge through the archway at the end of here. I haven't been here in ages. Not since I used to get drafted to fill in on our darts team. They don't have a snug, but the lounge is really comfortable.'

The pub was old. Crooked flights of stairs twisted upward

from dark passages, with darker flagstone floors dimly lit by yellow bulbs in hanging glass lanterns.

In the bar, the staff had already wound winking colored lights in and out of every available nook and cranny. Horse brasses, copper mugs, pots and jugs, candlesticks and candle snuffers, bellows, warming pans, trivets – all crowded along shelves – took on a shimmering luster.

'Christmas is in the air,' Tony said, steering Alex forward with a hand on the back of her neck. 'Bit early if you ask me.'

'I like it,' Alex told him. 'We'll have our new lights up in the next day or two. It's never too soon to brighten things up. Art and Dorrie Frampton do a nice job here. It always feels welcoming.' The Framptons had been licensees at the Chestnut for as long as Alex could remember.

Tony scanned the bar. 'Looks as if we're in safe territory. Don't know a soul except the Framptons. I'm glad we get Billy Joel and not Christmas carols yet.'

As he spoke, 'We Didn't Start the Fire' got some heads nodding.

Anxious to get on, Alex said, 'I don't want to be away too long. We'd better do what we came to do, or we won't have enough time.'

They made their way to the lounge, returning waves from the Framptons on the way.

Worn blue tapestry-covered banquettes and sagging armchairs. Thick oak tables were deeply scarred but brightly polished. The threadbare carpets might not survive many more seasons, but a Christmas tree in one corner would distract the average patron from other details. Illuminated with white lights, the tree was decorated with enough aged ornaments to all but obscure the branches.

'I did give Dad a quick call,' Tony said. 'But we should make sure we explain ourselves properly to him, and your mum. Maybe even later tonight if there's an opportunity. I was going to ask them to join us here but thought better of it. I told him we were coming to the Chestnut. He says he's never been here before. Funny how people stick to their own locals.'

'And we're glad they do,' Alex said significantly. 'We're lucky to have such a thriving clientele.'

'You earn it,' Tony said. 'You work at running a welcoming place to be. Or maybe not that. Word has it you're naturally charming to be with and I second that.'

'You're buttering me up.' Alex slid into a chair behind a corner table. 'But you're right, of course.'

She took off her coat while Tony set off for the bar to get drinks.

'We Didn't Start the Fire' slid into 'Piano Man'. Smiling, Alex rested her chin on a hand. She was relaxing for the first time in hours.

The ring felt foreign and obvious on her finger and she was surprised no one had noticed it earlier. Even more unexpected was the avoidance of any comments from their parents about the previous evening's sudden change of plans. But then she remembered how absorbed they had all been with their current issues, and wondered just how serious Mary and Harriet's money concerns were. Even more so, what was Major Stroud's connection to a murdered man and why was he behaving so aggressively?

Tony returned with a Courvoisier for Alex and a beer for himself. He sat down before noticing that Alex was gazing at their ring.

He gave her one of his completely happy grins – the kind that lit up his face – and stroked her cheek with the backs of his fingers. 'I hope we can start shouting our news really soon. And making plans. When you think it's time, of course. I'm sorry I made such a mess of last night.'

She took a large swallow of Courvoisier and coughed, then nodded, her face hot and her eyes watery. 'You didn't. And we'll make plans together. I think we're past the stage of making independent decisions about things that affect us both.'

'This seems as good a moment as any to say this,' Tony said. 'Barstwick – the solicitor – called. This sounds an odd thing to celebrate, but the death declaration came through for Penny.'

Alex shifted to the edge of her chair. She felt slightly light-headed. 'I never considered . . . never thought this was what we were going to talk about tonight.'

'It's not, not really, but I assumed you'd want to know we can carry on without that worry hanging over us.'

'You do know I'm sorry about Penny?' Alex replied.

Tony nodded and looked away.

There was more she wanted to say. What about the letter from someone saying she was Penny, and the threatening tone of what she – or he, Alex supposed – had written? From the mood Tony was in, this might not be the time or place for that discussion, but it had to happen.

'You know Doc James and my mum will ask about dates?' Alex said, picking up her glass. 'Before they ask about anything else, probably. They'll have to be the first to know when we have one.'

'It won't be long if I have my way.' He leaned to kiss her. 'Mm, you taste of brandy. Christmas might be too much of a rush, but New Year gives us a little longer. If you're sure you want to marry in the deep, dark winter.' He gave a wolfish grin.

Alex smiled back. 'I like frosty winds that moan and all the good stuff that feels a bit magical.'

'All right.' Tony sat up straight. 'I propose New Year's Eve. Everyone's still in the mood to celebrate and we could give them an extra reason.'

'Hm.' Alex considered. 'That could be lovely, but we'll still have to get a move on with arrangements – even if it is a small event.'

'I'll be disappointed if my future mum-in-law doesn't start throwing around her considerable organizing skills,' Tony said.

Alex flattened a palm on the table. Perhaps she was trying to steady herself – and that was silly. 'It's not as if this is a new idea, or as if we're in the bloom of young love!' she said without intending to speak aloud. 'Well . . . yes we are. That is, these *are* special circumstances and I'm so happy. Why didn't we do this ages ago?' She gave Tony a sidelong little grin.

'I'll let that pass,' he said, and looked about to say more but did not.

Alex took in a deep breath and blew it out slowly. 'All I want to do is talk about this good stuff, but it wasn't why I suggested getting away. I thought it would be good to talk somewhere without our locals showing up with anymore stories I'd rather not hear.'

'Always the practical one,' Tony said, but without rancor, looking around then giving a sheepish grin. 'Paranoia here. I think the coast is still clear.'

Alex took a swallow of Tony's beer. 'Thirsty,' she said. 'We've been backed into a corner . . . again. It's the old "keep this between us" routine. Which means we're not supposed to talk to the police   or anyone else – unless we're given the go-ahead. What comes next?'

'First question,' Tony said. 'What do we know about the Rum Hole? It's part of Mill House, where the Mill House Restaurant is. That's the restaurant. The Rum Hole is a jazz scene. It's a take-off on a London speakeasy – exposed brick, a lot of wood and a copper-topped bar. Cocktails rather than wine for most customers.'

Alex turned to him. 'You know a lot about it, Tony. You sound as if you've been there.'

'I have.'

There was no reason she should know everything about him, including where he had and had not been, but the idea of his going to some night scene she'd never heard of did cause a little rub. Jealousy? What an annoying thought. She sipped her drink.

Tony sat with his arms crossed, his beer in one hand. He appeared deep in thought.

'When were you there?' Alex asked. She should not have, but she was only human.

'Several years back. Harry Stroud pushed me to go with him – as his guest, he said. I put him off several times, but he wore me down. Seemed easier to go. Get him off my back.'

Alex made a face. 'Harry Stroud, of all people.'

'We were boys at more or less the same time,' Tony said. 'That's all we've had in common. He's one of those people you feel sorry for – without being sure why – and he's hard to like. For me, anyway. I shouldn't speak for other people.'

They both knew that Harry Stroud wasn't just 'hard to like'. He'd proved to be capable of frightening behavior. 'What was the club like?' Alex said.

Tony thought about it. 'Trying too hard to be special, I suppose. Could be appealing to a lot of people. I do think it's probably useful if you're looking to make business contacts in the area, but it isn't my scene. Not that I have a scene.

'I didn't appreciate the heavy sell of their "preferred guests" status. Harry made himself scarce and this fellow came over to me. The more "*valuable guests*" I could introduce to him, the more helpful he could be to me. He knew I was a vet and talked about all the animal owners who came in regularly. Funny really. But the main thrust was that goodies would come my way if I recommended someone who would be good for the Rum Hole. With more than one or two people, well, the sky's the limit. Free drinks. Peanuts on toothpicks gratis . . .'

Alex laughed.

'I should be completely honest,' Tony said. 'It's pretty plush if you like that sort of thing, but they're pretending they aren't running a modified pyramid scheme and I think they are. Or something that feels like that.'

Alex had held back from asking her main question, 'Is it just for men?' There, she had asked.

'There were women there.'

To press on or not to press on? 'Members? Couples?'

'It isn't exactly a membership club, or not as far as I could tell.' Tony gave one of his rare wicked grins. 'I'm sure they cater to all kinds of tastes.'

Alex elbowed him. 'Really?'

'Really.' Tony wasn't hiding his amusement. 'I bet they'd have whatever you asked for.'

'Yeah, I'm sure. Huge bar selection, hm? Do they specialize?'

'In the cocktails, yes. I had a "Squeaky Wheel", if I remember correctly. Different rums and licorice something, I think. Made my teeth itch.' He smirked at that. 'They're also heavy on single malts. More than fifty, I seem to remember. Seriously, I imagine it has some sort of dating scene, or whatever, but it's not obvious. What I'm trying to figure out is what Major Stroud could have meant about the dead man – Ricky Seaton – having enemies there.'

Bearing bowls of chips and cheese puffs, Art Frampton came into the lounge to ask if they wanted more drinks. They had hardly made a dent in the first round, but the nibbles were welcome. Short and broad shouldered, with a muscular physique trending soft at the edges, Art's gray hair curled forward under his ears to nestle on to his second chin.

'To what do we owe this honor?' he said, grinning and wrinkling up a shiny, red face.

'We're spying on the competition,' Alex said with a wink.

Art guffawed and sputtered, 'Don't blame you. Glad to see you anyway.' He left to make a circuit of his customers.

Leaning over the table, Tony said, 'So, any ideas what Stroud meant about Ricky Seaton and the Rum Hole?'

'Ricky Seaton probably went there.' Alex suggested. 'Do you think Major Stroud would go there? I can't imagine it. Besides, I can't remember a night when he wasn't at the Black Dog. We think Harriet may have seen the major with this Ricky Seaton.' She frowned and pushed her hands into her jacket pockets. 'At the Dog. Major Stroud admitted knowing who he is.'

Tony swung his beer glass by the rim and watched thoughtfully as the beer inside sloshed back and forth. 'That doesn't have to mean a thing as far as the murder goes though, does it?'

Alex slid back in her chair. 'No, but I don't see how we can keep the information from the police, even if it doesn't mean much. Not unless we can get Harriet and Stroud to speak for themselves.'

'Harriet's the answer. If she talks to Dan – and she does like him – but if she tells him what she thinks she saw, he'll be the one to deal with the major. After . . . I don't believe this. Look who just came in.'

Dan O'Reilly stood in the entrance to the saloon bar, surveying available tables. Inevitably, his gaze reached Alex and Tony and he didn't appear pleased to see them.

Alex bent over the table and stared into her drink. 'If I hadn't seen his face, I'd have thought he could be here to catch up with us.'

'Except we didn't tell anyone where we were going.'

'Good point, wise one.' She gave Tony a sideways smile. 'He's coming this way.'

The music stopped and, except for the crew around the bar, the volume of conversation dropped.

'Off your beaten track,' Dan said when he reached them.

'You, too.' Tony looked up, straight-faced. 'You're a long way from Gloucester.'

'I've moved,' Dan said, looking at his watch. He glanced toward the door. 'What brings you here? Hiding?'

'In a way.' He came too close to the truth and Alex felt irritated, as if she'd been caught out. 'How about you, Dan?'

'You could call this my new local. I live in Gambol Green now, have done for some weeks.'

Dan straightened. He slipped off his waxed jacket and folded it over one arm.

Tony said, 'Will you join us?'

'Er, can I buy you drinks?' Dan said.

That wasn't a *'yes, I'd love to sit with you'*, Alex thought. 'Not for me, thanks.'

Tony shook his head, no.

Dan looked at his watch again.

'What made you move to Gambol Green?' Tony asked. 'Other than it's a pretty place.'

'That was the first thing – next to how quiet it is. I'm pretty much right on the Isbourne and I can pretend I'm the only one around. And, just as important, it's good not to live too close to your work.'

'Your work seems to have followed you,' Alex said, and realized that might not have been politic. 'I mean . . .'

'Some think it was me following my work here, not the other way round,' Dan said, still without smiling. 'Not true. I did see this area for the first time – up close, that is – while I was on a case, but I like to think I'd have found it anyway.'

'You really like it here.' Tony finished his beer. 'Alex and I have been talking about the Ricky Seaton case.'

Since they were facing their cards: 'I think I saw him in a play at the tithe barn,' Alex said. 'With the Phoenix Players. Two or three months back.'

She got Dan's full attention. 'Why didn't you tell us that earlier?'

Why had she bothered to bring it up again? 'I did mention it at the Black Dog,' she said sharply. 'Then there was no opportunity to speak separately. I didn't want to open up a back-and-forth with that group who were all around us.'

'We're not in a group now. Think, Alex. You saw him at the tithe barn and had a clear enough impression to remember. Has he been to the Black Dog?'

'I don't know.'

'I find it hard to believe you wouldn't have noticed someone you remember from a stage play.'

'It was only when I sat with the picture, and Major Stroud
. . . was talking . . . We were talking about the picture.' Damn,
she had walked right into that.

She got very direct eye contact from Dan – before he checked
his watch one more time.

'Look,' Tony said. 'We're all tired. Can we go over this at
another time?'

'Why would we do that?' Dan didn't miss a beat.

Tony leaned against the back of his chair. 'To be honest; Alex
and I are in a difficult position. We need to figure out how to
deal with something carefully.'

'And I have problems that won't wait for anyone's finer feelings. I don't want added, similar problems. In other words, I do
not have time to be careful about whatever thorn you've got
under your saddle. You need to come clean now.'

'I've got nothing to come clean about – not personally.'

'Great. Then let's have whatever you're talking about.' He
checked over his shoulder and said, 'Excuse me. I've got to go.
We'll talk in the morning. You'll get a call.'

He turned away, turned back, 'Don't make any plans until you
hear from us.' And he left.

'Command appearance,' Tony muttered. 'I think someone
higher up's put a flea in his ear and he's taking it out on whoever's
nearest.'

'Could be.' Alex felt a little defensive of Dan, who was usually
in better control of his temper. While she watched, he greeted a
woman who had just entered. 'Perhaps he was just edgy,' she said.

'About what? Something other than his need to pull rank on us?'

'Yeah. About five nine, red-haired, with a terrific face and
body. I think he was afraid she wasn't coming.'

FIFTEEN

Could he justify leaving his calls on hold for a few more minutes – finally get a second morning cup of coffee – have a mental sort-out of the professional and personal crises crowding him? His brain felt like Speakers' Corner on a Sunday afternoon; filled with raised voices competing to drown out competition, and every one of those voices arguing a different point.

Beyond the windows between his office and the situation room, the desks were beginning to fill. Jumpers and scarves were in evidence. The heating had been playing up for days, damn it.

He put his elbows on the desk and rested his face in his hands. *'Do you want coffee, Dad? I brought you a cup in case.'* His son's voice that morning, trying to melt the frost that hung between them.

Calum must have heard the alarm go off at 5:15 a.m. Not long after, he had come to put a wary, slightly haggard face into Dan's bedroom, his expression showing how much he hoped his dad would start to relent about The Stunt (as Dan had dubbed it). Thinking about what might have happened on that journey from Ireland made the hair on Dan's neck prickle. He knew Calum wanted things to smooth over and for the two of them to be on good terms, but the situation was too full of potential explosives to be easily diffused.

His boy was more than half a man now. Dan scrubbed at his face. Half man but still a boy was the other way of looking at it – if that made any sense. Watching your son come out of the chrysalis was a time for fear as well as anticipation. God help them both.

The memory of last night at the Royal Chestnut slid in, a picture of Beth Wills sitting across from him with a gin and bitter lemon. They had talked easily enough, the way two people who were both raising children often did. He liked her, liked the way her face moved artlessly between emotions.

Yes, he liked her. How long had it been since he had felt that flash of genuine interest – and perhaps something more, more than basic sexual attraction? Not since Alex.

Dan skimmed over thoughts of Alex . . . Alex and Tony. Last night he had been brusque with them and he couldn't find it in him to regret that. In his profession, a line had to be drawn between the personal and the professional.

'Morning, sir,' LeJuan practically sang out as he burst into the office – without knocking – and put a coffee cup on the desk. He took a squished paper bag from beneath his arm, opened it and offered the contents to Dan.

'Good morning.' Dan extracted a slightly flattened jam donut, leaving behind a bright pink and yellow mess which had probably been a Russian Slice. 'What's this all about?'

His sergeant sat in a chair that creaked dangerously. 'I saw your car outside and decided you might have arrived too early to get your morning hit. In the interest of office relations, I hopped back quick to Costa.'

'Smartarse. Thank you, but you're still a smartarse. How did you know how badly I needed this?' Dan closed his eyes and smelled the coffee before sipping and savoring the rich, strong taste. The coffee at the station was worse than terrible.

'Sue at the shop said you hadn't been in yet today.' LeJuan raised his own coffee cup in a mock toast.

'Yeah. This is exactly what I needed. I was slammed this morning. Had to come direct.' Dan took a bite of his donut. 'Then I had an unexpected visitor waiting for me before I had a chance to get my coat off. Would only speak to me.'

'Harriet Burke, by any chance? I thought that might be her getting into a taxi as I arrived.'

'The very same,' Dan confirmed. 'Don't know what a taxi to and from Folly might cost but I swear those two sisters, or in this case the one sister, could've saved a good few pounds by just being up front when we were at the Dog last night.' Dan sighed and shook his head in frustration. 'I did offer to have her driven back, but Harriet wouldn't hear of it. Said she would be *mortified* to be dropped back home by the police.'

Dan drank some more coffee and ate another chunk of his donut – savoring the still warm raspberry jam in the middle. The two men sat in brief silence until LeJuan asked the question, 'So, you going to keep me in suspense here? What did the Burke woman have to get off her chest that was so important she needed to come here to see you rather than call?'

If it came up later, Dan would mention his brief chat with Tony and Alex the night before. Since he didn't want to bring up being out for a drink with Beth, it might not have to come up at all. He had already let Tony and Alex know he wouldn't want to talk with them this morning after all.

'Seems Harriet believes she saw Ricky Seaton with Major Stroud at the Black Dog a couple of weeks back. Wasn't confident enough to mention it last night but realized we needed to know. She sounded very sure this morning.' Dan drummed his fingers on his desk and looked at the window, where rain spattered in wind-driven bursts.

'That actually kind of fits with the major's caginess last night, doesn't it?' LeJuan said. 'He let us know he didn't want to answer any questions. Interesting how he reacts to pressure. He goes on the offensive instantly.'

'Exactly. I think Major Stroud needs to pay us a visit. Make it clear to him that we're moving beyond preliminary enquiries. No more friendly chats and taking no for an answer. His cooperation is required – no option.'

'I'm on it, sir. I'll send someone to pick him up.'

Already detectives were on the phone and stabbing at their keyboards. LeJuan stepped from the office and called out to Longlegs Liberty to bring in the major. Dan heard LeJuan suggest to Longlegs that the major not be given any special treatment. Longlegs could be intimidating for his height and dour expressions alone, but Dan chose not to point this out.

'It's good to have something – anything – new on the case,' LeJuan said as he returned to Dan's office and shut the door. 'I think it would take a lot to stop me combining the Coughlin and Seaton murders into a single case – not that it was hard to do.'

'Me, too,' Dan replied. 'Too many similarities not to. There's always the possibility of a copycat, but for now we keep the team searching for a connection between the two men.' He stood up and stretched his back. 'It's got to be there.' Walking around to the front of his desk he leaned against the edge while continuing to drink coffee.

'You're not going to like what I suggest next.' LeJuan looked wary. When Dan raised his own cup to indicate he continue, LeJuan did so. 'Leon Wolf might be what we need to help us get inside the killer's mind. This man – not many women could move those bodies – this man is smart. He's brilliant at getting in and out without leaving anything behind that he doesn't want there. At least so far. But setting up the scenes the way he has suggests neither of these murders was spur of the moment. Whoever it was, planned carefully. You've got to be wondering how long it took him to come up with it all. Supposedly different MOs but loaded with enough similarities to choke you. It feels as if he went about it coldly, then set the scene for an audience – or, to be more precise, for us. I get a feeling he may be trying to show us up, to prove how much brighter he is. He wants to make fools of us. Or am I trying too hard here?'

'No.' Dan threw his empty coffee cup into the waste basket. 'And we're all going to have to try a hell of a lot harder.'

LeJuan squeezed his eyes shut. 'We need insight into the type of killer who would do that.'

Dan grimaced. 'You have a point about Wolf, but I just don't trust the man. He never lets an opportunity pass to criticize me or question my decisions. If I didn't know better, I'd think he has it in for me. Not that I can come up with a reason why. Could be he treats everyone the same – everyone he doesn't think can do him any good. I agree on getting criminal psychological profiling, but Wolf isn't the only possibility. I'd rather approach someone else for help.'

'Well, at least you liked the general idea.' LeJuan smiled and settled down a bit in the complaining chair. 'How's Calum?'

'Making himself at home. Not sure he understands how much stress he caused his mother when she found out he had travelled all the way to my place from Ireland. He's focused on his imme- diate future. I was young once and I seem to remember being occupied with whatever was immediately in front of me. Calum wants to settle into a life here with me. How much of that is just because he doesn't want to go back to Ireland, who knows? If I would say I'm head over heels with what he's done and I'll fight to keep him with me no matter what, he'd be great. What a stunt.' Dan chuckled. 'Seriously, it's not funny, but my son perhaps inherited a bit of my stubbornness. And my intelligence, of course.'

'Clearly.' LeJuan rolled his eyes.

'At some level, that kid's proud of what he pulled off. I think the lectures from Corinne and me went in one ear and out the other. I may be putting a positive spin on it, but had I known before he showed up on my doorstep that he had set out on his own, I'd have been a mess, but I didn't know and neither did Corinne. I don't think that was an accident on his part. Thankfully, he timed his connections just right and had no delays. He told his mother he was spending the night at a friend's house. It says something about how preoccupied Corinne is that she didn't get suspicious about that; she knows Calum hasn't really made any close friends since they all moved. When I called, she sounded just as surprised as I felt when he turned up here. She actually asked me if I'd put him up to it, but then had the grace to apologize. She knows I'd never do that.'

'So, what are you going to do now?' LeJuan asked. 'Send him back after Christmas? He was coming for a visit, so he might as well stay.'

Dan rubbed the back of his head. 'Well, actually, Calum's going to stay with me for a bit even after that. At least through the end of the school year. That reminds me, I have to contact a school and see about getting him enrolled.' Dan realized LeJuan was staring at him, coffee cup half raised to his mouth. 'What? Seriously, sir? You don't talk a lot about your personal life, but I know how disappointed you were last Christmas when your ex-wife convinced you to let Calum go away with her new family for the holiday. I just assumed she would insist you put Calum on the next ferry or plane after this Christmas. That is, if she didn't say he had to go back immediately.'

Dan felt comfortable talking with LeJuan. He realized that his sergeant had become a friend over the past year, while they had been working closely together. 'Well, you're not wrong. That was Corinne's first thought, or "demand" is a better word. She was furious.'

'So what changed?'

'Corinne's new husband has accepted a job offer in California. She hadn't told me herself yet . . . looking for the right time apparently.' Dan sighed. 'Is there a right time to tell a father you want to take his only kid halfway around the world so that even the timing of phone and video calls is difficult, not to mention the logistics of visits?'

LeJuan looked appalled on Dan's behalf. 'That's horrible. Can she do that?'

'Actually, no, she can't. And I suspect that is more the reason she hadn't brought it up to me yet. The custody agreement requires my permission for Corinne to move Calum outside the UK. I agreed to Ireland, even though Calum didn't want to go, because it's at least the same time zone and Corinne deserves to be happy. But I won't agree to this. Not that it would just be me she'd have to fight.'

'What do you mean? Who . . .?' LeJuan saw Dan's raised brows and pointed look, 'Oh, Calum. So that's why he's here. Huh.'

'He told me – well, he yelled at me actually – that if she tries to move him to California he will run away again. He doesn't like living in Ireland. He misses his friends here. And me apparently.' Dan swallowed around the lump in his throat at the intensity of Calum's desire to stay with him.

'Don't look so shocked that he might want to stick around, boss. From everything I've seen, you're a great dad.'

'Thanks, LeJuan. Anyway, I think Corinne is regrouping to try and figure out a different way to sell this move to both Calum and me. In the meantime, he gets to stay for a bit. And I'm really happy about that.' LeJuan's look told Dan his partner understood the emotion was more than just happiness.

A text came in on Dan's mobile. Picking it up and reading quickly, Dan laughed. 'Speaking of the sneaky lad.' He turned the phone so that LeJuan could read the text. *Calum: Hey Dad. Ms Wills invited me to go over for lunch. I made progress cleaning up my room.* A photo of Calum's organizing efforts in the bedroom was attached.

'Like I said, making himself right at home. Ms Wills is my neighbor, Beth. She and her kids live in the cottage across from my place, Silky's Cottage.' No need to say more than that, he hoped. 'I'm giving Calum extra chores as punishment for what he did. The room he wants for his bedroom happens to be where the movers put a lot of the boxes, so he has to unpack and put the stuff away before he gets to move in there.'

LeJuan laughed. 'Well, not the worst outcome then. Free labor.'

'When you put it like that . . .' Dan laughed and let that hang. The phone on his desk interrupted the moment between the two men. 'What exceptionally helpful tip will I get this time?' Dan wondered aloud. 'My dog barked in the night – twice, once for each murder. My dog never barks . . .' Still smiling, he reached behind him and picked up the receiver without checking the readout. 'O'Reilly.' Any levity gone, Dan's eyes drifted briefly to the ceiling and he pinched the bridge of his nose with free fingers. 'Yes, sir. Be right there.'

Hanging up and looking back to LeJuan, Dan picked up his jacket, 'Looks like the shite finally hit that fan you mentioned the other night. I'm off to talk to the chief constable.' He waved off LeJuan as he started to rise from his chair. 'Just me. No need for you to deal with this. I would like a hint about why the chief constable is inserting himself into the chain of command. Chief super can't be thrilled. Do the rounds and find out if anything useful has come in. I'll leave this morning's briefing to you. When I get back, I'll want to know that Major Stroud is being brought in. Call me with anything I should know. And remind me of what needs to be done about Alex and Tony. I don't want them messing with this case.'

SIXTEEN

Conscious of promising himself to work on upping his fitness level, Dan took the stairs between floors two at a time – or at least for the first two flights. Almost tiptoeing past the super's slightly open office door, he arrived in the anteroom, where the chief constable's eagle-eyed watchdog had her desk.

'Morning, Beryl,' Dan said with his most charming smile. Beryl Harstible was short, 'comfortably' built, with gray hair tightly restrained in a bun at the crown of her head and small, glittering, almost black eyes that everyone in the building knew missed nothing.

Beryl took a significant pause before looking up at Dan. She didn't smile.

'Hi,' he said, still beaming. 'I was summoned.'

'Good morning, Chief Inspector. The chief constable instructed me to send you right in.' Despite her usual formal tone, Beryl surprised Dan with an upward twitch of her lips as she waved him toward the door to the inner office. He wasn't sure if he should feel heartened by her unaccustomed warmth or prepare himself for a bollocking.

Knocking on the door twice before entering, Dan mentally braced himself for what he expected to be a major dressing-down. He was not sure what to think when he found the chief constable was not alone. Sitting in one of the chairs in front of the desk was Leon Wolf. 'Good morning, sir. Morning, Wolf.' Dan nodded at the latter.

'Sit down, O'Reilly.' Not often one for niceties, as soon as Dan was in a chair, the chief constable went straight to the point. Dan felt as if he had been called into the headmaster's office. Winston Baily often took visible pleasure in cutting his juniors down to size. 'Two murders in two months and it's already in the news that they are likely related. Unless you made some progress overnight, you have nothing. Am I right?'

Dan bristled at the chief constable's phrasing. The unsubtle inference was that Dan was personally responsible for what the man saw as inconvenient failings. Pushing back on that would be unwise. But he was also glad to have something to report, no matter how tenuous it could be made to sound; something that nevertheless might move the case along. 'We have a possible lead as of this morning, sir. A witness believes she saw our latest victim in the Black Dog pub in Folly a couple of weeks ago. I'm having the person he was seen speaking to brought here for questioning. Just last night this man denied knowing Seaton – to me, directly.'

'I might have known Folly would be involved somehow. Isn't that the pub owned by the Duggins woman?' The ever-so-slight sneer on the chief constable's face let Dan know the man was aware he was being rude – and enjoying the fact.

'It is, sir.' Dan opted to answer the question without further comment.

'Based on your reputation for solving cases quickly I've left you alone, but I'm starting to regret that decision, O'Reilly.' The chief constable's tone oozed condescension. 'Do you believe there's a direct connection to the Folly or Underhill area? I thought we could hope you hadn't had the services of the ever-helpful Duggins this time. Tell me you didn't seek her out yet again.'

Dan was not sure how to respond to that without sounding defensive. 'I don't need to seek out members of the public for advice, sir,' he said, keeping any shortness out of his words. 'But I should show you something on a map, sir. The killings took place within two or three miles of each other. With the barn being so isolated and closed off in woods, it's easy not to immediately think of that entire area being what they've called the Playing Fields over the years. The time was when they were used for school field days, open days, fêtes and the like. They're about equal distance from Gambol Green and Folly, actually. Winchcombe's close, too, among other places.'

The chief's thin, gray hair stood in a sparse crew-cut and his face was long and thin – the rest of him was also long and thin. He kept himself in good shape and liked to make comments about the failure of any of his officers to do likewise. His habit of pushing his lips out, whistle-ready, only without the whistle, put anyone who worked for him on guard. It was a sign his mind was working on a takedown. Those lips were in position now.

'I suppose that means you're spending an inordinate amount of time on fruitless cruising around the countryside and asking questions that haven't done a damn bit of good so far. I would remind you that endless cups of tea and pieces of cake with the county gossip brigade do not, as a rule, produce much matchless information.

'Now we've got two dead men, the media are on our tail like rabid animals. I don't like it, O'Reilly. I don't like it one tiny bit. There'll be a press conference demanded before the day's out and *I am not happy!*' He'd worked up to a breathy roar. 'I hesitate to ask this, but do you think you're giving this case your best?'

'Always, sir. I always give my work top priority. One thing I do think we should be aware of is keeping what we tell the media streamlined. There are bound to be details about these cases that we don't want spread about – particularly to the killer, who doesn't need to know what we know.'

The chief constable grunted, and it was not a convinced grunt.

When Dan saw Leon Wolf open his mouth, a coil of dread formed in his stomach. Ever critical and snide, Wolf could easily make this sound so much worse. After all, he had been in on some of the conversation at the Black Dog the night before.

'Come now, Winston. That's not exactly fair to Dan, is it?' Wolf sounded reasonable.

Dan concentrated hard not to allow his mouth to drop open. On several occasions in the past, Wolf had agreed with similar thinly veiled opinions about Dan's connections to Folly, the spate of murders in the area, and to Alex Duggins. Dan was completely thrown by the man stepping up to defend him.

The chief constable's stare, which had been pinning Dan to his chair, shifted to Wolf. 'Leon, you're the one—'

Wolf cut him off. 'I've been critical of how some of the cases in Folly have been handled, but that doesn't mean I don't respect DCI O'Reilly's abilities. I would guess we have each had individuals who thought they could do our jobs better than we can. I cannot count the number of people I've met at parties who want to explain how they can 'do therapy' every bit as effectively as someone with years of training and two decades of experience. And Ms Duggins has a sharp mind, and she knows it.' Turning to Dan and giving him an encouraging smile, 'Isn't that true, DCI O'Reilly?'

Dan stared briefly into Wolf's eyes, looking for some trap, but didn't see anything but openness – which was unusual in itself. Maybe he had misjudged the man. 'Yes, that's true. Alex, Ms Duggins, seems to turn up around ongoing cases. Not that I think she goes hunting for trouble, but it has an uncanny habit of coming her way, and she can't seem to turn her back when it does. She means well, but she's put herself in danger several times. In spite of being warned off. I assure you I've never encouraged her. Quite the reverse.' Dan stopped himself from saying anything further. He flinched slightly at the traitorous feeling that he was betraying Alex. She meant well and had provided key evidence for several of his cases in and around Folly. But Leon had handed him the perfect opening to hopefully shift the chief constable's attention from Alex and back to the current case, not that he had any groundbreaking answers. This case was different from any past case.

Dan remembered LeJuan's suggestion from earlier. Something he wouldn't have seriously considered even fifteen minutes prior. 'Actually sir, I think Dr Wolf might be able to offer valuable assistance on the current cases.' Dan caught Wolf's slight smile before they both turned to face the chief constable.

The chief constable looked at each one of them in turn, smiled and then chuckled. Dan couldn't remember ever seeing or hearing him do so before. 'I'm starting to wonder if I actually woke up this morning. To have Leon here defend you, O'Reilly, and then to have you ask for his assistance, after keeping him at arm's length for the past year, well, it arouses my curiosity. Curiosity I plan to ignore for the time being as in this instance I agree with you.' He laced his fingers together, paused, and looked at each man in turn. 'Two murder scenes that appear to have been staged. Both victims male and of similar age. The second victim was actually posed on a stage. I might suggest you consider whether the killer is trying to let you know he's out to best you. And he's laughing at you while he does it. But a psychologist of Leon's caliber should definitely be an asset to your investigation.'

'Agreed, sir,' Dan responded, with more heartiness than he felt.

'Leon, are you still willing – and do you have the time – to work with O'Reilly and his team?'

Wolf took a few seconds to look at Dan, who felt as if the bulbous and intense stare was an attempt to read Dan's mind before the man said, 'Yes, of course. This appears to be my area of expertise. I'm glad to offer any help I can.'

'Good. It's settled then.' The chief constable rose from his chair. Dan and Leon Wolf did the same. 'Leon, shall we grab lunch?' said the chief constable.

'Actually Winston, I hope you won't mind if I beg off this time. Dan and I have been trying to find time to meet and get to know and relate to each other better. I've got a few things to catch up on first and Dan's obviously slammed, but late afternoon today seems like a good time to make that happen. You up for that, Dan?'

With the chief constable looking at him, Dan immediately felt back on the spot. Before he could agree or come up with an excuse to decline, the chief constable chose for him. 'Great idea as usual, Leon. You two should enjoy a pint and unwind a bit. Not usually so easy to do when you're on a difficult case.' Dan nodded and headed toward the door with Wolf on his heels.

As Dan opened the door, the chief constable, who had sat back down and didn't look up called out, 'O'Reilly, I expect movement in this case soon. Give it your full attention.'

Dan wondered briefly if the chief constable had heard about Calum's arrival, but dismissed that from his mind as unlikely. 'Yes, sir. Of course.' He wished he didn't feel suspicious of Wolf's sudden about-face toward him. He allowed the man to precede him out the door and then shut it after them.

As they walked through the outer office toward the hall, Beryl gave them both another of her pinched smiles and said, 'Good luck, gentlemen.'

'Thank you, Beryl,' Dan and Wolf said in unison, while Dan wondered why exactly she thought they needed good luck.

He was being paranoid; not a good idea in the company of a

psychologist who probably didn't like him but who had the ear of the big boss.

Once in the hall, Dan turned to Wolf, ready to give an excuse for needing to postpone their meeting again, but Wolf, perhaps knowing what Dan had in mind, spoke first. 'Before you come up with a reason to duck out on that beer, I think we could both benefit from working together. I know I can be heavy-handed at times, but I'm prepared to work on that. This case is nothing if not interesting. To me, that is. Probably frustrates the hell out of you. I'd really like to be involved – not to get under your feet, though. D'you understand? Can we meet halfway?'

Dan had already realized Wolf's knowledge could be useful to his team. Was it possible the man actually had good intentions? Surely, he could survive an hour or so with Leon Wolf. 'Of course, and I wasn't going to try and duck out on you.' Not exactly true, but Wolf didn't need to know that. 'Could we make it quite a bit later? We could touch bases as we see how the afternoon goes. My son's home alone – not that he isn't perfectly capable – but he's just settling in with me and I want him to know I'm available to him even if I'm buried by work. I'd like to do a quick drive-by and see how he's doing. Then I've got a couple of leads to follow up.' Bit of an exaggeration, but hey-ho.

'That would be better timing for me, too,' Leon said, checking his watch, then glancing through the windows at rain that was definitely mixed with snow. 'Might even manage to get home reasonably early afterwards. That would be a treat. I'm glad you've got your family priorities straight. Wish more people would pay some attention to that.'

'Thanks,' Dan said. Why did he find it hard to look this man in the eye? He had to concentrate on not letting his gaze slide away. 'Do you have a place in mind? I'll be ready for a pint and whatever they've got to eat by then.'

Leon Wolf smiled. 'Good to hear. Shall we try for your local again? I liked the look of it. And I believe that puts us close to the first murder scene—'

'Both scenes, really.' Dan cut him off and shook his head. 'Sorry to barge in. One of our sergeants, Cyril Chesney, grew up in a village out that way. He says when he was in school those were the playing fields for a lot of kids. Cricket, football, hockey, track and field. The barn where Ricky Seaton's body was found was used for school plays at one time. The two scenes aren't far apart, and they're definitely as close to Folly and Underhill as they are to Gumbol Green. Anyway, you were saying something.'

Leon pulled car keys from his pocket and worked out a small brown leather-bound notebook. 'If there's time, maybe you could walk me through your conclusions at the sites. And I do have thoughts about what kind of person we're looking for.'

Discussing the case with Wolf? Dan's jaw tensed at the idea, but he could do that. 'Yes. The Royal Chestnut in Gambol Green. I'll meet you there. Give me a jingle when you're ready to be on your way.' And he had never felt more certain that the jury on Wolf's intentions would remain out until the end of all this.

SEVENTEEN

Paying the taxi driver to wait for her would have been a step too far, Harriet thought. Really, she was not herself today. Making up her mind to go to Gloucester and see Dan O'Reilly had quite taken the stuffing out of her.

If her sister Mary could see her now, standing irresolute (Harriet was convinced absolutely no one could imagine her being irresolute), but here she was, irresolute. Well, first Mary would roll her eyes and tut, then she would laugh, loudly. 'Cackle' would be a better description.

Harriet turned quickly, a hand half-raised, almost certain she would signal for the taxi to come back and bear her home. The wretched thing was gone and her twenty-pound notes with it. And here she was at one end of the village green – in Gambol Green – looking from one building to another with no idea where to find Henry and Judith Childs, miniature painter and bookseller respectively, the latter: 'Mostly used but stringently curated.' She rather thought any sign would be tasteful, apparently too tasteful to be evident.

The plan on leaving that police building in Gloucester had been to go directly home. And she had – almost. The taxi, with Harriet peering anxiously between the two front seats as they reached the outskirts of Folly, had drawn to a stop to allow two mums with toddlers in pushchairs and two rather disreputable terriers of some kind trotting beside them, to cross the road. And, gosh, that had been that. 'I've changed my mind, driver,' Harriet had said. 'Take me to Gambol Green instead please.' And that had most definitely been that. After all, how often did she actually go somewhere on her own? And since she was out and there was somewhere she wanted to go . . . why not?

Gambol Green was only a few miles from Folly, but Harriet couldn't remember when she had last been there. At one end of the green stood St Hubert's Anglican Church, a beautiful golden stone Norman building – complete with impressive tower – and with a scrumptious half-timbered lychgate. It would be criminal for the gate not to be adorned with blowsy climbing roses – in the appropriate season, of course – but leafless vines looked promising in that regard.

A cup of tea was what she needed, and perhaps a toasted tea cake, hot with lots of melted butter. First, she had been up much too early that morning. Then she had tussled with Mary over the plan to take a taxi to Gloucester and talk to Dan. '*Tell him to come here,*' Mary had commanded, with no thought to the fact that Harriet had made a mistake in not talking to him at the Black Dog the night before. Not that Mary knew anything about that, and Harriet intended to keep it that way. Come to that, for once she would rather her sister didn't get involved with what might, with good fortune, remain a very insignificant issue between Harriet and Dan. In fact, it might be all over and forgotten by now.

So, the less attention drawn, the better. But whatever she had paid for the taxi was a small price in order to foil prying eyes from seeing her arrive back in Folly in a police car. It had been disquieting to turn down Dan's offer in that regard, and Harriet did hope she had not sounded rude, or ungrateful. She shuddered.

This wouldn't do, all this shilly-shallying about. The way she had behaved when she'd left Gloucester went to show how true it was that one's mind often had a will of its own. The extraordinary feeling that she wanted to do something construc-tive before going home had been irresistible. The miniature paintings had popped into her head, and so off she'd gone to find the Childs in Gambol Green to reach out a hand of friendship and let them know how serious she was about their little venture; and here she was. In fact, it was now getting past lunchtime. Perhaps a sandwich first would be appropriate.

A black-and-white sign set into a wall let it be known it was Duck Walk that ran between the village green and a terrace of three, three-story Georgian houses, bunched companionably together with three immaculate cottages on one side. They faced St Hubert's Church. Freshly resolute, as was only appropriate, Harriet perused the terraced houses and saw with pleasure that one lone, whimsical green and yellow board, decorated with painted flowers, announced: 'As You Like It'. Deli sandwiches, pies, soups, salads, fresh cakes, biscuits and fancies daily. Smoothies, best coffee and tea in the county. As joint proprietor of Folly's 'Leaves of Comfort', Harriet took issue with that claim, but everyone was entitled to a little creative license.

Watching where she stepped, Harriet carefully crossed the walk, her shoes squelching into shallow mud where she imagined many, many a duck had trodden before her. She glanced up to plan her heading and picked out another sign, white on black, extremely (overly) tasteful and extremely small, 'Get An Eyeful', almost hidden beneath a window. The sign screamed, 'Don't find our book and miniature shop unless you really want to.' How unfortunate.

Drawn to bow-fronted windows, she decided lunch could wait and made a beeline for the open cottage door. Business called.

Old books and linseed oil. Harriet sniffed the air inside 'Get An Eyeful' with deep appreciation. The first two rooms inside the cottage formed Henry Childs' gallery. She noted that, rather than crowd miniatures closely together – and she understood that the man produced an amazing number – the paintings were treated with the artistic respect they deserved. They were arranged mostly in groups, some by different angles on the same scene, others according to season but of different subjects, and still more to suggest mood, or by complementary hues; the pieces drew Harriet to them.

Standing in this shop, she was excited, glad for the opportunity to talk with these people. This was her kind of place, and books and paintings were her kinds of treasures. She was sure that when she found the books, she would be right about the whole shop.

There was no sign of life, or so Harriet thought until she heard someone singing along – suddenly belting out off-key – to what she immediately recognized as a recording of Vera Lynn singing the old World War II song, 'We'll Meet Again', on a radio. The voice came forcefully down the stairs. An arrow on one banister pointed up with the instruction, 'This way to Books and More Books.'

The vigor of the singing was a little intimidating, but after checking a second main-floor room and finding it empty except for more paintings, Harriet climbed the stairs somewhat hesitantly and emerged to see a woman on a ladder, shelving books – and singing.

Harriet waited until the piece finished before saying, 'Hello, there,' as firmly as she could muster.

The woman swung around, teetering alarmingly on the ladder. 'Hello, hello,' she said. 'I say, turn off the radio for me, would you?'

Locating the piece of equipment on a table, and mostly hidden by sheets of stock printouts, Harriet did as she was asked – quite reluctantly. 'My mother used to love Vera Lynn,' she said, too loudly now the radio was no longer in full voice. 'I think she was a real wartime sweetheart.'

'Yes, yes. And lately she's become popular again, but you probably know that.' She descended the ladder and bustled toward Harriet with an outstretched hand. 'Judith Childs at your service. Are you looking for something in particular?'

The woman's eagerness made Harriet pause before launching into the subject of the miniatures. On this floor, every inch of wall was covered with books. She looked around and spied a lovely little children's section, complete with three brightly painted miniature benches ranged around a small table piled with books and puzzles.

'I have a friend in Folly-on-Weir. I expect you know Folly.'

'I do indeed,' the woman said with alacrity. 'I'm Judith Childs, by the way.'

Harriet barely stopped herself from saying '*I know.*'

'Books are my department,' Judith continued. 'My husband, Henry, has all the talent in the family and paints the *plein air* pieces you passed downstairs.' She gave a nasal laugh. 'And up one, of course. He is so good, and so incredibly fast.'

'Erm, yes.' Harriet gathered her thoughts again. 'How nice to meet you. I was going to say that my good friend, Alex Duggins, collects children's books – whenever she has a little time to herself. She's very busy. I know she will want to come and look. In fact, I'll have you pick something out for me today so that I can take her a little present, just to whet her appetite.'

'Something old? Something new?' Judith rubbed her small, white hands together. She brought to mind a charmingly plump brown bird, with shining dark eyes and a pretty, round face. Her long, lustrous brown hair, plaited down her back, swung from side to side with her energetic movements.

Harriet's mind went blank. 'Surprise me,' she said, feeling like a failure.

Judith pinched her chin between finger and thumb and drew her brows together. Then she clapped her hands and said, 'I've got it. *Our White Violet* by Kay Spen. One of my regulars brought it in the other day. They say it was Agatha Christie's favorite childhood book.' In only a few moments Judith held a volume aloft. Worn brown-leather binding with gold lettering and a spine that had peeled in places, it immediately grabbed Harriet's attention.

'It looks marvelous,' she said. 'I know Alex would love it.' She hoped Alex didn't already have a copy but, if so, was sure it could be exchanged for something else.

'Published in 1869,' Judith said, leafing through the first pages. 'A treasure.'

'I'll take it,' Harriet said, then added a bit sheepishly, 'I should ask how much it is, though.'

'Forty pounds. But if that's too much, I can take some off for you.'

Not a seasoned businesswoman, Judith Childs. 'That will be fine,' Harriet said. 'And I've got swept away from the reason I came to see you. I'm Harriet Burke. My sister Mary and I own Leaves of Comfort. It's a tea shop in Folly.' She looked expectantly at Judith.

The other woman frowned, clearly puzzled. 'That does sound familiar. Henry is always painting so I don't get out very much, except to book sales wherever I can find them.'

'Perhaps I should be speaking to your husband.' Harriet crossed her arms over the book. 'A local businesswoman, Elly Fermer, brought a box of his paintings to us with a proposition that we consider selling them in our shop. I think they're going to be a big success.'

'Oh! Oh, yes, of course!' Judith tutted. 'That's what jogged my memory about your shop. Henry will be so put out to have missed you. He's somewhere in Chipping Campden, working, of course, and he turns off his phone. Can't bear to be interrupted when he's in the mood – or is that the *zone* these days?'

Harriet smiled, but thought that Henry sounded a bit

self-involved, superior even. 'Yes, well. My sister and I will be delighted to carry Mr Childs' miniatures. We think they will fit in perfectly at Leaves of Comfort. He should have our card – Mrs Fermer gave it to him, I think – but I'll leave another just in case. I came today on a whim. Didn't even know if I'd catch you, but I hoped to meet you and put our little joint venture on a firmer footing. Perhaps you could call us and we'll arrange a time to meet – with your husband, too, of course – and discuss things.'

'Yes!' Judith took the card. 'We'll phone this evening, if that's all right.'

'Absolutely. But I can't leave without telling you about a success we already had with Mr Childs' miniatures. We showed them to a dear friend – she's the one who collects children's books – and she insisted on buying the one we have of Tindale Tower just outside Folly. What do you think of that? And she's an artist herself.'

Judith bit her lip and her eyes looked suspiciously moist. 'He is so good,' she said with a little sniff. 'I'm very glad your friend likes that. Is it the one in the afternoon, in the sun? The sky is very blue?'

'Yes, that's it. Alex is going to hang it in the main bar at the Black Dog. And – and I think this could be wonderful – she wants to hang more of the paintings in the pub because she thinks people would really like to buy them. There would be little cards with the title, the artist and price on them. You know what I mean.'

'Oh, my. The Black Dog. I have been there and it's such a lovely pub.' Judith frowned and her bright eyes narrowed. 'You mean *that* Alex Duggins? Of course you do.'

'You know Alex? What a coincidence.'

'I don't *know* her, but most people know *about* her, don't you think? This is odd, Harriet. May I call you, Harriet?' At Harriet's nod, the other woman gave a quick smile. 'Yes, it's odd because I was only thinking today that I wouldn't be surprised if Alex Duggins is involved in these horrible killings.'

'Involved? What killings?' Harriet's breathing shortened.

'I suppose they are what they call *serial* killings, even though there's just two of them. I mean, two must be enough to call

them a serial, mustn't they? Gosh, that sounds awful. I have a
way of putting things badly sometimes. What I meant was that
with the man dying over at the cricket club – beaten to death with
a cricket bat' – she shuddered – 'and then this other poor fellow
stabbed so many times in that tithe barn in front of an audience
for some Shakespeare thing, it sounds bizarre enough for Alex
Duggins to be on the case. He must have got away or they
wouldn't be hunting for him, would they? Hunting the murderer,
I mean, not the dead man.'

Goosebumps popped on Harriet's arms. She wished the benches
were adult sized. 'That isn't quite right, you know. Dear Alex
has been helpful in a number of cases around Folly, it's true, but
she doesn't go around looking for bizarre, erm, *happenings*.' This
wasn't at all how she had imagined this encounter going. 'Alex
works things out. Says she isn't clever, of course. But that's the
sort of woman she is. Unpretentious. Mostly, she's determined
and brave, if a bit headstrong sometimes. Anyway, what were
you saying?'

'Too much. As usual. It's just that we aren't used to this sort
of thing around here. We're quiet, peaceful people. But with a
prowler shining his torch into windows at night, the way he did.
On the very night of the Shakespeare killing, one feels *personally*
involved, even though one isn't.'

Judith, Harriet decided, was a gentle woman given to the
understandable vice of gossip, and she had upset herself with
her own chatter. 'These things are upsetting,' she said soothingly.
'We've had far more than our share of nasty events in Folly. It's
been awful.'

'My friend Daphne,' said Judith. 'I know you two would get
on ever so well. I'm not supposed to share this – Daphne only
told me – but I feel a bond forming with you and it's not unreasonable to need someone to share such a thing with. Imagine
how she feels about a prowler shining a torch into the windows
in that little spot where she lives. So few of them there, you
know – very isolated. This prowler person could have been the
murderer, don't you think?'

EIGHTEEN

Dan opened his front door . . . straight into a wobbly stack of packing crates. 'Calum!' He pushed as hard as he dared and gradually inched open a wide enough space to step in sideways. 'Calum – you here?'

The boxes – apparently empty, thank God – tipped sideways before Dan could execute a catch. Or try to. The damn things went everywhere.

'Calum!'

Headed for the stairs, he kicked debris out of his path before he was met by Busy the Beagle, whose joy at seeing him might have been uplifting if the dog hadn't taken a running jump and left dust and white hairs all over Dan's suit.

Calum arrived behind the dog. 'Hey, Dad. What're you doing home?'

He quelled the urge to say that he lived here. No point in taking his short temper out on his boy. 'Meeting in Gambol Green a bit later – quite a lot later really. But I've got to follow up on something in Folly and check back in at the station. I'm on my way to Folly first but I wanted to see how you're doing. From the picture you sent, it looks as if you're making a lot of progress.' Calum's smile shamed him into adding, 'I thought I'd see if you fancy picking out fresh paint for your room. Looks as if you'll be able to move in soon.' He knuckled a box. Just what he needed, another room to paint while he had a tough case on.

'I'll paint it,' Calum said eagerly. 'I paint for Mum. It's a wicked room. I always wanted a dormer window. And there's a tree right outside. It'll be wicked if it really snows on it. I'm going to save up for stained glass, if that's OK. I'd ask you to help me choose. You pick out the pattern and colors and they make it before they bring it to you. They put it in, of course. Mum did it in the front windows in Dublin. It's the only thing I like about that house.' He turned a bit pink around the edges. 'I mean . . . this is a cool place, Dad.'

'Great.' How could he not react to the boy's enthusiasm? 'We'll see about the stained glass. We have to get you a new bed. Maybe one of those with drawers underneath to give you more storage. And we could build some bookshelves. Nothing fancy. I reckon we'd be after managing some of those with blocks you put the boards on.'

'That'd be wicked, Dad!' Calum punched a fist into the air and swept Busy into his arms. 'We can do it all, can't we boy? Mrs Wills says Busy likes it here best – in Canal Cottage, I mean. He waits outside and runs in when you open the door. I always wanted a dog. Mrs Wills makes killer lunches.'

'We shouldn't be luring Busy in with us,' Dan said. It was true that Calum had asked for a dog many times, but it was hard to do when there was usually no one home all day. 'I'm not saying I don't like having him. He's a fine little fella. But it wouldn't be good if the owners were to think we were encouraging him away from his home. It's always best to get along with your neighbors if you can.'

'They let him run on his own all day, Dad,' Calum said. 'Mrs Wills said so, too. They've been gone all today and he's shut out. He's got a doghouse in the garden, but he doesn't like it. Doesn't like his mucky dishes, either.'

Dan laughed. 'Told you that, did he?'

'You can tell when a dog's bothered.' Calum turned the corners of his mouth down and narrowed his eyes. It was a look Dan remembered too well – ready to argue if necessary. 'I did try to take him back but, like I said, they were out and the weather's rotten. He wasn't about to go in the doghouse. He followed me and made a giant ruckus at the gate, so I let him out and kept him with me so he'd be safe. I used a piece of string as a lead and got him out for a couple of walks. He's great company, and how can we not be doing those people a favor by keeping him happy when we can? He likes being around me and he's a smart one. He's wicked.'

Wicked? Word of the day. Dan was getting old – or tired. He'd take tired.

His mobile rang and he answered, 'Yes, LeJuan.'

'How's it going, boss? You on your way back?' His partner's deep voice sound unenthusiastic.

'Just stopped by home. I'm going into Folly for a quick word with Alex and Tony. After my meeting with the chief constable, I think I'd better make sure they understand that they won't be doing us a favor by sticking their noses in.'

Dan heard LeJuan mutter something that might have been, 'They've done us favors before,' but he chose not to engage on that. He continued, 'Late afternoon I'm meeting Leon Wolf at the Royal Chestnut. Supposedly we're having a bit of getting-to-know-you time. If it sounds unlikely to you, it sounds more than that to me. Could be your idea about psychological profiling might be in the works.'

'Yeah?' LeJuan gave a short laugh. 'I hope you'll have time to give me a report afterwards.'

'You bet. But don't hold your breath in case it doesn't go anywhere. Did anything useful come up at the briefing?'

'Not really. But I think having a few more tidbits brought up the team's spirits.' He cleared his throat. 'We didn't get anything useful from talking to the Phoenix Players. Mostly they were annoyed at being questioned again, although they were pretty upset about Ricky Seaton. He was the glue that held it all together, by the way. Fundraiser in chief, principal thespian, final word on all decisions, including about which plays they put on. But, like I said, nothing too useful.

'I went to see the farmer who found Ricky Seaton's body to see if he could tell me who had access to the barn. Little bit more interesting there. He said he'd heard one of two sets of keys went missing a few weeks back. He knows because someone from the theater group asked him if he had a set. He didn't and he didn't hear any more about it. It's probably nothing.'

Dan thought for a moment before saying, 'We'll file that just in case. Anything else?'

'Major Stroud's still being a pain in the arse.'

'I haven't forgotten Stroud. I intend to be back at the station to talk to him—'

'You might want to hold up on that until you hear from one of us,' LeJuan said quickly. 'Longlegs is hanging around Folly waiting for the major to show up. His wife said he was due back a couple of hours ago. We're thinking she may have told him the police had come calling and he's gone to ground. Legs is at the Black Dog grabbing a bite and staying close. Mrs Stroud told him she'd call as soon as the major showed.'

Stroud was an arrogant man. 'Sod him. We don't have time for messing around. The chief constable's champing at the bit. I was going to Folly anyway to poke about a bit. I'll see if I can help Longlegs scare up Stroud. I might drive by his house. The fool's playing us, don't ask me why. Could be we should be looking at him harder.'

'I'm going to drive through Underhill on the way to Folly. They're only a couple of miles apart – with a hill in between.' Dan grinned at Calum, who looked overly pleased to be in the passenger seat of the Lexus and on his way somewhere . . . anywhere, if Dan read his son's expression accurately. 'You need to orient yourself anyway. I'll drop you in Folly and you can poke around a bit. There's more there than you'd think from just driving through.' Something more to eat would probably be a good idea, too. His son had a reputation for his hearty appetite.

'That'll be great!'

At least it was not 'wicked'. 'We'll have to look into a new bike for you. When I moved I brought your old one, but it's too small.'

'It was too small before I left.' Calum chortled at the thought. 'Jack Wills doesn't have a bike. We could put blocks on the pedals and give my old one to him. If he doesn't have a helmet, my old one might do for him, too.'

'Nice idea.' Dan glanced at his boy sideways. He sounded happy and interested. It was pleasing to hear him looking out for the Wills boy, never having had a younger kid in his life before.

There was more snow mixed with the rain now, Dan decided, not that he minded. Winter was his favorite season. Watery snow, like globs of cuckoo spit, swelled in the joints of twigs and branches along the roadsides. The sky and the land melded together into a viscous haze, and flakes of graying snow swarmed the windscreen, melting on touch.

'It's nice out here,' Calum said, wiping at condensation on the inside of his window. 'Quiet. I always thought I liked living in busy places best, but that was when we were in Gloucester.

Dublin's OK but it never felt like home. This feels right to me, this place. You don't have to worry about me, you know, Dad.'

Dan cast him a rapid look. 'It's normal for parents to worry about their kids, Calum.'

'That's not what I mean.'

A motorbike overtook, spraying a noisy fan of gritty slush across the windscreen. Dan slowed down and let the wipers deal with the mess.

'I meant I'm OK. I'm here because I want to be and I don't expect you to run me around all over the place or entertain me . . . unless you have loads of spare time to use up, and you want to entertain me.' Calum laughed. 'Year and a half and I'll be driving.'

Dan didn't say how the uncertainty about their future weighed on him. 'Scary thought,' he said lightly. 'You'd better start saving for a clunker in perfect condition.' There would be rough days ahead before he and Corinne got Calum's living arrangements settled. He wanted to keep things level between them, for all of their sakes, but he couldn't agree to Calum living in California.

'Perfect condition and clunker? Oxymoron there, Dad. The perfect clunker, I mean. I'm gonna get a job. You said you didn't think I'd go back to school until January, so I've got time to look for one.'

Calum was clearly planning ahead, as if Gambol Green had become his permanent home. Dan made a noncommittal noise. He wasn't ready to move on to the deeper issues facing them. If he was honest with himself, there didn't seem to be a reasonable resolution to the dilemma that was keeping him awake at night.

'This is Underhill?' Calum peered from his side window then leaned forward to look through the windscreen. 'I hope it looks better when the sun shines. Looks like a village everyone forgot.'

'Good people live here,' Dan said. He felt honor bound to speak up for underdogs, even underdog villages. 'It is a bit run-down, I'll give you that.' A row of gray houses on either side of the road with peeling paint around most windows and on doors. Cottages, some well-kept if a bit shabby; some just shabby. A bargain store, its sagging striped awning open: 'The Polka Dot', with some of its many large turquoise dots peeling off its sign – baskets of cheap plastic clogs, tennis shoes, kiddies' clothes, kitchen gadgets, crockery, brooms and garden rakes on the pavement in front.

They were almost to Folly when Calum said, 'Look at that place,' with awe in his voice. 'It's huge.'

'Yes, indeed.' As luck would have it, *that place* was The Vines, home to Major Stroud and his wife, Venetia. 'I'd forgotten how close it was to Folly. I know the people who live there. Or one of them, anyway – Major Stroud.' Dan closed his mouth on any other comments he might have made about the cantankerous major.

He slowed a little to look at the multi-angled stone roofs and tall chimneys of The Vines, which were all that could be seen of the Strouds' mansion on its grassy knoll. Spike-topped green iron fencing and soaring yew hedges surrounded the property.

Just as a stone gatepost came into view, dramatic wrought-iron gates swept inward. Curiosity made Dan pull to the side and idle while a Range Rover nosed its way out.

Alex Duggins's Range Rover.

Holy shit. One way or another, Dan decided, he was going to need a few pointed words with Alex. Her visit to the Strouds' home might have nothing to do with the current investigation, but as far as he was aware, Alex was not on chatty terms with the couple; in fact, there had once been an incident when things had turned decidedly nasty between Venetia Stroud and Alex.

'Sit tight,' he said, pulling the car higher on the verge and getting out. He tapped the horn to get Alex's attention and she looked startled. 'I need a word with this lady.'

His shoes sank into spongy grass and the snow-laced rain drove straight into his face and down his neck.

Alex rolled her window down. 'I'm just leaving now,' she called. 'Won't take me a minute to get out of your way.'

You won't get away that easily. 'I'd like a few words, if that's OK.' *Or if it isn't.*

He made for the driver's door but she waved him around the bonnet, 'Get in. You're going to be soaked.'

Grateful, he did as she suggested – after almost slipping backward down the bank. He sat beside her, trying to ignore the wet knee of his right trouser leg.

'Are you arresting juveniles today?' Alex grinned and indicated

Calum's wavy shape behind the wet windscreen of the Lexus. 'Is that your son? I think it was someone from Gambol Green who was in this morning – at the Black Dog – and mentioned he was staying with you.'

Dan wasn't in the mood to joke, least of all about the overactive local gossip machine. 'That's Calum, yes. Are you a friend of the Strouds – I mean, other than owning the pub the major frequents?'

'Why would you ask, Dan?' She raised her eyebrows. Despite his irritation at seeing her in this venue at this particular time, she had the same effect on him as always – he felt he knew her and liked what he knew. He sat back and looked straight ahead. This was strictly business and he must make sure he conveyed that impression.

She touched his arm and he stiffened.

'Dan, what is it?'

'That was a simple question. I didn't mean it to sound abrupt. I was surprised to see you here.'

'Venetia Stroud phoned and asked if I'd come down and chat,' she said. 'That's all.'

'The last I knew, you weren't on chatting terms exactly.' He kept his gaze on the opposite side of the road.

'No. That was all an odd time. Unpleasant. Venetia has apologized for it, but I know she was in a very difficult space and trying to do what she thought was best for her son.' Alex grimaced.

He cleared his throat and looked at her again. 'I'm going to have to talk to her myself. Do you think it would help if I knew why she phoned you?'

'I've told you. She wanted to . . . talk.'

'Was it anything to do with her husband?'

Muscles around her mouth tightened. 'Yes.'

He didn't like this anymore than she did. 'OK. I'm sorry if I've made you uncomfortable. Thanks for talking to me.'

'She's worried because you sent someone to pick up the major and take him to Gloucester for questioning.' The words came in a rush. 'She wanted to know if that meant you suspect him of a crime – something to do with the men who've been murdered. She's very worried.'

'Yes.' He crossed his arms and considered. 'Did she mention

that Major Stroud is suddenly nowhere around? One of my officers has been trying to meet up with him for most of the day.'

'I think you should ask them about this.'

'You're right.'

'Please go a bit lightly with Venetia – if you can. I don't think her life is particularly easy and she's had a difficult day. She wouldn't have called me, otherwise.'

'Why did she call you – really?'

Alex closed her eyes. 'Because, and this isn't a good or a right reason, she thought I would have some idea about the way you might be thinking. As far as the major's concerned. Silly, I know, but—'

'It's not your fault.' He cut her off, but he meant what he said – for now. For a moment or two, he thought quietly. 'I think I'll put off going to see Mrs Stroud. There's something else I should do first.' Not really, but he could make an argument for having a few words with Legs to get his report so far.

'I'd love to meet Calum,' Alex said. 'You've mentioned him so many times, I feel I know him.'

Dan drew in a slow breath. 'I'm going to the Dog. My officer's there. I'll get Calum to wait in the restaurant and you can meet him there – if you're going back now.'

'He can go in the snug. We often use that as a family room.' Her car phone rang and she switched on. 'Harriet. How are you?'

'Not wonderful, I'm afraid,' came Harriet Burke's voice over the speaker.

With his fingers on the door handle, Dan paused and reached down to tie his shoe. If Harriet said anything of interest to him, he might have to stall getting out.

'What's the trouble?' Alex asked.

'You're the only one I can talk to. The only one who will understand and know what I should do next. I don't want to . . . I've been in Gambol Green. To meet the people with the miniature paintings. I met the wife, Judith Childs. Lovely person. But she told me something that's really got me all bothered.'

Dan struggled against what he knew he should do – get out of the vehicle. He took his mobile from his trouser pocket and went to put it inside his jacket. The mobile slithered from his hand to the floor.

'Can this wait a little while, Harriet dear?'

'They've had a prowler in Gambol Green. He was there the night that second poor man was murdered and some of the locals think he – that's the prowler – could be the murderer.'

Alex gave Dan a meaningful look, which he ignored. He grabbed up the phone and made no further attempt to get out of the car.

'I called you because you always know the best thing to do about these matters,' Harriet said. 'Do you think I'll have to go and speak to Dan O'Reilly again? After this morning, I'll be mortified if I do.'

'Where are you, Harriet?' Dan said. Giving her a shock might not be strictly by the book but could sometimes yield an incautious, and honest, response.

Silence ensued. He met Alex's eyes and got the kind of annoyed look he expected. At least she didn't attempt to interfere.

'I'm walking to the Black Dog,' Harriet said finally. 'I was about to ask Alex when she plans to be back here. As I assume you heard, I have something to discuss with her. May I take it that's not against the law – talking to Alex, that is?'

'You can,' he told her. The vehicle's windows were now completely steamed up, but he could feel the temperature dropping. 'I'll give you time to do that. Very shortly, I should think. Afterwards you and I should meet for a chat. *Another* chat. And that will also be short. Silly gossip can get dangerous. It needs to stop.'

He leaned to flip off the speaker.

NINETEEN

D an O'Reilly infuriated, rigidly controlling his temper but not so well that it didn't glitter in dark eyes that had turned ice-sharp, and in a muscle that twitched in his cheek – this was not the Dan O'Reilly Alex wanted to be around.

'Look,' she said tentatively, and cleared her throat. 'Please hold on, Dan. Stay calm.'

'Stay calm?' He pushed open the car door but didn't take his eyes from hers. 'People don't usually tell me to stay calm, Alex. I'm a calm man. But I do have limits to my patience and you Folly people could be about to push through those limits.'

'Yes.' She kept her tone contrite but was starting to feel royally ticked off. None of this was her fault. Sure, she would shoulder part of the blame just because she was in the wrong place at the wrong time, but she wanted him to give her a chance to speak her piece.

'Yes, what?' His voice had gone soft, soft in a way that could be intimidating if she let it be.

What did Lily always say? '*You have to lie down to be a doormat.*' Well, Lily's daughter was no doormat. 'Yes, I'm aware of the authority that goes with your job and your position. I know you're good at that job. And I truly regret any annoyance I've caused you . . . but I haven't done anything for you to make me a target of your frustration.'

He chose that moment to dig his ever-present bag of sweets from a jacket pocket and work free a sticky sherbet lemon. He slid it inside his cheek and sucked thoughtfully.

He didn't offer her a sweet.

He did let the door swing shut again – unfortunately.

'I want a discussion with you and Tony.' An order, not a request.

'In Gloucester?' she asked. 'When?'

'This afternoon, after I've talked to Harriet Burke. I'm here so it might as well be in Folly.'

'I should really get back to work, then,' she said, and cracked her window open to let in some air, even if it was icy. 'I told Hugh I wouldn't be gone long and that was too long ago. And I must have a few words with Harriet, first. She's a good person, kind, generous.'

'You do find positive qualities in your village friends, don't you?'

She ignored that. 'So you're meeting Harriet at the Black Dog, too. I'll make sure my chat with her is short.'

'I didn't say I was meeting her there. I intended to get together with her at Leaves of Comfort. Probably fewer distractions in her flat.'

'You didn't mention going to Leaves of Comfort. I think Harriet wants to meet you at the pub because she doesn't want Mary to know she's talking to you again.'

He took a notebook from an inside pocket and turned pages. 'I must have hung up before I got her subliminal message.'

She said she was on her way to the Dog. Alex took a deep breath and breathed out through pursed lips. 'That would be after you hijacked my conversation with Harriet. And around the time you terminated the conversation; yes, that would be when you switched off my phone.'

'On the hands-free, yes. Miss Burke and I had finished what we had to say, or I thought we had. It was automatic on my part. Sorry about that.'

He didn't sound sorry. 'I know something of the way Harriet thinks. She'll be on her way to the Dog now and she'll wait there for you after we've talked. If you go to Leaves of Comfort and alert Mary, you'll embarrass Harriet and accomplish nothing.'

'And it would be petty? Isn't that what you're implying? Do you think of me as petty, Alex?'

'No, I don't.' *But you sound high-handed now. And self-righteous – and perhaps just a touch petty after all.* 'We don't always read other people very well.'

Snow flew in through her window and she closed it. 'This is turning into a blizzard,' she said.

He grinned. 'I can hope. This is my kind of weather.'

Dan O'Reilly was full of surprises.

'I shouldn't say this, but elements of the current case, or cases, have me gnashing my teeth. There are too many outside elements distracting. The last thing I expected was for any of it to be played out in Folly but it's looking more as if it may be.'

'As I've already said, you're very good at what you do. And I don't mean to be patronizing. Just honest, from what I've known of you. If I've irritated you, I'm sorry.' In truth, she valued this man, considered him a really interesting friend, even. The thought stopped her, unsettled her. 'You remember Scoot Gammage? And Kyle?'

'Of course. Doc Harrison – with your mum's help, of course – he's doing a great job with them. Giving those boys a stable home at such a formative time in their lives.'

'They're really good kids, Dan. Every morning before school, Scoot works at the Dog. And Kyle wouldn't give up helping out at Tony's clinic for anything. He still wants to be a vet. Tony loves that idea.' Tony loved children, full stop.

Dan tucked the notebook back into his jacket pocket. 'Their dad isn't a bad man. He made wrong choices for the right reasons. Let's hope he can pull things together and make a family for them when he gets out of the big house.'

'I was going to suggest Calum might enjoy having his tea with Scoot. Kyle, too, if he gets there in time. They often eat at the pub. They could eat early and see if they can melt the ice a bit. It's not always easy for kids to break down barriers – especially if they know that's what adults want them to do – but we could try it. The restaurant won't be open yet – if at all on a night like this one promises to be – so they could be in there. That way it would be easier for you to chat with Harriet in the snug.'

'We'll see how that goes.' With a wry smile, Dan hitched at his wet trouser knee. He opened the door and got out. 'One of my men is waiting for me in the bar. I need to talk to him first. If Miss Burke is there, would you mind having her wait for me in the snug – as long as it's empty?'

'I will, and it will be,' she said. 'And I'll let Tony know you want a word.'

He had started to shut the door but looked at her first, and smiled.

Such a smile.

*   *   *

'What's going on?' Tony's arrival behind her at the counter startled Alex. 'Who's the boy with Scoot and Kyle in the kitchen. And I don't know – or don't remember – that copper sitting by the window. How do I know he's a copper? Holes in his shoes.'

She laughed. 'He does not and you couldn't see them from here anyway. Detective Constable Liberty. He came in a couple of hours ago – looking for Major Stroud. I got the impression the police were interested in him last night, too. The Strouds are worrying me.' She told him about the panicky summons from Venetia Stroud.

Tony stood beside her and rested his elbows on the bar. 'That was all she wanted? To ask if you knew why the police were looking for the major?'

'Basically, yes. She sounded desperate on the phone, which was the only reason I went scuttling down there – and she could have asked her questions about my supposed superior knowledge of police procedure when she called, too.' Alex paused for breath. 'The detective constable is nice. He had something to eat and he's been drinking coffee ever since he got here. I don't know why he's sticking around now Dan O'Reilly's arrived. They already talked.'

'They seem to hunt in pairs,' Tony remarked and glanced at the officer.

The bar was almost empty but she felt she had to keep her voice down. 'What a day.' She gave an involuntary little shudder. 'I'm hoping we can get out of here early.' Not early enough if Dan kept his promise to talk with them after Harriet.

'Me, too.' He bent to kiss her quickly. 'As soon as we can will be too late for me. I'm desperate for time to ourselves.'

She didn't say that she wanted them to be alone but, almost more than that, she wanted to be away from the cross-currents that had surrounded her all day – and didn't show any sign of easing soon.

Tony nudged her. 'Who's the boy in the kitchen?'

'Sorry. Calum O'Reilly, Dan's son. He's staying with his dad. A bit quiet but a nice kid. My mum's going to give them some tea in the dining room.' Lily was behind the counter, taking pies and cakes from their glass cases and putting them on plates. The pies she slid into the microwave.

'Where is O'Reilly? Did he drop off his boy – or did the other copper bring him?'

'That's one of the things I'll tell you all about. Just not here. The weather will keep the numbers down but there'll be regulars in anytime.' She dropped her voice even lower. 'Dan's in the snug with Harriet.'

'Harriet? Oh, something about her seeing that man with the major, the one in the picture?'

'Dan's fuming about her coming to me for advice about what to say to him. She called me and he overheard the conversation.' She swished several spirits optics in a bowl of soapy water.

'And he's in a touchy mood about that?' Tony put an arm around her shoulders and eased her against him.

'And other things.'

'OK. Later, then.' His frown belied an even tone.

She would let Dan break his own bad news about wanting to talk to them. If he still wanted to. They might get lucky and he would decide against another interview today. There was no doubt Harriet would repeat what she'd told Alex in detail, so Dan would have plenty to think about.

Lily waved at them before hefting a laden tray and walking into the kitchen. The dining room could be reached from there without going through the pub. 'Do you ever think about how your dad and my mum will feel when the boys go back to their dad?' She hadn't intended to ask that. The question just popped into her mind.

'I started worrying about it almost as soon as Scoot and Kyle moved into Dad's. It's a heartache waiting to happen, has to be. But knowing my dad, he'll already have tried to make peace with them moving away eventually, and Lily's a pragmatist, too.'

Alex's tummy felt funny and not in a nice way. 'I hope you're right, but I know it's going to hurt, at least for a while. It won't be easy for Sid Gammage to get work after being in prison and I expect he'll want to start somewhere fresh, not in Folly.

'I feel as if something heavy and dark is about to roll in and obliterate all the good stuff. I've been happy thinking of . . . well, I've been happy, that's all. Does everybody worry it's dangerous to feel good, that it won't last? I suppose that's superstition.'

Tony bumped her shoulder with his arm. 'I've made up my mind I'm not letting things I can't change mess with our lives. What we've got now was a long time coming and we're grabbing it and holding on. Is there really any reason we can't duck out now? It's not going to be a busy evening. Look how dark it's getting already. Driving won't be fun. You can't see across the road from here and the snow is really coming down. The sooner we head up the hill, the better.'

There was no option but to explain why they shouldn't just leave. 'I think Dan wants a word with us after he finishes with Harriet.'

'Why, sweetheart? I sure as hell don't want any words with him, not about his case, if that's what it is. We have nothing to do with it, thank God.'

'He'll let us know soon enough,' Alex said. 'Or I hope so. I don't like to think of Harriet being put on the hot seat. She hasn't done anything wrong. None of us has. I read in the paper that the police wouldn't say if there were any leads in these murder cases, or whether there was anyone helping them with their investigations. That's code for there aren't any.'

'Right. We've seen Dan get nasty before when things weren't moving the way he wanted them to.' Tony straightened. 'Battle stations. Here they come now.'

Harriet rarely approached the bar, preferring to be helped at her fireside table. This afternoon she walked purposefully toward Alex and Tony while Dan took a seat at his DC's table. The two men leaned close together to talk.

'Only saying goodbye,' Harriet said, buttoning up her green tweed overcoat and avoiding eye contact. 'Mary will be wondering where I am. What a day.'

Alex almost told her she'd just said the same thing herself. 'Yes. And not in a nice way, hm?'

Harriet looked straight at her then, her lips pressed together in a straight line. She didn't comment.

'We're getting company,' Tony said. 'Good afternoon, Dan. Or it isn't, is it? Nice, that is. It's nasty out there.'

Dan gave a nod. He must have left his raincoat and hat in the snug. Not a good sign for those hoping to leave the pub quickly.

'I almost forgot,' Harriet said, reaching into the tote bag she carried over one arm. 'That shop I told you about. In Gambol Green. I got you this book for your collection. *Our White Violet* by Kay Spen. Judith Childs – she owns the bookshop – she showed me this and I had to get it for you.'

'How lovely,' Alex said, taking the book and looking at it from all angles. 'Isn't this the one Agatha Christie was supposed to have loved as a child? Thank you. I've looked for a copy but never come across one. I need to get my books out of boxes and on to shelves again. It's too easy to put off finishing your unpacking.'

Apparently watching the exchange between the women with little interest, Dan shifted from foot to foot. When he crossed his arms, the message was that he was impatient to get to whatever his own business was.

'I'll get out of your way,' Harriet said a little acidly.

'I'll run you home,' Tony said at once. 'It's really foul out now and it'll be slippery underfoot—'

'We need to have a chat,' Dan cut in. 'And I do have another appointment after that.'

So, what did that mean? That elderly ladies must walk through ice and snow rather than cause DCI O'Reilly to wait a few minutes? Alex hid a smile when Tony said, 'I won't be long – or would you rather talk another time?'

'Constable Liberty can take Harriet home,' he said, as if she weren't standing in front of him. 'And she needn't worry, he has an unmarked car so she won't be embarrassed.'

Tony didn't rise to bait easily, but when he opened his mouth with that certain light in his eyes, Alex prepared for words along the lines that he'd do what he damned well liked. Fortunately, or unfortunately, Harriet took charge. 'Thank you,' she said. 'That's very kind.'

'In the snug all right with you?' Dan said, already in motion. 'I'll just have a word with my officer.' And he returned to the tall man by the window, who was zipping himself into a dark rain jacket.

Harriet patted Alex's cheek, squeezed Tony's arm and smiled. 'I think he's not a happy man at the moment,' she said quietly. 'And I'm not excusing him, just more concerned with your blood pressure. Good luck in there.'

'Yes,' Tony said. 'We'll catch up later.'

In the snug, Dan made no attempt to sit down or to suggest Tony and Alex might like to. He ducked his head, apparently to look at his shoes, then raised his chin sharply. 'Let's get to the point and keep this short.'

They did not answer him. Tony pushed back his Barbour jacket and stuffed his hands in his pockets. He glanced at Alex then met Dan's gaze steadily. There was a virtual crackle of antagonism in the room.

'We have a situation on our hands.'

'Not as far as Alex and I are concerned,' Tony put in at once.

Dan looked at his watch. His notebook and pen were on a table and he picked them up. He leafed through pages, more to give himself time to think – and to settle his irritation, Alex thought. 'I wouldn't need you here if I didn't assume Alex shares whatever's on her mind with you,' Dan told Tony. 'I don't like this anymore than you do, but I don't have a choice. I'm going to be blunt. I have bosses. I answer to them, and their instructions are explicit – no locals interfering in this case. Your history of landing slap in the middle of anything police-related is an embarrassment. My neck is on the line and I don't like the feeling. In case after case, seems whichever way I turn, I'm up against someone who has already talked to one or both of you before talking to me. Or, as you have to admit we both witnessed today, Alex, someone who doesn't intend to talk to me until they get the all-clear from you. It's bloody infuriating and it's got to stop. Anything you'd like to say about this?'

Her legs felt slightly shaky. She didn't do confrontation well and Dan O'Reilly was confronting her. Whatever the reason, she was glad Tony was here so he would have the full picture without her having to make a report later.

Dan rolled his shoulders back and Alex felt his tension.

She crossed her arms and looked directly at him. 'Maybe the question should be, is there anything *you'd* like me to say about whatever's on your mind. I'm not going to stab around in the dark trying to figure out how I can make you happy, Dan. Sorry, but I don't think I'm being unreasonable.'

He checked his watch again. 'Do you know the Parker-Rains of Gambol Green? Coincidentally my neighbors.'

'I know Daphne very slightly from local Historical Society meetings. I've met her husband, Simon, nothing more. I think Daphne said they work together. A law firm in Gloucester.' She didn't ask why he was asking since she already knew. Before Dan arrived, Harriet had shared the information she'd gathered at the Gambol Green book shop.

'Has Mrs Parker-Rains ever confided in you about . . . about unusual personal events?'

Alex barely contained a smile. Dan was trying to extract information without giving any hints in the process. 'Nothing like that.'

'But Harriet has.'

The flat statement didn't leave her any wiggle room. 'Some.' She didn't want to add to any antipathy Dan felt toward Harriet. Why not risk trying to divert this thinly disguised interrogation? 'I hope you and Calum weren't too put off by whoever was around your cottage the other night. I'm sure it was unpleasant, but perhaps you've already found the culprit.'

Pages slid together as Dan turned them then wrote in his notebook. So much for trying to divert him. She met Tony's eyes and he raised his brows a fraction.

'You don't need to waste your detecting skills on that,' Dan said at last. 'All under control.'

'Good,' she said. 'Glad to hear it.' He was edgy about the case and letting them know he didn't want any helping hands this time around. OK, he was right, intrusive civilians could get in his way, but she couldn't control what neighbors, especially neighbors who were good friends, confided in her. But she could make an effort to discourage any potentially uncomfortable confidences. Still, O'Reilly didn't need to be so bloody prickly.

'Major Stroud told you he knew Ricky Seaton. The man in the photo we showed you.'

'Yes, he did. But by then it wasn't news to you.'

'Not because Major Stroud attempted to give us any help.' There was no doubt he was furious. 'And you didn't share what Stroud told you with us – in case there was something we hadn't heard. Do you begin to see what I need to get straight with you?'

She began to feel pressured – and cross. 'I think we can shorten this meeting, Dan. A lot. Let me get something straight with you.' She took a sharp breath. Heat suffused her face and neck. 'Whether or not Major Stroud chooses to share information with you is nothing to do with Tony and me. The fact that he indicated to us that he knew Mr Seaton also didn't make it our responsibility to check whether or not he'd told you exactly what he told us. It never crossed my mind.'

'Or mine,' Tony added.

Dan looked steadily at Alex. 'I think you were aware that Major Stroud hadn't told us everything he told you about Seaton. You were standing there when we asked him if he recognized the man and he wouldn't give a straight answer. I've spoken to Mrs Stroud and she indicated that she and her husband knew Mr Seaton. He was an acquaintance of their son, Harry. Seaton went to the Strouds asking for a large donation to the Phoenix Players. Mrs Stroud brought all this up to you when you visited earlier today, and you told her the major had already discussed these facts with you.' He paused, outwardly calm again, if quietly seething.

'And which part of this points to wrongdoing on either Alex's or my part?' Tony said.

'The people of Folly have installed you as their local investigation team. That's . . . it's a bloody nuisance. It's getting in the way of this case, in my way and that of my officers. I'm asking you either to refuse to listen to what may be police business, or to come directly to me if you're told something you know damn well I should know too – even if it's possible I could have been given the information already. Is that clear?'

A sharp rap on the door was a blessed interruption.

Alex rubbed her upper arms and waited for Dan to respond to the knock. She did intend to be circumspect about any conversations relating to police business, but not to make it easier for him to crawl from beneath the nasty diatribe he had just delivered. There was always more than one way to get a point across.

He swiveled away and threw open the door to LeJuan Harding. 'Yes?' Even with his back to them, Alex could imagine the hostile expression on his face.

'Boss.' LeJuan gave Alex and Tony a brief wave. 'Sorry to interrupt but we may have another one.'

Dan paused for an instant then said, 'Holy shit!' He grabbed his coat and hat and strode from the room. 'Where?'

'Gloucester nick.'

TWENTY

'Alan Dimbleby's that furniture salesman who's running for the county council,' LeJuan said as he ducked into Dan's car outside the station. 'Or I suppose he owns the shop. It's in Winchcombe but he lives in Guiting Power.'

A smattering of rain and snow entered with LeJuan who had driven his own car from Folly-on-Weir.

'This day's too long already,' Dan said. The conversation with Alex and Tony had done nothing for his mood, or for the fact that he was exhausted. 'Why does this man want to talk to me and nobody else?'

'Mystery to me. The officer who spoke to him said he thought at first that Dimbleby was just in asking for votes. He talked about running for the county council and put a stack of pamphlets on the desk. Seemed determined to be noticed as important. That was before he got around to what was supposedly his reason for coming. Not that he said much about that. He reckons he was almost a victim of what he called the Playing Fields killer. The desk officer called me. You weren't picking up, so I talked to Longlegs. I was almost home so I carried on to Folly.'

Dan drummed his fingers on the steering wheel. 'OK, let's get to it. I do wonder how he picked me out for the honor.'

'Evidently he didn't – or wouldn't give any more information. Not anything helpful. He did say it was a disgrace the killer hasn't been caught and if he had been—'

'If he'd been caught after the first death, there wouldn't have been a second one,' Dan said, cutting LeJuan off. 'A man with original lines, hm?'

They got out and started for the building. 'How did you make out with Alex and Tony?' LeJuan asked. 'You didn't look happy. Neither did they, especially Alex.'

'I'm still not happy. I like both of them, but this business is evil. God knows what I'll do if they get caught up in the middle of this case. I'd say it couldn't happen, but history says different.'

The building lobby swarmed with activity, and from some raised and slurred voices it sounded like closing time at a local pub – only it seemed a bit early. Dan scanned chairs lining the walls, looking for a candidate who might be Dimbleby, and picked out a hefty man in tweeds, a raincoat over his knees with a hat balanced on top.

A familiar figure cut off Dan's view. 'Bill,' Dan said, slapping his ex-partner's back. 'Where have you been keeping yourself?'

Bill Lamb threaded his fingers through his sandy crew-cut and crossed his eyes. 'I'm telling you, Dan, I fuckin' hate drugs. Staked out half the day waiting for a drop that never happened. Bum information.'

Other members of Bill's team trailed across the lobby and he nodded to each of them as they went.

'This is none of my business,' Dan said, 'but I got a little warble in my ear that you're living in Folly these days.'

LeJuan, ever the diplomat, had edged away to talk to another uniform.

'You heard right. Almost right. My address is Trap Lane.' Bill smiled and glanced away. 'And I'm happy.'

'Radhika is one fabulous woman. You couldn't have done any better. Beauty, brains, generosity, and I think she may even love you. Who could ask for anything more?'

'Right. No arguments here. I fought against moving into her house, but she wouldn't move into mine so, hey, we found out I'm a weak man. Not easy, but I can be had.'

Dan grinned. Bill Lamb had been the best sergeant a man could have and now he was a darn good DI with the frequently difficult sergeant Jillian Miller as his bagman, or should that be bag woman – bag person? He smiled at that. He'd gone through some difficult days after Bill was promoted, dreading that he might have to take her on himself.

'Any progress with the Playing Fields bloke?' Bill asked.

'Now you,' Dan exclaimed. 'Second time I've heard that tonight. Playing Fields. Where'd you hear that?'

Bill's light blue eyes turned innocently blank. 'Around. Just today, I think. Does the old saw about needing three to make a serial killer still hold?'

'Interesting question with this one. I think it's the same

offender. That makes it serial in my book and I don't want to see another one turn up to prove I'm right. I'd better do what I came to do. Some oddball witness who says he only has words for me has come forward. I think I'm supposed to be salivating to hear what he's got to say. See you, Bill.'

Bill gave him a high five and headed for parts deeper in the building. If anything, the lobby was even more chaotic. He caught LeJuan's eye and started edging around the gabbling crowd. 'Is our gentleman the one in tweeds?' he asked when his sergeant joined him.

'The very same, boss. I'd be worried about him sitting there so long only he seems happy enough. Looks as if he's taking mental notes for something.'

'Right.' Dan walked over and stuck out a hand. 'Mr Dimbleby?'

The man sprang to his feet immediately and with more alacrity than should be expected from such a big fellow, although a slight grimace and a hand passed around the neck suggested he could be in pain. Well over six feet, broad shouldered and built like a former rugby forward, he plastered on a smile, took Dan's hand and pumped it.

'Detective Chief Inspector Dan O'Reilly,' Dan said, 'and this is my sergeant, LeJuan Harding. You asked to speak to me about something important?'

'You'll want us to talk privately,' Dimbleby said, glancing in all directions. He was good looking with sharp, even features and thick, greying hair worn on the long side. Steel-rimmed glasses emphasized piercing hazel eyes.

Dan had to look up at him. 'My office should do. It's up a flight.'

He led the way upstairs and along the corridor to the squad room. His visitor actually managed to shake one or two passing hands on the way and announce his candidacy for Gloucester County Council.

Few people remained at work in the squad room, but Dan's visitor scanned around with avid interest – before looking at LeJuan and saying, 'Forgive me, Sergeant, but this is a very private, a very important matter and I need to speak to the Detective Chief Inspector alone.'

'Let me know if there's anything I should be interrupted for,'

Dan said, knowing LeJuan would be more than happy to miss this one.

'Can I offer you tea?' Dan said when Dimbleby was seated in front of the desk. 'Or a coffee. Frankly, tea is better than coffee around here, though not much.'

That got an unlikely, gurgling chuckle, and Dimbleby found a silver flask in the pocket of his raincoat. 'Laphroaig.' He held the flask aloft. 'Warms you up on a freezing night. Can I tempt you?'

Mentally tasting the whisky, Dan shook his head, no. 'Still on duty, but I'll give you a glass for that. Not very salubrious, I'm afraid.' He wasn't about to pull out one of the Waterford goblets Calum had sent him from Ireland after last Christmas. Mr Dimbleby got one of the worn water glasses.

'How can I help you?' Dan settled back in his chair, barely resisting the temptation to put his feet on his desk.

LeJuan appeared at the window in his door, a grimace in place. He tapped and waited for Dan to beckon him in.

'It's Dr Wolf, boss. He's downstairs.'

Dan screwed up his eyes. 'I've done it again. This is ridiculous. What does he say' – he held up a hand – 'no, I'll go down.'

'A word, boss?'

Dan excused himself, stepped outside the office, and walked LeJuan a few feet away and, he hoped, out of Dimbleby's hearing.

'Wolf says not to worry about missing the appointment. He's had a bad day, too. He tracked you down and someone told him you were interviewing a man about the case.'

'Who is this someone?' Dan almost shouted. He closed his mouth and rested his chin on his chest. 'Too many loose lips. Go on.'

'He'd like to come up and sit in.' The look on LeJuan's face suggested he was waiting for another barrage. 'He won't inter-rupt, he says, but thinks it might help him start to get a handle on what he can do to help with the case.'

'Bloody wonderful.' Dan whistled out a long breath. 'He's right, of course. Ask him to join me, please.'

Wolf must have followed LeJuan up. They passed in the doorway to the squad room.

'Sorry I didn't call, awful day,' Dan said when the psychologist reached him. 'This is Alan Dimbleby. He's running for the county council. Says there was some sort of incident he thinks was related to the ongoing case. There were moments when I thought he was going to turn out to be another body, so I'm grateful for small mercies.'

Back in his office, Dan braced himself to fend off Dimbleby's protests at seeing Leon Wolf but none came. 'I'm Alan Dimbleby,' he said, standing up and putting his glass on Dan's desk. 'I'm running for the county council. I think we've met.'

Wolf looked puzzled. 'Leon Wolf. I'm a colleague of DCI O'Reilly's.'

'Dr Wolf is a psychologist.' Dan pulled a spare chair into neutral territory between himself and Dimbleby. 'Now, sir, I understand you know there's been a possible second murder related to the one at the cricket club.'

'Oh, yes. It's all over the place. Everyone's talking about it – the Playing Fields killer and so forth. Not that there's any real information about, or any suggestion that you've made any progress.' He clapped Wolf on the shoulder – something Dan could never imagine doing. 'Got it. I saw you at a Merilee Sterling charity thing.'

'Ah,' was all Wolf said as he sat in his allotted chair.

'Why don't you tell us exactly what brought you here, sir?' Dan said.

'Alan, please. I was door-knocking in The Slaughters. These little villages don't get enough attention. They will from me. Fly tipping, mind you. They've started their own night watch. You would think these lowlifes would avoid dropping piles of rubbish in a place they can't easily get away from, but they don't. They do it regardless. And would again but for these upstanding and sensible people out there in all winds and weathers – freezing off their small parts, I shouldn't wonder – but they're protecting their property. When I'm on the council, I shall make fly tipping one of my primary missions. Stopping it, that is.'

Dan took a long breath in. 'When was it you were there?' he said. 'When something happened to bring you to us?'

'Earlier in the evening. It was quite dark already. Not pleasant, but you have to let the little people know you're there for them, too. Not just for the important people. They're reliable and they know what they want. And they should be able to walk in the evening in small places like that. And be safe.' He leaned toward Dan with laser focus in his sharp eyes.

Wolf had braced himself with a hand on each knee. He concentrated on what Dimbleby was saying, as if each word should be memorialized.

Dan was too tired and too irritable for this. 'Excuse me, Mr—'

'I'm Alan. And I hope I can count on both of your votes.'

'Alan,' Dan said.

'I didn't see it coming. Just like the other two, I'm sure, only I was more alert. I'm supposed to be dead by now, Chief Inspector, and I expect action.'

Dan caught Leon's gaze and he rolled his eyes. Before either of them could say anything, Dimbleby continued. 'Minding my own business, I was. Talking on my phone while this fellow came out of nowhere and started yacking on about having a problem getting into his car and how his mobile was inside on the seat – locked in there, you see. Had the flippin' cheek to ask to borrow mine. Told him where he could go. You can count on that. We were beside a car then and he said it was his and could I use the torch on my phone to help him see what he needed to do. The window was a bit open, he said, because something or other wasn't working and the windows got steamed up on the inside if he closed them all. He had a piece of wire – reckoned he'd had to get in like that before and as long as I held the phone light steady, he should be able to hook the wire around the button and bob's your uncle, it would open.

'I don't mind telling you I was browned off by all this but, well, docsn't do to upset potential voters. I gave him a pamphlet and a sticker for his car first, I can tell you that.'

Finally, he took a breath, and a swig from his glass. He coughed and wiped his mouth with the back of a hand. 'He had to have been this Playing Fields killer chappie. I got lucky, not that I didn't do all the right things, I can tell you that.'

'Playing Fields killer?' Dan wanted to know where that had started.

'Heard it on the radio when I was driving here. Someone phoned in to talk about it. This maniac's picking on public figures and dragging them off to the Playing Fields. I used to go there when I was a lad – for sports days, cricket, football and so on.'

'I think a lot of youngsters around here went there,' Dan commented.

'Do you think he injects them with something to knock them out? The fellow on the radio thought so.'

'Too early to say yet,' Dan said, aware that they would already know if that had been the case.

As he made notes, he wondered what Wolf was making of this. The man was not using a notebook. Maybe he had a photographic memory. Dan had the thought that he could use one of those.

'Carry on with your story, Alan,' Dan said, although it was beginning to seem feasible that there wasn't much more to tell. More wasted time and dead ends.

'Well,' Alan said. 'He popped open that door with no trouble. There was no mobile on the seat. 'Shine your light on the floor for me, would you?' he says. I did that and he gave me a good old shove while I was leaning in. But he hadn't bargained with me, or with me being hard to push if I don't want to be. He was about as big as me, or he seemed it. One of those tough, muscular types. I grabbed the roof and held on, but he gave me some good old thumps to my shoulders and back. But he wasn't getting me inside his car with whatever he had in mind after that.'

Dan speculated on the size of this assailant, since Dimbleby was a pretty big bloke himself, if not in the best shape. 'So you fought him off.'

'Not bloomin' likely. He could have had a knife – or a gun. These types have got all the gear now.'

Dan kept his attention on Alan Dimbleby's face, watching for signs he was getting nervous. So far he'd been completely sure of himself.

'So,' he said, 'what did you do next?'

Alan cleared his throat and, if anything, looked increasingly sure of himself. 'Well, I gave him a shove back and I think he fell, so I ran while I had the chance, I can tell you that. Didn't want him coming at me again. I got to my car, hopped in and locked the doors.'

The vision of Alan Dimbleby hopping nimbly into a car didn't

come easily to mind. 'Did you get the number plate of his car?'
Dan sent up a silent prayer that the man had.

'Are you kidding? It was dark, raining when it wasn't
snowing, and I didn't have time for any of that.'

'How about the make of the car?'

'No.'

'How about a description of your assailant?'

'My build, maybe a bit thinner. Must have been a big fellow
to push me like that. I don't think I'll forget I was attacked for
a day or two. Sore shoulders, I can tell you.' He crossed his arms
to rub his shoulders and arms. 'My neck isn't too clever, either.'

Dan suddenly longed for a shot from the bottle of whisky in
his own bottom drawer. 'How about his face?'

'Had one of those wool hats on, I think. Pulled down over his
ears and so on.'

'If we show you some pictures, do you think you could pick
him out?'

'Well.' Alan puffed out. 'No. Who could in the dark and the rain
and with my needing to run? He was ordinary, I can tell you that.
I expect you to do the legwork, Chief Inspector. I didn't believe
what that fellow said on the radio about your record being bad.'

Charming. 'My record being bad?'

'Mentioned you by name. Said he had a good source who told
him all about you.'

'And what does that mean?' Dan said.

'The radio fellow tried asking the caller a question or two
more after that. He faffed about a bit then hung up. Bit of a
blowhard, if you know what I mean. Probably made up most of
what he said, but I checked out that area we talked about, and
it is known as the Playing Fields, just like before. I wouldn't be
surprised if schools still used it. Not this time of year, I don't
suppose, which would make it pretty deserted. Our nasty man
would like that. Anyway, the caller mentioned your name a few
times and here you are, so everything he said wasn't all wrong,
was it?'

Alan became silent, studied his hands, did a couple of side-
to-side neck stretches.

'Perhaps you should see the duty doctor,' Dan said, but the
man shook his head emphatically.

'Might not hurt just to get checked out,' Dan added.

'It's not that bad,' Alan said. 'Don't want to sound like a ninny.'

'Is that all then?' Dan asked him and got a nod. He gave the man one of his cards. 'Very well then. Don't hesitate to call me if you're concerned about something. Thank you for coming in. Leave your contact details with one of my officers and we'll be in touch, Mr Dimbleby.'

Dan showed him from his office and a young officer hopped up to take him back down to the lobby.

'I don't know what to think about that one,' Dan said, shutting himself inside his office with Leon Wolf. 'What was your impression?'

Leon gave one of his rare smiles. 'Other than thinking you might like to kick him as far as you could see him? Yes, well, I think Mr Dimbleby is looking for a way to raise his profile. The headline would read: *Local politician outwits would-be murderer.* Then, if you're really unlucky, it will be: *Failing police chief inspector shrugs off council hopeful Alan Dimbleby's fears for his life.'*

TWENTY-ONE

Tony tucked their packages of hot fish and chips under an arm. 'I'm keeping them warm,' he said and chuckled. He felt something close to relief, just being away from the tension that hung around the Black Dog – at least for him, and he thought for Alex, too.

At least the wet snow had stopped falling and pinprick stars punctured a velvet black sky wreathed with scarves of cloud.

'Our dinner is keeping *you* warm, you mean,' Alex said, slipping a hand beneath his free elbow. 'Our local chippy seems to do quite well. He always has a queue.'

He took a sniff. 'Mm. Glad about that. There's nothing like the smell of fish and chips when you're hungry.'

'Makes me hungrier,' Alex said, and leaned closer to him. They matched their steps, although Alex took alternating skips to keep up the pace. 'Good idea to go to your clinic to eat rather than drive home. The food might stay almost hot that long, although we should probably have brought my car from the pub.'

'Don't forget we can drive home from the clinic in mine,' Tony said.

Katie and Bogie trotted happily at their sides, toenails scrunching into cold gravel along Pond Street, past cottages with pungent woodsmoke curling from chimneys. Ahead, soft light glowed through rosy curtains in the Burke sisters' upstairs flat. Downstairs in the tea shop, all was dark. On a clear and snappy night like this, Tony was happy to walk but glad they didn't have too far to go.

Their breath sent diaphanous vapor billowing into the still and freezing air. The deep, dark sky turned to old silver around the moon.

'Christmas weather,' Alex said. 'Cold and clear and filled with promise of things to come.'

He glanced down at her sharply. Every comment she made seemed to have hidden meaning. Or was it that he invented meaning because there was so much he would like to hear her say?

Passing Leaves of Comfort, Tony thought of Harriet. She had finished with Dan quite early and gone home, but the sisters hadn't come into the Dog later, which was unusual for them. On a different occasion he and Alex might be worrying that Harriet or Mary was sick, but this time the reason for their absence was obvious – Harriet didn't want to risk running into Dan again. If he had been in a similar mood with her as he was at his discussion with Alex and Tony, little wonder Harriet chose to avoid him.

Alex gave his arm a tug. 'I thought Harriet would come back with Mary, didn't you?'

'You read my mind.'

They reached the car park beside the parish hall and crossed over from Pond Street toward the end of Meadow Lane. A tiny stream ran beside the lane, only feet from the doors of another row of cottages. 'Let's go in the front,' Tony said. 'But watch your step.'

Late in autumn he had placed a single flat stone into the stream, just in front of his cottage clinic. He stepped on the crackling grass of the bank, then on to the stone. 'Icy,' he said, feeling the slippery surface beneath his foot and holding her hand. He was quickly all the way over with Alex beside him.

A hallway led from the front door of the clinic straight through to the kitchen and a waiting room at the back of the cottage. Stamping their feet, they went directly to the kitchen where they shed their coats. Tony found plates while Alex got out silverware and napkins.

'There's a bottle of Bordeaux in the cupboard by the refrigerator. And there's a corkscrew somewhere here.' He started sorting through drawers.

'Screw-top,' Alex said brightly. 'Useful, even if you think you don't like them.'

In the waiting room, they scooted two chintz-covered armchairs close to a low round table used for magazines, and a gas fire with a bulbous black iron surround.

'I think we're running away,' Alex said. 'I like it. I could decide not to go back for days, if at all.' She piled the magazines on the floor.

Tony opened and closed cupboard doors until he found glasses. Then he produced a moldering box of yellowing utility candles, some matches and a saucer. He lit a wick, waited until he could drip hot wax on to the saucer, and fixed the candle upright.

Alex held her hands to the flame and smiled. 'You've done this before. So have I, but it was a long time ago.'

'I was a boy scout. We had to learn these complicated survival tricks.' He started the gas fire which spat and popped in a very satisfying manner.

Alex unwrapped newspaper from the fish and chips and slid them on to the plates. 'I am so hungry. Did I have lunch?'

'I wasn't there.' Tony hopped up from his seat. 'Wait! Vinegar! Do you want any sauce?'

'Vinegar and pepper. I'm a purist.'

When Tony returned with the vinegar, pepper, and salt, he switched off the overhead light but left on two shaded lamps. 'Do you suppose we really are trying to run away?' he said. 'I feel bad about the meeting with Dan. He constantly seems uptight and I don't like to add to that, but he was in a foul mood.'

Alex slid to sit cross-legged on the floor in front of the table. She drowned her chips in vinegar, picked one up and nibbled thoughtfully. 'Mm. It isn't as if we haven't felt the sharp side of his tongue before, but this was different, I think. And he's tired. Someone said Calum, his son, showed up late last night – from Ireland – and Dan wasn't expecting him. That's got to be hard for Dan to handle when he's got a job that doesn't exactly give him a lot of time to deal with personal surprises.'

'I thought of that,' Tony said. Katie wriggled beside him and stuck her nose under his elbow. She eyed his plate longingly. 'One chip and that's it. You're getting fat and that won't help your joints.' He gave her a chip, which she inhaled, then gave her another and made her lie down.

Bogie remained where he was, curled up in front of the fire. He didn't do fish or chips. Now, had there been steak on offer . . .

Tony could smell the smoke wavering up from the candle. They had drunk the first glass of wine quickly and he poured again. Alex held her glass by the stem and rocked it back and forth, her eyes lowered.

'What are you thinking?' he asked her.

'About us.' The blunt answer surprised him. 'I suppose we could go on exactly as we are and it wouldn't matter. Or it wouldn't have to matter, but I think it would.'

'It would to me. And I agree it might to you, Alex.'

They ate in silence for a while. Bogie turned around as if he were toasting both sides.

'It would matter very much to me,' Alex said at last. 'I don't want that.'

He watched her in silence. You could come to take someone for granted, even someone who meant more to you than anyone else. The way they spoke fascinated you, and the way you assumed they thought. You cared about what mattered to them and how they responded to the things that mattered so much to you. Even the way they looked and moved . . . and laughed. The laughter was really important. No, he couldn't afford to waste a moment with this woman by taking her for granted.

She glanced at him, smiled a little, looked into her wine glass again.

His chest tensed, and his stomach. His skin felt tight. She loved him – he had no doubt about that, and the realization was both a pleasure and a burden. This woman was special. She was sensitive, intelligent, compassionate, and she was sexy. He smiled slightly. Alex was so much and she would be too much to lose. And therein lay the great big rub; he still feared losing her, yet it was unreasonable to imagine anyone could guarantee their future in the way they wanted it to be forever.

This was the time. He needed to know how she would react to what he wanted to suggest, and there was never going to be a better moment to lay everything out. His breathing shortened and he felt the beat of his heart.

Now. 'I know we've talked about New Year's Eve for a wedding. I want to be sure. Are you really up for getting married soon? I'm pushing again, Alex. Can we think about doing it as close to immediately as we can? I'm going to be straight with you. The death declaration for Penny means we're in the clear and I'd like to get on with it.'

She set down her glass. 'That's romantic.' She gave him a quirky little smile. 'You've decided not to worry about that email anymore?'

Putting everything on the table – everything he thought about almost constantly – felt the right thing to do, and doing it tonight felt right, too. 'I promise you as much romance as you'll allow.' He leaned to run a finger down the side of her face. 'But yes, I've decided to put that aside. With the official documentation received, there's no question of our marriage not being legal right now, and I want to do it before anyone can come up with an argument. I'm so sure this is right for us, Alex.'

Would she say no? That they must try again to find out if there was new information on Penny? Up until now she had not said anything like that. Alex looked away and stroked Katie, long, slow strokes.

He drank from his own glass, sat back and crossed his arms.

'Hello.' Her voice surprised him and he realized she was looking directly at him. Green eyes turned darker by the strange light in the room. The face he knew best yet still found amazing. 'Tony?' She leaned forward slightly. The candle highlighted glints in her dark curls.

'Sorry,' he said. His voice sounded rough. 'I was only looking at you.'

'What are you thinking about now? Really?'

He had to say it. 'If you didn't love me. If you found out you'd stopped loving me, but I asked you if you still did, I think I'd want you to tell me lies.'

Startled. He had startled her. Those eyes widened but softened almost at once and looked far away. 'Well then, you'll never have to ask me to do that. And I'm with you. I'm always with you. I think we should include our folks in the arrangements, but let's get married. As close to now as possible.'

He wanted to hold her but couldn't seem to move. She moved for both of them, got to her knees, reached her arms around his neck and kissed him.

TWENTY-TWO

He had mixed feelings about being in Folly's parish hall again. At least it wasn't raining or snowing today, but it was cold as hell and the famous radiators were spitting toasted dust again and sending an unpleasant smell into air that had been closed inside for too long. The team was still setting up portable situation boards and assembling computer stations, and, try as he might, Dan couldn't completely ignore the grumbling. Grumbling hacked him off.

At least he could blame it on the superintendent who had instigated the move. He'd said he noticed, *'These Folly shenanigans seem to move faster when we have a local presence.'* Not the description Dan would have chosen for any of his cases – and at odds with the messages the chief had been issuing, Dan would have thought. He had been tempted to point out that although the current crime scenes might be closer to Folly than Gloucester, there hadn't been any actually in the village – so far. It seemed likely that the chief constable had pressed for more action and faster results and the super saw moving Dan and his team away from Gloucester as a means to ease the focus away from himself. The media was leaning hard on them, causing the usual tension. It paid to be as open as possible with members of the press – that way there was a better chance of controlling at least some of what was aired or printed.

'Open the fucking doors,' someone yelled, the voice echoing up into exposed rafters. 'And fucking leave them open. It's cold as hell in here but we can't breathe for all the stinkin' dust.'

'Aye, aye.' LeJuan this time. 'Calm down boys and girls. Seems counter-intuitive, but air quality will improve with occupation.'

More grumbling and a few jeers.

'You mean we'll be choking on different aromas,' Longlegs said, but mild as ever. He had just returned from the Black Dog and was in the middle of ferrying coffee and tea urns from a van in the car park. 'I opened the doors for you, look. My civic duty for the day.'

Moments later Alex Duggins came in. 'Forgot to send these so I drove them over,' she said, peering around the cardboard bakery tray she carried to see where she was walking. 'Doughnuts and biscuits.' She stopped when she saw Dan and he wondered why the sight of him would make her flush.

He took the box from her and slid it on to one of a row of computer desks. 'We could have sent someone for them, but thanks.'

Her waxed jacket was too big. Perhaps it wasn't hers.

'I grabbed Liz Hadley's coat by mistake.' *She had known he was staring at her.* 'I was trying to catch up with Longlegs.' She gave a little, awkward laugh and drew up her shoulders, which only made her look like a kid wearing her mum's clothes. 'Shouldn't be in such a hurry, I suppose.'

'You look cold.' It *was* cold, for God's sake. 'Sit down and have some of our good Black Dog coffee. And a doughnut. Might help that coat fit you better.' He closed his mouth. *Bloody brilliant, O'Reilly.*

'Um.' Her expression said she didn't know whether to stay or leave. Or should that be whether she wanted to stay or leave. Or, she definitely wanted to leave, but hated to be rude and didn't know how not to be, or seem to be.

'Yes, then,' she said in a way that gave him the impression she'd heard every word of his rambling thoughts.

'Warmer in the gallery,' he said. 'Coffee or tea? Doughnut or biscuits – or both?'

'Only coffee, thanks. I need the caffeine. Black, no sugar.' She followed him to the coffee urn and picked up the first mug he poured.

On the way to the gallery stairs, she waved to LeJuan who gave her his best, glad grin. Dan wondered if inviting her to stay, even if only for coffee, was such a good idea. He was supposed to be encouraging less contact, not more.

'I keep looking for signs of renovation here,' he said. 'They've cleared out that old storage room and there's a bit less junk in the kitchen, but that's about it.'

In the gallery they sat with an empty chair between them and

Alex set her coffee there. 'They hope to make the kitchen usable again, but that will take more money than the village has got so far.'

'Right.' Either he worked, grabbed a few minutes with Calum, or he was alone. Nothing there was conducive to practicing the art of small talk.

'I almost called you earlier. Before I found out you were moving into the hall again.' She picked up the mug but didn't drink. Or say anything more. He glanced at the ring on her finger – glanced away again.

Voices, punctuated by scraping noises, sounded from the main floor, and the repeated ring of phones.

'Something on your mind?' he said. 'Can I help?'

'Yes,' she said, so low he leaned closer to hear. 'I wonder if I've got information you don't have. If I do, it's by accident. I'm not sure it's worth bothering with, anyway. Just bits of talk for the sake of making conversation, probably. You know the way people do.'

He knew. 'Why not tell me what you've heard, and I can decide how important it is. If there's nothing useful, well then, no harm done.'

The coffee must be getting cold but she sipped at it. 'All right.' She set the mug down again and leaned hard against the back of her chair, laced her fingers so tight in her lap the knuckles whitened. 'I'm only here because I don't want to find out I've impeded your enquiries by not coming. And while I'm fessing up here, I might as well say I made an excuse to come because I was trying to make myself talk to you. And now I'm really embarrassed.'

He would have smiled, had he dared. 'Fair enough on the explanation, Alex.'

'OK.' She sat on the edge of the chair again. 'I talked to Harriet before you did and there wasn't time to talk again afterwards. Which was probably a good thing. In my car you heard her mention the prowler and Gambol Green. And a Mrs Fermer, whom I've met but don't really know.'

'All true about what I heard.' He'd wait to see which way she took her remarks before telling her the prowler had been Calum. Best not to interfere with her train of thought.

'Do you know . . .' She paused, brows drawn down in a troubled frown. 'If this is any of my business, I should go and ask Harriet what she said to you. That way I'm not destroying a trust. Crikey, I don't know what to do.'

'I can't make you tell me anything, but it'll be unfortunate if there's information floating around that could help us catch a killer, or killers, but it's not being brought to light.'

'Harriet has said she told you about recognizing the man in the photo that night at the Black Dog, right?'

'Right.' No need to elaborate on how unfortunate it was that the woman hadn't come forward as soon as she saw the photo.

'You know the Parker-Rains?'

'Yes. They're neighbors of mine.' He hadn't expected that name to come up again, but he was on alert now.

'The prowler came around the area where you live on the same night as the second murder happened, and, well, it felt as if there must be some connection. That's what Judith Childs at the bookshop in Gambol Green said to Harriet. And Daphne Parker-Rains told Elly who told Judith, but I expect you already know this. It sounds as if the story could have got a bit bent in repeated tellings.'

Harriet had talked about the 'prowler', torches shone through windows and potential danger to local inhabitants.

Dan made up his mind how much he needed to say. 'There wasn't a prowler.' He smiled at her. 'Other than my son, Calum. He arrived late from Ireland and I didn't know he was coming so I wasn't in. He had never been to the cottage before – we were still in Gloucester the last time he was here – so he was looking for addresses in the dark.'

Alex laughed, and immediately donned a serious expression instead. 'I shouldn't laugh,' she said. 'You must have had a shock.'

'I did. But it was great to see him.' No need to elaborate on the circumstances of his boy's arrival.

He felt Alex relax a little and knew he was striking the right note.

'Did Major Stroud come to see you?' Alex asked.

The anxiety was back. 'Not yet. As I said before, we've been having trouble contacting him, but we decided it's best to give him space and let him come in on his own – as long as he doesn't take much longer.'

'He knows . . . knew Ricky Seaton,' Alex said. 'He said Ricky was a friend of Harry Stroud, the major's son.'

'The one in prison, yes.'

Alex really could blush. Her discomfort was painful to look at. 'Harry made a lot of really terrible decisions but he's paying for them,' she said. 'Major Stroud made a point of telling Tony and me that Mr Seaton was always trying to raise money for the Phoenix Players. He asked the major and Mrs Stroud to contribute and I think it's been a problem between the two of them. Poor Mrs Stroud.'

Alex had a wide streak of empathy in her, had to have, or she wouldn't be able to forget Venetia Stroud's past ill-treatment of her.

He didn't attempt to prompt. If she had anything else to say, she would get to it on her own.

'Do you know the Rum Hole at Mill House?' she said. 'It's part of what's left of the Mill House estate. In that Playing Fields area. Near Underhill.'

'I know it.'

'Major Stroud said something strange. He was angry about a lot of things he didn't actually spell out. You were in the Black Dog with the photo of Ricky Seaton, you'll remember. Stroud told us we could find people at the Rum Hole who didn't think kindly of Ricky Seaton. Or that they didn't like him there. Something like that. There was so much going back and forth.'

He had better, Dan thought, not make further efforts toward stopping Alex from listening to the people around her. What would it take to get them to open up with the police directly? These rambles through second-hand accounts wasted valuable time, time when their killer could be setting up to attack again.

'I'm very grateful to you, Alex. It can't have been easy to come here and tell me this. No one will know we've had a chat, or not what we chatted about, at least.'

'Thank you,' she said, and smiled at him – a relieved smile as she got up. 'I don't think there's anything else I should tell you, so I'd better get back.'

He stood aside, then followed her downstairs.

As they reached the vestibule, the front door was scraped open by DS Cyril Chesney, one of Bill Lamb's men. Thin sunlight gleamed on his shaved scalp. He gestured to someone outside.

'Excuse me, DCI O'Reilly?' Chesney said. 'You want this one here or in Gloucester?' He steered Major Stroud into the entryway.

TWENTY-THREE

Alex muttered a greeting, a muffled greeting, and slid sideways through the doors and outside, but turned back to give Dan her mug. *Of all the rotten timing.* Dan wondered how long it would take Stroud to make some snide comment about Alex being cozy with the police.

'Morning, Cyril. Glad you could finally join us, Major. Over here, please.' He went to the corner of the hall under the front window where he had put his desk, and hauled out a couple of folding metal chairs from a pile against a wall. 'We might as well do the honors here. Take a seat.'

He left the man there and caught up with the sergeant as he was about to get into his car. 'Hold up, Cyril,' he said. 'What's the story with you and Stroud?'

'He phoned Gloucester from his home and asked for my boss. Reckoned he thought that's who wanted to talk to him.' Cyril shrugged. 'Don't ask me what gave him that idea. Message got re-routed to me on the road and since I'd heard he's been too shy to come and see you, I drove by that castle of his and picked him up. He wasn't well pleased, I can tell you. Not that he said more than two words coming from his place.'

'Probably rather talk to Bill than me. They've got less of a history, although . . . yeah, that's probably it. He's a thorny fella but I'm about to shave off some of his pointy bits if I have my way. Tell Bill I'll be in touch and thank him for me.'

Back in the hall, a raised voice greeted Dan. 'I have no interest in discussing my private business in the middle of a big open room with every Tom, Dick and Harry listening in.'

Ah, yes, Major Stroud was behaving true to form. Presently he was haranguing LeJuan, who stood with his hands clasped behind his back and his head on one side. LeJuan looked jaunty in a black leather bomber jacket and black jeans, with a dark green polo-neck jumper. Yes, very jaunty. And long-suffering.

'Major,' Dan said, a bit more loudly than he might have if he weren't setting the tone he wanted. 'Coffee or tea? It's fresh from the Black Dog.'

'No, then,' the major said. 'I want nothing from that place. And I don't know why the constable brought me here.'

'Sergeant Chesney was following instructions,' Dan told him. 'He knew I was the one who wanted to see you and that I'll be working here for the immediate future. He also thought you'd be better pleased not to have to go to Gloucester. So, let's get to it.'

He walked around his desk but when he sat down, Stroud remained standing. 'I'm not having a conversation in front of a roomful of people,' he said. 'Not that I can think of anything I'd have to say to you.'

'Right.' Dan thought of his options and could only come up with one. 'It's here or the storeroom at the back. That's been cleared out but it's filthy and loaded with dust. Still, we can stick in a table and some chairs if you'd prefer that.'

'Allergies, dammit,' the major said, producing a voluminous white handkerchief and giving a good blow. He placed one of the chairs where his back would be firmly to the room and sat down. 'Have a nice visit with our local publican, did you? Cozy little chat in the gallery?'

Here we go. 'You're with me, LeJuan,' Dan said, ignoring Stroud.

His sergeant took a spare chair to Dan's side of the desk, but sat at a distance behind him, notebook and pen at the ready.

'This is an informal meeting.' He slid a folder in front of him. 'Think of it as an opportunity to clear up any misconceptions.'

That got no response. Stroud rested an elbow on the opposite forearm and smoothed his iron-gray mustache with a finger and thumb. The mottling of broken capillaries across his nose and cheeks seemed more pronounced these days, and the pouches beneath his sharp eyes were puffy. Blue veins stood out on the backs of his age-spotted hands. He was thin, Dan realized, thinner than he had noticed in the past.

'You always have the right to a solicitor, Major. Even though this isn't formal. If you can't afford—'

'Don't be impertinent. I don't need my solicitor.'

'You will recall visiting the Black Dog the night before last and being shown a photograph.'

Stroud gave a single nod.

'You said you didn't think you knew the man in the photograph.'

This time Stroud crossed his arms firmly. 'I said I needed to think about it.'

'Which is it? That you didn't know him – or that you had to think about it?'

'The light wasn't good. My eyes aren't what they used to be.'

This sort of fencing with words got very boring. 'Does that mean you're not sure? Or that you now think you know the man?'

Stroud crossed his legs and jiggled a foot. 'What difference does it make?'

'It makes a difference,' Dan said, working to keep his tone even. 'Do you think you know the man in that picture? Take another look.' He slid the photo of Seaton out of the folder and pushed it in front of Stroud who barely glanced at it.

No reply.

'Do you know him?' Dan heard LeJuan huff. He let the pause stretch before asking, 'Are you sure you wouldn't like to have your solicitor with you?'

The major cleared his throat, took out the handkerchief and blew his nose again. He muttered something unintelligible.

'Could you repeat that, sir?'

'I said he looks familiar.'

'More familiar than you thought at first, perhaps? Have you met him in the past?'

'I really don't see what difference it makes one way or the other. You meet people in pubs. That's a fact. I could have met this man, but it wasn't anything momentous – the meeting, I mean. Probably just a "how d'you do" thing and that was that.'

'How long ago did you meet him?'

Stroud crossed his legs in the other direction, studied the cream-painted and moist brick walls, then the rafters. The rafters held him rapt.

Dan glanced at LeJuan who sent him a raised-brow look and went back to doodling in his notebook.

Seconds ticked by. Damn the man.

'Like I said.' At last the silence was broken. 'I could have met him.'

'And like I said, how long ago might that have been?' Dan asked, deliberately softening his voice.

Stroud puffed up his cheeks and rolled his eyes. 'A month. Two months. Six. I don't know.'

'Would it help your memory if I told you someone remembers seeing the two of you together at the Black Dog? Talking and drinking together?'

Stroud picked up the photograph. 'It's not very good, is it?'

'Someone saw you talking to this man. Ricky Seaton, that's the name.' There was probably no advantage, but Dan would rather not say Seaton was dead.

'Ricky Seaton!' Stroud's exclamation, delivered with almost comical amazement, didn't amuse Dan.

'That's right. Remember now, do you?'

The major reached beneath his tweed overcoat to take glasses from a jacket pocket and put them on. He brought the photo close and tutted. 'See how you flummoxed me, DCI O'Reilly. Completely forgot to get out my glasses. Probably because I haven't had them that long. Extraordinary eyesight for a man of my age, that's what the eye-place fellow said, but not so good for some things. Like photographs. Yes, yes, that's Ricky Seaton.'

'And you met him at the Black Dog?'

'Erm, yes.'

'How long ago?'

'I'm still not sure about that.'

'The person who remembers seeing you together thinks you weren't too happy with Ricky Seaton. Is that true? And if it is, why was that?'

'This person . . . I can imagine who it was, and I'm not impressed. You need to watch out for people who think they can do your job better than you can, Inspector.'

'I'll bear that in mind, sir. What did you and Mr Seaton discuss?'

Stroud spread his hands expansively. 'Well, this and that, I suppose. It isn't as if I really know the man. Different generation, really.'

'More your son's age, was he?'

Pushing out his bottom lip, Stroud snuffled into his mustache and gave his head a deliberate shake. 'Hard to say. Y'know, I think he was waffling on about something but I'm damned if I can think what it was. Unless . . . no, just a casual meeting.'

Dan decided there was nothing for it but to dig in and reference what he had already been told. 'Perhaps I can jiggle your memory. The Phoenix Players. Out at the old tithe barn in the Playing Fields area.'

'Wonderful old place. Simply marvelous. Yes, I know that's there, although I've never been to see a production. Not my cup of tea.'

He would enjoy, Dan decided, rattling the man's bones for deliberate obfuscation. And why? Surely he knew these details would have to come out – sooner or later.

'Did Ricky Seaton talk to you about making a donation to the Phoenix Players? There's been a suggestion that he may have.'

'Has there? I read a piece about this recent murder being connected to the cricket-bat murder. In this morning's paper. Must rankle, that, having it all set out for the public. Everyone knowing nothing's moving on the first killing and now there's a second one. I should think you're desperate by now.'

'You didn't answer my question,' Dan said, staring directly into the man's eyes. 'Ricky Seaton asked you for a donation, didn't he? A simple yes or no, please.'

'Nothing's simple, Inspector. You know that.'

'What I know is that you're wasting my time by avoiding my questions. You're here voluntarily, but if you continue to avoid whatever question I ask you, that arrangement can be changed to something very official.'

'Why? Because you can charge me with some heinous crime? Not unless you want to make a total arse of yourself. I knew Ricky Seaton. I met him a couple of times at the Black Dog and we had a drink together. Make something out of that, if you can.'

'He was a friend of your son's, wasn't he? Harry?'

'Who told you that?'

Dan leaned back in his chair. The snappy answer told him he was right, but he was not about to say he got the information from Venetia Stroud, among others. Certainly, there could be no mention of Alex, which meant he might have to wait before poking around the Rum Hole connection.

'Things have a way of filtering out,' he said when he decided

Stroud was fidgeting nicely. 'Listen, two men have died and we're working day and night to try to make sure they're the only deaths. You want that, too, don't you?'

'You don't have anything on me,' Stroud said. 'This is one of those fishing expeditions and I intend to make it known that you're inept. So much so, you're dangerous.'

'I'm asking you once again, do you have any information you believe would be useful in this case?'

'Have you ever thought that if you were better at asking questions, you might get better answers? I think I know what you're after and I'll see if I can help you, since you don't seem able to help yourself. Ricky Seaton came around to The Vines a few times when he and Harry were boys. Strictly not our type and not a suitable friend for Harry but, as you'd know if you had sons, the best way to make them go against you is to tell them what you want them to do.'

No need to muddy the waters by mentioning his own son. Dan waited.

'All I said at the Black Dog was the simple truth: that Harry knew Ricky Seaton. And I may have mentioned that Seaton wasn't liked at the Rum Hole which, as you probably know, is popular among the up-and-comers these days.'

'But you go there, Major? That's how you know Ricky was disliked.'

Stroud puffed and pushed out his lips before saying, 'I have never been to that place and I never shall. But Harry used to like it, and I recall his saying that Seaton was forever annoying other customers by trying to cadge money for his theatrical nonsense. Nothing more than that.'

'Thank you,' Dan said, while LeJuan scribbled away in his notebook.

Major Stroud stood up. 'You've wasted enough of my morning—'

'You will be brought in for a formal interview.' The man's bluster satisfied Dan that he had done his job. 'At that time, you will want to have your legal representative present.'

Stroud's eyes narrowed. 'Your chief constable, Winston Baily, is a friend of mine. We both belong to the same golf club. I shall be talking to him shortly.'

TWENTY-FOUR

I f he had his way, he and Alex would snag two witnesses from the street outside the registry office in Cheltenham and get married with only Katie and Bogie representing the families. Not that he didn't love their respective parents, and their great – and even their irritating – friends, but his spirit screamed out for simplicity and all he truly needed was Alex at his side and a chorus of 'I do!' spoken resoundingly by the only people who mattered in all this: Alexandra Duggins and Anthony Harrison.

Tony ducked to give the Black Dog a sideways look as he drove past on his way home from the clinic. From the few cars parked, it seemed they were having a quiet night. Good. That had made it easier for Alex to agree to leave early. He had suggested she come now but she insisted there was still work only she could do.

The dogs were in the back of his Range Rover and he would leave them at the house when he came back for Alex. Her vehicle was in the garage for repair and should have been returned in the afternoon. They must have more work than they could handle, but it didn't matter – he knew Alex was a good driver, but he still preferred to drive her himself when the roads were as bad as they were tonight. He smiled. He had better not say that aloud to Alex or he would be accused of being 'such a man!'

Several hours ago, the two of them had gone to the registry office and given notice of their intent to marry. He couldn't help another, wider grin. They had been told the notice was only good for twelve months and he had taken pleasure in saying that six weeks would have been enough.

A thought about Penny did not surprise him – similar thoughts came too frequently. He wished she were alive and happy somewhere, but hoped he never got another email with her name on it. How did you go from loving someone to feeling something that must be close to disgust for them? He and Penny had always ridden an emotional seesaw, but he couldn't have guessed, even in the really down times, that their marriage would end as it had, with long stretches of silence and avoidance, and eventually in estrangement. Did he still feel sad about such a spectacularly failed relationship? Almost. Sometimes. But if he were totally honest, Penny had become someone he barely recognized from their early days: disgruntled, disenchanted with their life and – as detailed in the email – a woman who didn't want what her husband had wanted, what she herself had pretended to be excited about until it was in their grasp.

Every time he checked his email, he half-expected to see something more from her. The idea made him feel sick and tense. The solicitor, with whom he had been honest about the contact, told him that even if Penny made a sudden, dramatic appearance, her behavior in effectively deserting her husband and then playing threatening games years later, would cast her in a bad light. Barstwick assured Tony the situation would come straight in his favor. 'I hope you're right,' he muttered.

He turned on to the road leading uphill toward home and felt the front traction check sideways. Slush, the mixture of snow and rain that had fallen since late afternoon, spread a slick glaze. A degree or two more on the downward slide and it would become black ice. Now that darkness drew in so early, this kind of weather was treacherous.

It was an unfriendly night, the conifers on either side seeming to reach toward each other over the road. No moon or stars, no visible meeting of land and sky. Flat, surly obscurity. The windscreen wipers squeaked and juddered back and forth in front of him, pushing a scattering of wet flakes aside. He reached to touch the glass. Freezing.

The high beams of a following vehicle hit his rearview mirror, dazzling him for an instant. He tapped his brakes and flashed his own lights, but the tailgater either didn't notice, or didn't take the hint. Muttering under his breath, Tony tipped the mirror down. It was too bad there were no lights on this road.

There had been a call from the people contracted to build the new conservatory off the side of the house. Alex had grinned like a kid at the news that they could start within two weeks, and he had decided against suggesting a postponement until the weather got better – and the wedding was safely behind them. The construction plans had been approved ages ago; she had waited long enough to start replacing what had been her favorite room in the house she was selling.

Behind him, the headlights swung to the left as the car took off on the narrow road leading farther up into the hills. Living where he and Alex did would be too isolated for many. The two of them appreciated the peace, and the largely unspoiled surroundings. With Alex at his side, Tony thought, he could be happy if theirs was the only house in these hills.

He drove around the final curve before passing Alex's all but sold property. Only half a mile to go. Sensing where they were, the dogs stirred, their leads clinking, and they both started making 'we're home' noises that got louder and more agitated by the second. 'It's OK, boys and girls. Almost there.'

As he parked on the downward slope of the driveway, huge, sloppy flakes of snow started to fall in earnest again, splattering the windscreen. By the time he got out of the Range Rover and opened the tailgate for the dogs, half an inch of slippery mush coated the ground. He was glad of the automatic lights illuminating the pathway.

These conditions could get much worse and very fast, probably before he had intended to set off for the Black Dog again. The instant he had unlocked the front door, Bogie and Katie burst into the house and romped joyously toward the kitchen at the back, spreading filthy footprints and sprays of muddy water as they went. Tony followed. They would want food and fresh water before he could even get his coat off in peace.

He filled the electric kettle and switched it on for tea. An unopened packet of Jaffa Cakes taunted him from the biscuit tin and, although he hated to give in, he took them out and ate two in quick succession, savoring the orange filling and chocolate coating. After all, he needed all the help his energy level could get . . . he had paperwork to get through and wanted to be sharper than he felt right now.

Katie set about finishing the dry food left in her bowl from the morning, but Bogie trotted to the back door and looked at it expectantly. It was his ritual to come in through the front door, dash to the kitchen and demand to be released into the gardens.

Tony made him wait until the kettle had boiled and the tea bag was steeping in a mug. Then he let the dog out and watched him hare off toward his favorite spot among a group of yew trees.

He left the door open and went to finish making tea. Katie was already on her way to the sitting room where she would be disappointed not to find a fire alight.

A whistling gust of wind surprised him, blowing snow into the kitchen and slamming the door wide open. He could smell the biting, pine-laced air. The lights flickered and he groaned – starting a fire would be a good idea since mini power failures often heralded the real thing. Grabbing a torch from the window ledge and stuffing it into a pocket, he went to shut out the snow – and heard Bogie yipping outside.

'Come, boy,' he called, zipping up the liner on his waxed jacket and closing the snaps over the top to foil the wind. 'Come on, now. It's too cold for messing about out there.' There was nothing Bogie enjoyed more than a game of 'you can't catch me!'

He hunched his shoulders and dug his hands into his pockets. Bogie kept up the barking but did not come to the door. Tony walked outside and took a few steps away from the house. He listened to the dog. The barking speeded, became quickly frantic. Switching on the torch, he strode rapidly toward the yews. 'OK, Bogie. I'm coming, boy.'

Once between the trees, their dense foliage blocked the snow. As he walked, the wind whipped twigs and fallen leaves into mini tornadoes. There was too much debris on the ground. He should have had a proper cleanup done by now.

The stand of yews petered out and Tony was confronted by pitch darkness contrasted with dirty, mostly half-melted snow and, at the far end of the garden, the three fine old oaks he and Alex never failed to admire. That was the direction Bogie's barking seemed to come from, he realized. 'Bogie! Come, boy. Come.' It would have been wiser to take a light with a broader beam. The torch was not strong enough and he had to range it back and forth, then in front of his feet to avoid stumbling over a stray rock or root.

Even with their sturdy branches bare, the oaks formed a

crowded canopy. Tony had to duck in places to keep moving forward, while rotting mulch beneath his feet made the going slower than it should be.

Then he saw Bogie, or he saw his solid little body jumping, and falling into the slimy leaves again. His bark was a panicky, high-pitched croak.

'Bogie – it's OK, Bogie. I'm here. Stay boy, stay.' And the dog tried to do as he was told but he whimpered and squeaked and danced – at the end of a rope.

With the hair on his neck standing up, Tony looked around while he ran and reached the dog, and the rope that tied him to the middle oak that was farthest away from the house. He dropped the torch beside the tree and went to work on a series of knots. Whoever had tied them was guilty of overkill – they could have held a cow captive.

Finally giving up on leaning over, and cursing himself for not carrying a knife, Tony dropped to his knees, cradled Bogie in the crook of an arm and struggled with rope that felt stiff and oily.

Where were his wits? *Take the collar off!*

The beam from his discarded torch projected upward and he felt as well as saw a moving shadow against the tree trunk. 'What the hell . . .?' Solid, overpowering pressure landed on his shoulders and he pitched forward. A boot came down on the hand he reached toward the torch, his only possible weapon, and he saw a second shape moving, swinging.

A noose.

He yelled, not knowing what he yelled, and fought to get free of the weight on his shoulders; a man knelt on his back and those knees moved to form a vice on Tony's head. There was nothing to get a hold on but handfuls of slick leaves. Still he scrabbled, tried to get his legs beneath him and push up.

An unyielding arm closed around his neck, but he managed to almost stand while he tore at the feet grinding into his sides. He was being ridden, piggy-back, by an assailant he could not see. The arm yanked at his head, turned it sharply to the side and, at the same time, what he knew was that shadow noose fell past his eyes and mouth to his neck and was drawn back mercilessly.

He fell then, hard, with the entire weight of his own body and the madman on his back throwing him into the tree.

The blow to his forehead snapped his head backward, crammed his face into scouring bark. Blood in his eyes. So much pain. Pain like fire; fading to nothing.

TWENTY-FIVE

'I should have left with Tony,' Alex said to her mother. 'We'll be getting there almost as soon as he does anyway.'

Lily kept her eyes on the road and speeded up her wipers. 'You weren't to know the temperature was going to drop the way it has. And more snow is coming – sooner than we thought.'

'Tony will say I shouldn't have let you drive me home in weather like this.' Alex looked sideways at Lily and chuckled. 'And I'm going to blame you for being impossible to argue with.'

Her mum laughed with her. 'You do that. I had to move my car anyway. And I need more time with you to talk wedding.'

Alex couldn't help her smile. She hadn't expected to get excited, but since she and Tony had visited the registry office earlier in the day, she had to admit that her tummy had been jittery in the nicest of ways. 'We've gone in circles about the date. We just want it to be soon. At first I thought about Christmas, then we decided that although it'll be very casual, the extra week until New Year would be better.'

'Very nice of you,' Lily said sarcastically. 'Of course, we're never too busy over Christmas – only a few weeks away, in case you hadn't noticed – so there will be plenty of time to plan and do all those things a wedding means.'

Alex didn't rise to that. 'I'm glad you're coming up with me tonight. Tony's almost more excited than I am.' An understatement. 'He'll be only too happy to discuss cakes and flowers with you. Not that we're doing anything fancy.'

When her mother didn't comment, Alex twisted in her seat and said, 'I'm thinking we could do lots of cupcakes. They do all these spray-on icings in bright colors; we could pile them up. A rainbow of colors would be fun. Cupcakes are all the rage now and they're easy to eat—'

'Stop right there.' Menace entered Lily's voice. 'Just reel it right back in and keep your DIY wedding ideas to yourself.'

'But—'

'Ah, ah, ah,' Lily interrupted. 'I'll make one statement then we'll be at your place and I'll discuss all this with Tony. You're welcome to listen and give positive comments.'

'Mum!'

'OK, I'll make two statements before we observe silence on the subject. One, I am the wedding planner and, although I will entertain suggestions, I am the only one with veto power. Two, George's has been supplying baked goods to the Black Dog forever and doing a fabulous job. I've seen their wedding cakes and they're equally fabulous. I'd like you to design your own cake – nothing less than three tiers, with plenty of extra cake to allow for the groom's cake we'll send out. I happen to know that George's loves to execute individual designs for one-of-a-kind wedding cakes. Any cakes, for that matter, and they do it beautifully.'

'Take a breath, Mum!' Alex didn't know for how long she would keep thinking her mother's takeover bid was funny, but for now she'd roll with it.

'I'm done. For now. I'm still glad I got this SUV. James insisted this one wouldn't be good for hills and bad weather. I think it's great, don't you?'

Neat change of topic. Lily was crazy about her RAV4. She had been driving it since midsummer and still treated it like a new toy. 'People seem to like their Toyotas. I like them. This is a good vehicle for you.' Alex was not a car enthusiast. She would happily drive her Range Rover until the wheels fell off.

A freshly furious bombardment of snow all but halted the wipers. Lily pumped her brakes gently and slowed to a crawl. She flipped on her hazards and peered over her shoulder. Alex looked, too, in time to see the rear wipers struggling with sliding snow and sludge from the roof.

'Call Tony,' Lily said. 'In case he thinks he should set off to pick you up before the weather gets any worse. There's no reason for him to go out in this again.'

Alex felt around in her bag and found her mobile. She called Tony but his phone went straight to messaging. 'Hi, you,' she said. 'We did have the discussion about not turning our phones off unless we're in the middle of surgery or blow-drying our hair, didn't we, sweetheart? I'm almost home so don't worry about driving to get me. Love you.' And she hung up.

'Blow-drying *our* hair?' Lily said.

'That was just to pretend we might both be capable of leaving a mobile off when someone needs to reach us.'

'Uh-huh.'

Home lay at the next bend in the road and Lily leaned forward to watch for the gates. She turned the defoggers on high, slowed and checked in all directions, at least for as much as she could actually see. And she swept across the narrow road somewhat faster than Alex might have, unless she was completely sure no vehicle would burst out of the snowstorm and flatten them.

They came scarily close to the passenger side gatepost . . .

Lily had resumed her snail's pace and inched down the steep driveway to park beside Tony's vehicle and in front of the garage doors.

'A spare bed is always made up, Mum,' Alex said, opening the door and gathering her bag. 'I can't let you drive home in this tonight. I have plenty of nighties.'

'Pish. It'll ease off and I'll be fine.'

The temptation to talk about invoking her own veto power was strong. 'We'll see how it goes,' Alex said instead.

She zipped her wax parka and slid to the ground, sinking into inches of powdery snow. Lily joined her and they linked arms to trudge to the front door.

'Katie!' With her slightly creaky gait, Katie came from the side of the house and walked ponderously to greet them. 'Sweetheart. What are you doing out here in the cold? She must have gone into the gardens to do her business and got shut out of the kitchen. Poor baby.' Alex crouched to hug the dog and accept a sloppy kiss. 'Or perhaps she heard us coming and came to investigate.'

'Right,' Lily said. 'Let's get in and warm us all up.'

Once inside, Alex shut the door with a solid thump and breathed in warm air gratefully. 'We're home, Tony!' She hauled off her boots while Lily did the same. 'Tony can't have been home long. I bet he's outside getting wood. Come on in and sit down by the fire. She led the way into the breakfast-cum-sitting room and turned the corners of her mouth down. 'Well, I was half right. He must be fetching wood but there's no fire yet. Rats. I'll make sure there's a kettle on.'

A cold draft met them before they made it all the way into the kitchen and Alex stopped, frowned around. A mug filled with what looked like tea stood on the closest counter beside the electric kettle. Automatically, she gave the kettle a quick tap with the flats of her fingers. It was quite warm.

The door to the gardens stood wide open.

'The veterinary business must be good,' Lily said.

Alex went to the door. 'Why do you say that?' Tony didn't leave outer doors open, ever.

'Nothing really. I was going to make a crack about heating the outdoors. He'll be in soon enough.'

'Right.' She stepped outside, instantly soaking her socks with icy slurry and called, 'Tony? You OK?' and added, 'He's had too much on his mind.' The last thing he would want was for her to tell someone, even her mother, about the email supposedly from Penny, but Alex was certain it was still bothering him. 'I'll heat the water again.'

'I hear Bogie barking. He's probably having a great game in the snow.'

'He loves it,' Alex said. 'Ploughs through it like a dolphin if it gets deep enough.' She braced herself on the doorframe and tugged off the sodden socks, then she slowly straightened and leaned outside.

'What is it?' Lily came to lay a hand on her shoulder.

'Mum, does Bogie sound . . . he sounds frantic to me. I think he's in some sort of trouble.' She stuffed her feet into a pair of wellies just outside the door, trying to ignore the cold wet insoles, and started forward, listening to the dog. His barks were scratchy shrieks. Her stomach turned over.

'That's not right,' her mother said, sounding breathless. 'Tony!'

The sound of his name, shouted like that, jolted Alex, and she started out across the snow-laden grass at a jog. 'Tony? Where are you?' Her own breath caught in her throat with each inward puff of frigid air. She looked from side to side, turned a circle to see in all directions. Nothing – other than the distressed barking.

'Bogie's over there somewhere.' Her mother panted. 'Somewhere on the right side.' The wellies she'd grabbed were too big and they hobbled her. Snow drove into their faces, their eyes.

'Tony!' Alex shouted again.

'Why isn't he answering?' Lily said. 'He has to have heard us, doesn't he?'

'I don't know. He could be helping poor Bogie. He concentrates completely when he's working.' She could blame her smarting eyes on the snow, but it was tears that prickled and made her squint. Some use in an emergency, she was.

What emergency? As far as they knew nothing awful had happened. Bogie had probably got himself tangled up in something. They had talked about how they needed to get the very back of the garden sorted out – especially around the trees. It was a mess and Bogie was probably paying for that. Weren't there some lengths of wire out here that had been pulled from around dead vines.

'I see him,' Alex cried. 'Under the oaks. He has to be injured or he'd come running.'

'He's jumping around,' Lily said breathlessly. 'You can tell he's caught up in something. Bogie, boy, we're here now.' Running side by side, they made it across the virgin snow as fast as they could.

'Someone's tied him up,' Alex said through gritted teeth. She looked in all directions. Nothing moved. 'They must have just come into our garden and done it, then run away. Can you believe that? Were they hoping he'd freeze to death on the end of their stinking rope? God, I hope Tony hasn't gone after someone in the dark like this.'

She stumbled a few more steps and grabbed Bogie, held him close while he whined and made little sobbing sounds into her ear. There wasn't just one knot in the rope. Knot after knot had been tied. 'This makes no sense,' Alex said, discarding a glove to work the damp rope undone. 'Do you have a knife by any chance, Mum?'

'No, but I'll run back and get one.'

'What's the matter with my brain?' Alex said. 'I'll take his collar off.' The frozen buckle caused her numb fingers to ache. 'I'm getting it done now. I think he's more offended than hurt. How dare some horrible person do this to you, right, Bogie? Hey, look at that.' All but buried was a tennis racket, the kind with a big head.

Lily picked it up and gave a shake. 'Brand new. Did one of you leave it out here?'

'No. No reason to, but it doesn't matter. Nothing matters but finding Tony now.'

'Alex.' Lily's voice caught. 'There. Look. Oh, my God.'

Bogie came loose and burrowed deeper into Alex's arms. Lily hurried past, her feet plunging deep with each step.

Then Alex saw what Lily had seen and for an instant she was sure her heart had stopped. A wide swathe of flattened snow swept into deep shadow that stretched behind one of the three great oak trees. She swallowed a scream. Tony, in his denim shirtsleeves, lay face down and very still on the ground,

There was blood on the snow.

She could not allow herself to think about that other time when another man, Bogie's first boss, had lain, dead, on just such a frozen carpet.

'It's Tony,' Lily shouted.

Alex couldn't speak. She couldn't breathe.

They stumbled until they stood over Tony's still body. His head was turned to the side, his chin driven down, and his face covered with blood.

'Mum, look, they tried to hang him!' She heard her own scream. Around his neck was a stiff noose that stood up against the back of his head and a coil of rope had been thrown over a thick tree branch. 'They stopped. Oh, my God. They were going to hang him.'

Lily's face was ashen. 'Why would they do that if he was already . . .' She clamped her lips together. 'Did they stop because they heard us?'

'Don't touch him,' Alex said, ignoring what she knew her mother had been about to say. 'Ambulance! Call an ambulance! We have to try to keep him warm.' She fell to her knees, stripped off her coat and spread it over him. 'Where are his boots? Mum, help me. Blankets, we need blankets.'

Lily was already through to emergency. While she talked, she bent to press fingers beneath the noose at his neck, moved them and pressed again. She didn't meet Alex's eyes, but stood up again. 'Yes,' she said into the phone. 'It's a steep driveway. The doors are open. We're at the end of the back garden on the right.'

Alex swallowed and swallowed. She put a cheek to Tony's

and felt wet blood on her skin. This had not happened long ago. 'That's good, isn't it?' she shouted. 'The blood's not dry.'

'The ambulance is on its way,' Lily said, the phone still at her ear. 'Here's my coat, Alex. I'll get blankets. And I'll call James. He'll want to be here.'

Alex put Lily's coat on top of her own. She wanted to cover his head but didn't dare in case she caused more damage. 'Whoever did this heard us coming and stopped,' she whispered close to his ear. 'Hang on, love. Why didn't I just leave everything and come home with you?'

TWENTY-SIX

Dan checked his mirror with little hope that he might have lost Leon Wolf on the way from Gloucester. Snow fell more heavily but, sure enough, there were the headlights of the psychologist's glittering new Jaguar XF, bumping across an old cattle grid inside the gates. Present for another chat with Winston Baily that afternoon, Major Stroud having kept his promise to kick up a fuss with the chief constable, Wolf had ever so kindly volunteered to keep Dan company for this evening's exploratory visit to the Rum Hole. Evidently there were further enlightening theories to share. This had been a shitty day and it was not getting any better.

Already he was beating himself up over leaving Calum to rattle around in the cottage so much, never knowing when Dan might turn up again. He called when he could grab a few minutes, but it wasn't often, and there was too much going on for that to change any time soon. Calum seemed happy enough, though, and he had already conned Beth Wills into driving him to buy paint for his bedroom. The boy's choice of off-white ('small rooms don't need a lot of color, Dad') had surprised Dan. And he was glad of the choice – and the boy's enthusiasm.

Beneath a leaden, grey-black sky, Mill House sat amid two acres of slightly ragged gardens tinted by yellow-tinged lights that sullied snow-covered lawns. From Dan's brief online reading about the place, several generations of former owners had gradually sold off large parcels of farmland, leaving the house looking too big for its grounds.

If they didn't get turned away from the Rum Hole for want of a secret password, he could hope for pointers to why Ricky Seaton might not be smiled upon at the club. Was it really only because he had tried to solicit donations there?

Why the hell anyone thought a Prohibition-style speakeasy was a good idea in the Cotswolds evaded him. They worked well in London, or so he was told, but that was, well, *London*. What had started as a spur-of-the-moment idea for a recce – mostly to have something to persuade Winston Baily that the case wasn't completely stalled – might, if nothing else, have offered an opportunity for a pint quaffed in his own company at the end of a busy, often frustrating and mostly fruitless day. But that was not to be, since Dan was sure Wolf had his own agenda and it would entail conversation to be carefully negotiated. Each time they spoke, Dan couldn't help looking for veiled meanings and potential traps. Probably not fair since, in the main, Leon Wolf seemed a somewhat reformed man and anxious to mend bridges between them.

Mid-1700s, Mill House (why, one wondered, was it called Mill House?) was built of red brick and clearly Georgian. Spotlights shone on the front face and illuminated a balustrade edging the front roof, and three symmetrical lines of windows across the flat façade. At the top of a central flight of stone steps to the building, white marble pillars flanked an imposing, and open, front door.

A broad drive and a line of bare sycamores separated a car park from the house. Dan waited for Wolf to park beside him before leaving his car to walk through shallow drifts of slush with fresh snow starting to pile on top.

'Have you been here before?' Wolf asked, raising his usually quiet voice a notch. 'Did you know it was here?'

If I've been here before, I know it's here. 'No. I understand this is one more part of the area that used to be called the Playing Fields.'

'Still is, by those of us who've lived here a long time. Look, Dan, I didn't mention this at the station because . . . well, you'll know why when we speak about it. No point in ruffling already ruffled feathers by raising questions that might not have come up. It's about the man, Dimbleby. Any insights into what went on with him? If anything did?'

Dan wiped his wet shoes on a mat to make sure he didn't go skating on the marble tiles inside the hall. Rooms on both sides appeared to be part of Mill House Restaurant, and the hum of music and voices, the rattle of dishes and silverware, suggested business was brisk. The lobby was decked out for Christmas, complete with skyscraper tree and acres of colored lights.

'If he believed he was attacked, and by our man, I would have expected him to make more of a fuss. You saw the piece in the papers?'

'Oh, yes,' Wolf replied. 'And I heard him on the *Andy Preece Morning Show.*'

He'd missed that, damn it. 'Did you? You mean he called in?' Someone on the team should have caught the broadcast and brought it up at the team meeting. He'd have to see who was supposed to be on that.

'He was the main guest. People were calling in to ask him questions. You might want to think about putting a lid on him somehow. He's using whatever did or didn't happen to whip up attention. Sounds more and more like a PR stunt to me. Mentions running for the county council every few moments. When he's elected, so he says, he'll stay on the backs of the police and make sure this is a safer area to live in. He'll get results, fast results. And in the process of all this, he's whipping up fear.'

Bloody nuisance. 'He declined the offer to see our doc for a check-over. Reckons all he wanted was to let us know what happened just in case it was helpful to our investigations. As long as he doesn't remember anything useful to the case, the sooner he can forget all about it, the better.' Dan took off his raincoat and draped it over an arm. 'Although I don't suppose we can hope he'll stop yacking about it on the radio every chance he gets. Politicians! He's even less subtle than most and he's the kind of nuisance we can do without.'

'No one on reception,' Wolf remarked when they'd waited at the desk for too long. 'We might as well make our own way.' He pointed to stairs where a brass plate stated, Rum Hole. and pointed upward. The banisters were tinsel-draped to match a similarly decorated Christmas tree on the opposite side of the lobby.

Leon started up ahead of Dan and tapped the tinsel. 'I can see someone with a few drinkies inside grabbing this stuff by mistake and taking a header downstairs. Hope they've got good insurance.'

Such a positive guy. 'Cheery thought,' Dan said.

They reached the Rum Hole, where no one greeted them with

a request for the password . . . or an offer of a table. The room was wide but not so deep, wrapped around in dark wood with groups of leather chairs and green-shaded lamps. In alcoves there were low tables and double settees set well back for privacy beneath large but dim pendant lights. The place wasn't busy although there were sporadic bursts of raucous, maybe forced-sounding laughter. Surprisingly, traditional jazz was the music of choice. Dan noted that some of the clientele, especially singles, seemed well-oiled, then remembered it was close to nine o'clock and many of them might have been here for hours.

A waiter swanned past, decked out in a red and white striped waistcoat, rolled-up white sleeves, natty bow tie . . . and a black bowler hat. Dan had never been to New Orleans but thought this was a takeoff of something that might be found in the French Quarter, muddled with gentlemen's club accoutrements. Speakeasy? He still couldn't see it.

'Would you mind finding us a table with a reasonably good view of the place so we can watch the action?' Dan asked Leon. 'I'm going to see if I can find out who to talk to.'

He left without waiting for a response. The truth was that he would be far more relaxed and into this if he did not have a hanger-on. LeJuan intended to meet up with them after he finished coaching basketball with a group of twelve-year-olds from a local school. He was dedicated, made it a weekly priority.

After waiting several minutes, during which a barman polished glasses and served no drinks, Dan cleared his throat and leaned on the counter. 'Excuse me.' He took out his warrant card and introduced himself. 'Couple of questions, please.'

The bloke sauntered over. 'Yeah?'

'Do you recognize this man?' He proffered the photograph of Ricky Seaton and Kelly leaning on the MGB. 'We understand he was a regular customer here.'

'A lot of people are regulars.'

Dan swallowed a retort and decided to wait the man out.

'Yeah, I've probably seen him.'

'When was the last time?'

'Oh, mate, I don't know. Like I say, this is a busy place. A helluva lot of people come and go.'

'There's a good few people nursing drinks alone tonight,

though,' Dan commented. 'It's loud in here but you aren't exactly overrun with customers. Is that an anomaly maybe?'

'Look. I just work here—'

'I'll talk to someone in charge.' Dan cut the man off. 'I'm going to do that. You've got a manager?'

'Yeah. He's out. Don't know when he's getting back.'

'Do you have table service, or do we place an order here?'

'Suit yourself.'

Dan was past getting uptight about negative reactions to the police. He turned away and located Wolf at a table in a far corner. His mobile rang as he got within hailing distance and he answered. 'DCI O'Reilly.'

'LeJuan.'

'OK. Hold a moment.' He held the mobile to his chest and said to Wolf, 'Fancy mixed drinks are the specialty in these places. See if they can scare up a pint of good bitter. Otherwise a single malt. It's on me.' He indicated the mobile and turned away to find a quieter spot.

At the top of the stairs outside the club, he leaned against a wall and went back to LeJuan. 'Sorry. We're at the Rum Hole. That's Leon Wolf and me. He's determined to stick to us like glue. If you never see this place, you probably won't have missed much. Are you planning to come here?'

'No, boss. There's been an accident. No, I mean an attack. No accident, I assure you, or that's what the uniform I spoke to told me. Apparently, Tony Harrison was attacked in the back gardens of his house, and whoever did it probably has the same playbook as the killer of Edward Coughlin and Ricky Seaton. Don't quote me on that, but from where I'm standing that's how I see it.'

Dan realized he was holding his breath. 'And Tony?'

'He'd been taken away by the time I got there. They were waiting for CSI. You'll want to be in on this.'

Masking what he was feeling, Dan turned back into the club and located Wolf. He gave him a wave and hunched over his phone again. 'How's Tony?'

After too long a silence, LeJuan said, 'Not quite dead yet. One of the medic's words, not mine. Alex and her mother found Tony. Alex has gone to the hospital, but her mother agreed to remain here and answer questions. Doc James went with Alex. Boss, it doesn't look good. I thought Tony was already dead and I wasn't the only one. He's been beaten around the head and shoulders. There was a rope. It's still here.'

'A rope?'

'Yeah. Looked like they were going to string him up. Hang him from a tree. And another thing. Think cricket bat and dagger. A brand-new tennis racket was lying in the snow. At first Alex said she couldn't think of any connection, but then she remembered that Tony had been the leading light on his school tennis team at one point.'

'Shit. This only gets worse. Our man is deliberately scattering breadcrumbs for us, then laughing because we're not too bright at his game. I'll be there. Don't be surprised if I've still got my psychology companion. And you can thank the chief constable for that.' He switched off and went back to get Leon Wolf.

But he stopped so suddenly, he almost tripped. A man came through swinging doors from what Dan thought must be the kitchens. He walked behind one of the bar counters, pulling a black beanie from his blond hair as he went.

Slowly at first, then with more purpose, Dan headed toward him, his heart beating hard. Oh, yeah, oh, yeah, indeed.

'Excuse me,' he said when he was close enough. He was already fishing out his warrant card. 'Excuse me, sir.'

He had raised his voice to combat the music and increasingly loud shrieks of laughter. The man looked up at him, his face tense but not anxious – at first. That changed when he took a closer look at Dan.

'You work here?' Dan said.

'Manager and part-owner,' came the clipped answer.

'And we've met before. You're the friend of Kelly and Ricky Seaton. It was at the Seaton house.' Dan could picture him now, hovering protectively around the just widowed Kelly Seaton – she who had insisted she and her husband had no friends.

The other man stuffed his hat into a pocket and his blank look was almost convincing.

'Gordon Dulles,' Dan said. 'You and I need to talk.'

TWENTY-SEVEN

How could she be freezing, but hot at the same time? A dry heat that roasted her face, prickled damply along her spine. Alex looked at her hands. She couldn't stop them shaking, and the palms were red and itchy. Her feet were numb.

Please let Tony come through this. Let him wake up and look at her so she would know he was alive, that he was coming back, that he was who he had always been. He had laughed when he'd tried to coax her into going home with him late in the afternoon but, just as jokingly, he had added that he knew she was with her first love so he would stand in line. And she had laughed with him. *God, don't let it be true that he thinks the pub is more important to me than he is.*

Why didn't I go home with him when he asked? She couldn't get the question out of her head.

They wouldn't let her travel in the ambulance, even though she had kept her voice as steady as she could when she asked to go with Tony. The medics didn't say as much, but it was obvious that there was too much to be done for him to have space wasted on a useless onlooker. Doc James had insisted on driving her to the hospital while Lily followed in her own car.

After three hours in Emergency, they had transferred Tony into the main hospital. Doc had been allowed on to the ICU but not Lily or Alex. She knew nothing, absolutely nothing, apart from what she had seen with her own eyes. The injuries must be terrible . . . so much blood. She heard the raking sound that escaped her throat and swallowed – as if she had any control over it, over anything.

Lily stood facing a night-black window in a waiting room for relatives of ICU patients. Snow had turned to hail. It blasted the glass, driven by fierce winds that rattled the frames. Alex didn't think her mother saw anything, but looking was something to do.

I can't stand this any longer.

'I'm going to ask if I can watch through the windows into Tony's room,' Alex said, although she did not move. What she had said was for Lily's benefit, to judge how she would react. 'I've seen what it's like on the television, they have windows all around. I can't bear being here and doing nothing.'

'I'll go and find some tea,' Lily responded. 'Sit down and close your eyes. If you must think, think. But if you could concentrate on relaxing your muscles, seeing something that makes you feel good, letting yourself feel as if you're floating, so much the better.' She threw up her hands, let them fall. 'What am I faffing on about? You know all the right stuff to do. Tony needs you to be the best you can be. You haven't got time to fall apart, or not now. Later you can do that if you still want to.'

'Later, after Tony's dead, you mean?' She heard her own voice rise and break. Lily didn't say anything. She came to Alex and put an arm around her shoulders.

'I'm sorry, Mum,' Alex murmured. 'I don't know where that came from.'

'I do. It came from being afraid and you've got a right to be. Tony needs positive thoughts coming from all of us, but mostly from you. The doctors and nurses are giving him everything they've got. We have to hold it together for all of them. I know James will come and talk to us as soon as there's something to say.'

'How long do you think Tony was out there like that before we found him?'

'Not long. You know when the two of you last talked – just before he set off for home.' Lily took her arm from Alex's shoulders and started to pace slowly. The silver in her dark hair had become more plentiful. It glinted under the overhead lights. 'I wanted to get you home because, well yes, there was the weather, but I know the two of you need more time together, alone. You haven't had much lately. Thank goodness I did think about it and thank goodness you agreed. Maybe it was forty minutes from when you and Tony last talked and when we got to the house. About fifteen minutes to drive up there. He could have been home for twenty minutes or so, but we don't know when he went into the back garden. He'd made tea. I expect he let Bogie out. Don't you always do that?'

'Yes. Bogie likes to run around out there as soon as he gets home, and he loves snow. I was trying to think how long Tony might . . . just how long, that's all. What they did to him took time, didn't it? They must have surprised him, I think. They'd have to. He's a strong man. He would fight back. His fingernails are all broken and bloody. And his face.' She touched her own cheek. The blood was still there but now it was dry. 'I wanted to hold him, but he looked as if I could break him.' It hurt her throat to talk.

'You were right not to move him at all. They immobilized him on a backboard before they put him in the ambulance.'

Alex felt she might be sick. She sat with a thud on an orange plastic-covered couch and bent forward over her knees. Her head contracted inside. Standing again was out of the question – her legs would not hold her.

'There are pillows,' Lily said. 'And blankets. I think you should lie down.'

'I can't, Mum.'

A nurse came through the door with a paper cup in each hand. 'Sweet, milky tea. That may not sound very nice, but it will do you good.' She gave Lily a cup and went to stand in front of Alex on the couch. 'Drink this,' she said quietly. A comfortably built woman with very red hair, she wore startlingly pink scrubs.

Alex nodded her thanks.

'When did you eat?'

The desire to scream that she didn't want food was strong. She buried it. 'Thanks, but I'm not hungry. Do you know if there's any news yet?'

'Not yet. A doctor will come and talk to you when there is.'

'It's been hours.'

'I know, love. I don't think it'll be too much longer before you hear something.'

Hear whether he was going to live or die. Hear if he would recover and be completely healed, or impaired in some horrible way. She picked at the knee of her jeans. Tony did surgery, often on very small animals – he needed his hands to be strong and sure.

'I'll check back on you,' the nurse said and left, quietly except for the squeak of her rubber-soled shoes on linoleum.

Lily sat beside Alex and they sipped at the unappetizing tea. 'How long has it been now?' Alex said. 'Since he was brought into the hospital, I mean.'

'I don't know.'

If she could just see him, even with the medical staff working on him, because at least that would mean he was still alive, and they were still trying to save him. 'They would have come to tell us if he'd died,' she said.

Lily slid her arm beneath Alex's.

Squeaky footfalls again, coming toward them this time.

Alex looked at her mum and blinked rapidly to stop stinging tears from working free.

Doc walked into the room with an extremely tall man. He wore a white coat over green scrubs, his scrub cap pulled down to bushy blond eyebrows. He had intensely grey eyes nestled into dark puffy skin – the eyes, Alex thought, were probing. She felt uncomfortably as if he could see her mind.

'Are you the fiancée, Ms Duggins?' he asked, extending a hand. 'Mr Morgan. I've been looking after Tony Harrison. He's been through the wars.'

He made Tony sound like a ten-year-old given to rough games. Alex didn't know how to respond.

'Scans show he sustained a pretty shocking blow to the occiput, the base of the skull. But he's a lucky man. There's a subdural hematoma which may or may not resolve on its own; we'll cross that bridge when we have to. He also has a hairline fracture at C4 – spine at the neck, where that knobby bone is. Damn lucky, a bit higher and we would have been having a very different conversation.'

'What's happening now?' Alex struggled for the right questions.

'There's some swelling of the brain. We're not surprised by that. If necessary, we'll help that to go down. It's quite common to operate and drill through the skull to remove blood clots. I would be very comfortable doing that. I'm telling you all this so you won't get surprises later, but it may not be necessary. Meanwhile, we're putting him into coma to help that, and to help his condition in general. It'll be easier on him.'

'How long will he be in . . . in the coma?'

'That will depend on him. People take different lengths of time to regain consciousness once we start to bring them out. Try to be positive. He's a strong man and in excellent health.'

Alex crossed her arms tightly. 'When can I see him? May I sit with him?'

'Not quite yet.' The man smiled. It transformed his face and showed lines that proved he had smiled a lot in the past. 'Keep the faith, Ms Duggins.'

'Alex.' She felt jumpy, panicky, somewhere between hope and despair.

'Alex.' He nodded. 'I don't know how long it will be before he's settled but you might want to go out and get something to eat now. Drink a glass of wine. Try to relax.' He looked from Doc to Alex's mum and smiled once more.

When he had left, the three of them walked into a hug. With the strength of their strong arms around her, hope nibbled at the edges of Alex's fears.

Food still sounded impossible, but she went into the corridor with Doc and her mum. They pushed through swing doors into a reception area where a scattering of mostly seated people looked up at them hopefully, only to glance away again when they met her eyes. So many evolving dramas.

'There's nothing like questionable timing,' Doc said quietly. 'Here comes trouble.'

Through yet another set of swing doors came Dan O'Reilly with the man, Dr Leon Wolf, at his shoulder. Alex had thought she couldn't feel any lower. She was wrong. No, they shouldn't be here anyway. This wasn't a murder investigation.

'How is he?' Dan said as he reached them. 'This is a helluva thing. I'm so sorry. Got here as soon as I could.'

The door he'd just used swung open behind him again and a uniformed policeman approached. He went directly to Dan. 'Evening, sir.'

'Are you relieving someone?' Dan didn't sound pleased.

'No, sir. I think I'm first on.'

From his expression, the officer had said something Dan didn't want to hear. 'For fu— Get on with it, man, and I'll want to know why you weren't there from the moment the ambulance pulled in.'

'Yes, sir. I just got the word I was to come. Thank you, sir.' And away he went in the direction of ICU.

'Bloody incompetence,' Dan muttered, aiming the comment to Leon Wolf.

'Incompetence is a large part of the human condition, isn't it, Dan?' Leon responded, unctuously, Alex thought. 'Or should that be unconsciousness?'

'We're going out for a break,' Doc said. He didn't look happy with what felt like an intrusion. 'We all need to catch our breath then get back to waiting for Tony. That's all we're concerned with.'

'How is he doing?' Leon asked.

'Not well at the moment.' Doc said. 'They feel that although his injuries are serious, he's probably been . . . lucky, as the surgeon put it. He has a head injury and a hairline fracture of the cervical spine that won't cause catastrophic repercussions if all goes as the medical staff think it may. But for now, they're putting him in coma. There's a subdural hematoma and the expected swelling. They may have to operate to deal with the hematomas.'

Alex could have kissed Doc for explaining things with such calm reason. She wasn't ready for a question-and-answer session – least of all with the police.

She could feel how anxious Lily and Doc were to get away. 'I'm sure you have more important things to do than talk to us,' she said, and instantly knew her mistake.

'It was all of you we came to see,' Dan said promptly. 'With luck the cafeteria won't be busy at this time of night. I'm sorry to press you but I do need to ask you a few things. Shall we go down?'

That wasn't really a question. Alex pinched the bridge of her nose, stared at her shoes. What was she supposed to say?

'What's he doing here?' Dan said in a lowered voice.

Alex glanced up and frowned. 'I think he's an old friend of Tony's. He came to the Black Dog with him a few days ago. You were there that night, Dan.'

They fell silent and watched the man spot and close in on them. He checked his stride as if he didn't know whether to keep on approaching. 'Oh, my God,' he said in a low, pained voice, then came tentatively to them. 'Tell me he's not dead. I got here as soon as I could figure out where to come. I was at the Black Dog when the news came in.'

Alex moistened her lips. What was his name? He was quite tall, broad, and fit-looking, with thick brown hair. A pleasant but unremarkable face. She stared at him while he stood before her, his dark brown eyes filled with desperation – and suspiciously moist.

'Oh, you poor dear,' he said to Alex. 'You have no idea who I am. We met at your pub. John Ross. Tony and I were at school together. He looks after my Beatrix now. My sweet cat. I decided to stop in at the pub – been promising myself I would. Such a lovely place. Those nice sisters were hanging more of the little paintings from somewhere – Gambol Green, I think. Charming ladies. I met their cat, Max, so we clicked immediately. Cat lovers do, don't you think? But you don't want to talk about that. What's the matter with me? I'm shocked. That's it. So shocked. Please, give me news of Tony. He's such a special man.'

Doc started to speak but Alex put a hand on his arm. 'I can do this.' He shouldn't have to carry them all. 'Tony's being put into a coma to give his brain a chance to heal. Or that's what I understand from what the surgeon said.'

'Oh, I've heard of that.' His hand went to his mouth. 'It's as serious as they said, then, isn't it?'

'Who said?' Dan asked immediately. He didn't look pleased.

'At the pub. I told you I stopped in for a drink and after a bit they started talking about Tony and what happened. I'm not sure who mentioned it first. Several people had just come in. And you, Alex, you poor thing to find him like that. But he's still alive, so there's hope.'

She wanted to get away. Now.

'I had to come. I called the parish hall in Folly to track Tony down and an officer said he'd been brought here, Chief Inspector, so I decided I could find him if I was lucky.' He ducked his head. 'I admit I told the officer I was a friend of Tony and Alex's and that's probably why he told me where to come. I wouldn't want to get anyone into trouble.'

'This isn't the best time,' Leon Wolf said, surprising Alex. He gave Ross a cold stare. 'Not good at all. Best duck out and wait for news, old son.'

'But it may be my fault, don't you see?' Ross cast his eyes from one to the other of them, apparently beseeching. 'The rope. God, the rope. They were talking about how a rope was – a rope and noose. Over a tree branch. Around Tony's neck.' He choked and covered his face with a hand, rocking back and forth while he muttered unintelligibly.

Leon reached out to rest a hand on Ross's shoulder. He looked meaningfully at Dan. 'Let me help you back to your car,' he said. 'You've had a shock and being here isn't helping you. Brave of you to come and try to comfort Tony and Alex, but you're making yourself ill.'

John Ross gave the psychologist an unfriendly stare. 'I don't know who you are, but this has nothing to do with you. I'm talking to Alex about Tony. I owe it to both of them. This won't take long,' he added, giving Alex his full attention. 'History is repeating itself for me and this time, like I've said, I'm sure it's my fault. I'm the one who told Tony about the death of our friend, Malcolm Loder, and I knew he took it badly. He was devastated.'

'Should we find a quieter place to talk?' Doc said.

Ross continued as if he hadn't heard. 'Malcolm died six months ago. Suicide. He hung himself from a tree and I told Tony that.' The voice got higher again. 'Why did I tell him? It didn't bring Malcolm back. And I think   do you think it could have given Tony the idea, right when he was feeling so desperate about difficulties in his own life?'

Stunned, Alex couldn't formulate a response.

'How do you know he was in a bad way emotionally?' Doc said. He glanced warningly at Alex, who knew he didn't want her to interrupt him.

'Tony told me he was feeling low,' Ross said. 'He said he didn't know if he could go on. I'm sorry to bring this up, Alex.'

TWENTY-EIGHT

D an drank his espresso fast and intended to have another. He was certain that if she were on her own, Alex would have stayed close to the ICU rather than go to the cafeteria.

She settled for a cheese and tomato sandwich on thin and floppy white bread. Dan didn't think she particularly noticed what she ordered and that she only had it to stop anyone from telling her she ought to eat. At least Doc and Lily were adventurous enough to go for vegetable soup – also thin – and bread rolls. Lily opted for a glass of white wine and got one for Alex, too, while Doc ordered a beer. Like Dan, Leon stayed with coffee. Thank God they'd grabbed a couple of hamburgers on the way to the hospital.

Dan got up to go for the espresso. 'Can I get anybody anything?' Leon, his legs crossed and a toe bobbing, shook his head, no, and the others appeared not to hear Dan's question.

He liked this hospital cafeteria less than the one at the station – not a good recommendation. Fortunately, there were few people in the glaringly lit and cavernous room, but still there was the sense that voices and clattering noises ricocheted around its off-beige walls. Whatever currently fell from the skies bounced on the glass roof. Hail had taken over from snow with gusto.

Coffee was about the only thing that smelled appetizing, and Dan ordered a double shot.

From the corner of his eye, he saw Alex walk to stand beside him. 'Hey,' he said without looking at her. 'More wine?'

'I'll take what you're having,' she said. 'But I want to talk to you. On our own. I don't know what you *weren't* saying upstairs, but there's something. Can we sit at another table for a few minutes? I told them what I was going to do.' She inclined her head toward Doc and Lily, and Leon, who would be gnashing his teeth at being excluded from the action. He really was getting into the case – even had some insightful comments to make –

and showed himself willing to put in the extra time it took to work a case hard. 'I don't think Dr Wolf appreciates my splitting up the party.' Alex gave a wry smile.

'Double espresso for you?' Dan asked.

'Sounds good. I don't have time to be tired.'

Once they were served, she led the way to a table just about as far from the rest of the group as possible and took off her coat before sitting down.

'I understand you and Tony spoke before he set off for home.' Better to get straight to the point. 'Can you give me the gist of your conversation?'

'He let me know he was leaving the clinic and asked me if I wanted to go up the hill with him. That was all.' She moved her coffee closer, crossed her forearms on the table and stared down into her cup. 'If I had gone then, we wouldn't be here now.'

The strain she must feel showed in the tight set of her face. 'You can't know that, Alex.'

'I think I can. We would have been doing things together, for one thing. And I would never let him go outside without a coat, or . . . oh, Dan, I can't stop thinking I could have stopped this – just by being with him.'

Alex wasn't a crier, but the corners of her mouth jerked down.

And Tony's coat was missing. Officers at the scene made certain it wasn't in his car or the house. Of course, Alex had no way of making a connection to the other two murdered men, both of whom had been found without their coats or shoes.

'Tony isn't dead, Dan,' Alex said in a tight voice. 'Why are you here when this isn't a murder?'

Again, she didn't know everything he knew, and he wasn't certain how much to reveal. 'It's precautionary. With the recent events in the area, we've got to be extra careful. Are you keeping Tony's wallet for him?'

'No. Why would I? I didn't even think about it. He puts it in a back pocket when he's working and it's probably still there – or it fell out. You think whoever murdered the other two men intended to kill Tony tonight, don't you?'

He couldn't take too long to come up with an answer. 'Anything is possible at this stage of—'

'You do, Dan. That's why you're here. It's why there's a

policeman guarding Tony. You think he's in danger still, that someone will try to come back and make sure he dies.'

This coffee was more bitter than the last cup, but he drank it anyway while he thought of what to say for the best.

'Do you know why the two men were killed? Is there something that makes you think Tony is like them in some way?'

'Nothing definitive.' If he were honest, he would say he'd never worked a case with so few meaningful leads. 'There's no apparent evidence to tie the three together. They went to the same school, but so did a lot of boys from the area, and that was more than twenty years ago. Their lives and occupations are completely different. They didn't live close to one another, or, as far as we know, have common interests.' He wouldn't tell her he believed the injuries in all cases were too similar not to suggest the same killer and, in Tony's case, attacker. So far.

'John Ross shook me up,' Alex said. 'He's like an unexploded bomb. I think he's really cut up about Tony getting attacked.'

Dan considered that before saying, 'Yes. He made some pretty wild assumptions.'

'Like Tony trying to commit suicide by hanging himself in that oak tree, you mean?' She shook her head, brushed at her hair with a shaking hand. 'Why wouldn't he wait to know more facts before jumping to a conclusion like that?'

He would prefer to hear Alex's theories on that than to prompt her. 'What do you think?'

'If Tony had mentioned what John said about his friend's death, I might not think this, but he didn't. And he was in a good mood that night when he met me at the Black Dog. But it does seem to me John was sincere when he came here, and really unnerved that he could have given Tony the idea to kill himself – or made him so depressed he might have done that.'

Her green eyes rose to lock on Dan's.

'Tony was beaten, wasn't he? Viciously? I saw the blood on his face, his nose bleeding, his hands mashed around the fingernails and knuckles where he must have fought. Yes, there was a noose around his neck and the rope was over a big branch, but he didn't do that himself then pass out and have a horrible fall or something. That's the only explanation for it working the way John thought, isn't it?'

'It didn't work that way. I spoke to the doctor in A&E and the surgeon who admitted Tony, and the implications are clear. He was severely beaten up – a violent attack. Our people on the scene and the medics all insist this was a beating and the rope looked like window dressing.' What no one was in a position to know was whether the assailant had knocked Tony out with the intention of hanging him from the tree afterwards. Was that how he had been slated to die?

Alex was quiet for a moment, still looking at him. 'Someone who saw the scene talked about it, Dan. They put out a story and John – and probably other people – heard it. But that's how John Ross got the idea that sent him rushing over here. I'd like to know exactly what was said.'

'So would I,' Dan said. He put a hand over Alex's on the table. She was trembling. 'I intend to find out. If it was deliberate meddling, I need to know.' He didn't add that anyone planting a story like that could have reasons for wanting to steer the narrative.

Alex gave him a tight little smile. 'Thanks, Dan. I'm going to be here with Tony but I'm not going to stop trying to work out a few things. Somewhere in this mess there's an answer. I mean to find it.'

It could be hard not to say too much, but he couldn't let that pass. 'You're a fearless woman, Alex, but sometimes that scares me. Could I have your word that you won't do anything that could put you in danger – or compromise the case I'm trying to build?'

'As if I could.'

'You have in the past and you probably could again. We both want the same thing now. To get through this for Tony – and the previous victims, of course.'

'OK,' she said, not meeting his eyes this time. And that could mean she'd do as he asked, or simply that she understood what he'd said. There was no point in pushing the issue further.

'Dr Wolf can't make himself sit there any longer,' Alex said. 'He's on his way over.'

Dan managed not to look behind him and only nodded.

Alex stood up. 'I want to go back upstairs. Will you let me know if there's any news I'd want to know?'

'I will. Of course, I will. And you'll come to me with anything you want to make sure I know?'

'Yes, I will.'

He was on his feet as she walked away, and his phone rang at that moment. He answered and watched Leon bearing down on him at the same time. 'LeJuan,' he said, seeing his sergeant's name come up.

'Evening, boss,' LeJuan said. 'I wanted to let you know why I haven't caught up with you yet. Our councilman-in-waiting showed up at the station several hours ago. Dimbleby himself.'

Leon arrived but stood apart, signaling he had seen the phone. Dan covered the mouthpiece. 'Come on over. Just catching up with LeJuan.' He sat down again and Leon joined him. 'Fill me in, LeJuan. He can't still be there.' And if it were important he, Dan, should have heard about it earlier.

'He came to see the doc, who apparently wasn't in at the time. They only got together about a couple of hours ago and the doc sent him for X-rays.'

Dan covered the mouthpiece again. 'Dimbleby went to the station. Hurting apparently. He's been there for hours. Our doc finally saw him and ordered X-rays.'

LeJuan continued. 'We may have to take him seriously. He was complaining of upper back pain and bruising. Said he wished he'd taken us up on our offer for him to see the doctor when he first came in.'

'I wish he had, too, even though we may not get enough out of him to be useful. There was nothing concrete in what he offered. I had the feeling he was holding something back under all that bombastic tripe. But who knows why he'd do that, after he'd come in the way he did? What do you think?'

'If you'll remember, I wasn't in on that one, boss,' LeJuan said, and Dan was glad Leon couldn't hear what was said. 'For what it's worth, I'd put money on Dimbleby's only interest being to make as much as he can out of a publicity opportunity, with or without having actually been attacked. But I'd also take about the same flyer on the attack being real. That's the damn way this case is going. Any evidence keeps shifting under our feet.

'Speaking of evidence, what did Alex say about the tennis racket?'

'It hasn't come up so far,' Dan said. 'I didn't think the timing was right, but we'll get to it soon enough.' Dan looked at his watch. 'You're working very late, LeJuan.'

'Yeah, well. With Tony lying in the hospital, I think we all feel extra pressure. I want to get this bastard, whoever he is. He feels like quicksilver – sliding away and no way to get a hold on him. I've been hanging on, hoping for word on Dimbleby's X-rays. And anything else they come up with. Or don't.'

'Give it up till tomorrow. But we need to go over my chat with Gordon Dulles at the Rum Hole. Odd chap. Another one who isn't easy to pin down.'

LeJuan didn't answer immediately, then he said, 'Gordon Dulles is the man who was with Kelly Seaton at her house, right? They seemed chummy. Was he with someone when you saw him at the Rum Hole, a date?'

'He's a manager there, and part-owner,' said Dan. 'He was also working behind the bar. Not pleased to see me, or not once I reminded him who I was.'

'He seemed aggressive toward us when we visited Kelly Seaton. And protective of her. It made me wonder if there was something between them at least on his side.'

'I got the same impression, and now I'm as good as sure of it. He didn't like Ricky Seaton. Said he was an ass with a one-track mind – acting, and how brilliant he was at it. According to Dulles, Ricky neglected his wife. His preoccupation with himself drove her away and I had a feeling Dulles came very close to saying it drove her to him and he was glad. But I'm jumping the gun. However, that does raise a little flag in the motive area – getting Ricky out of the way to free up Kelly. Not very original, but who said crimes of passion were ever original?'

Dan couldn't shake the idea that Dulles wouldn't be much help to them. 'The obvious question is, if we're thinking of one offender for two killings, potentially a third, what reason would Dulles have for Coughlin and Tony? Tony being only "attempted" at this point?'

'Yeah,' LeJuan said. 'Unless something changes, I see no potential connection either.'

Dan ran a hand around his neck. 'He also said he spoke to Ricky on multiple occasions about making a boor of himself looking for doners for the Phoenix Players. At the Rum Hole, I mean. Whenever he was there, the man accosted everyone who came in – and he was persistent. Dulles regularly asked him to lay off.' This case felt as if it was closing in. And he wasn't ready for that to happen until he got a bigger break.

'You want me to put someone on taking a longer look at Dulles?' LeJuan asked.

'Yeah. I'm not hopeful we'll get anywhere with him, but let's batten his story down. Put Longlegs on it. And while you're at it, John Ross needs checking. He showed up here at the hospital today and I'm not comfortable with him. He's an oddball. Twenty years or so and he doesn't lay eyes on Tony Harrison, or contact him as far as I know, then he turns up talking as if they're close. And he mentions dropping in at the Black Dog as if it was his local. No, none of it rings quite right. Or it could, but I want to find out either way. Y'know, I'd prefer to let you check him out. And get someone to look into the death of a chap called Malcolm Loder. John Ross's late pal. Around six months ago. Supposedly a suicide by hanging. We need all the details on record. You OK with that?'

'Yep. I'll get on it, but hold on a minute.' Dan heard another voice in the squad room and waited for LeJuan to give him all of his attention again.

'Busy, busy day,' he said to Leon, who glanced at him with a raised eyebrow.

'OK,' LeJuan said, and from the lift in his tone, Dan had the feeling there could be constructive news. 'They walked the doctor's report over, including X-ray report. Oh, boy. Dimbleby has heavy bruising across his shoulders. They're surprised he chose not to go for an examination right away.'

'I don't get it,' Dan said. 'He didn't seem in bad shape when I saw him.'

'Boss, X-ray report says he doesn't have any boney injuries, but they think the pain comes from a cervical sprain. Ligaments. Can take several days to fully develop. Consensus is that he sustained an injury to the neck – could be from a fall, overuse, awkward posture of some kind – or a blow.'

TWENTY-NINE

Alex walked into the Black Dog kitchens and hung her coat on the back of the door. She flapped her arms and rubbed her hands together. The temperature was plummeting and beyond ice-rimed windows, bare tree branches were coated with glittering white. Mid-afternoon was usually their quiet time but there were plenty of raised voices in the bar. She was on autopilot, and feeling dissociated, even from the familiar.

She didn't know who was working today, other than Hugh. He would try to help her decide how to go forward – if she asked him. Why did she feel overwhelmingly responsible for keeping Tony safe, for stopping the horrible things that were happening? Alex didn't know why, but while she never thought of herself as brave, she had become able, and willing, to step into danger for a reason too important to ignore.

Scoot Gammage brought a loaded tray of used dishes into the kitchen. Seventeen, blond, over six feet tall, lean but well-built, Scoot had the kind of openly friendly face and grin that attracted a trail of teenaged girls with excuses for talking to him – or just looking at him.

'Alex!' He pushed the tray on to the nearest counter and started toward her in a rush, then hesitated as if he wasn't sure what to do or say next. He made up his mind and strode to give her a bear hug with just the faintest hint of awkwardness. 'Tell me how Tony is. Please. It's been awful here. People come in for just about no reason and find ways to ask about him – and you. We're in bits waiting for news.'

'He's holding his own. Badly beaten up and with some serious injuries, but late this morning they thought the swelling in his brain might be down just a little.' She should have called someone here to give them an update.

The tightening in her throat, the gathering tears in her eyes, were becoming familiar. She couldn't think of Tony lying there, unconscious, and not feel desperate. It was true that Mr Morgan had almost, but not quite, said he was optimistic that he would not have to operate on Tony's head.

Scoot surprised Alex by putting an awkward arm around her. 'I bet you're tired.'

'I'm coping – more or less. I waited all night and this morning for someone to say I could see him. That didn't happen until one or so, but then I got to sit with him for a few minutes. It felt hopeful just to look at him and hear all those machines doing their thing. I have a sense he'll come back to me . . . to all of us. He's determined and he's strong.' And she wasn't going to say that her current biggest fear was that there was someone out there trying to work out how to get to Tony again, and this time make sure there would be no recovery.

Alex patted Scoot's shoulder and straightened away from him. 'How come you're not in school?'

'We're finished for Christmas,' he said with an indulgent grin. 'Remember Christmas?'

'Not so clearly. There must be masses to do. I'd better see how much I can get through before I have to go back to the hospital.'

'You don't give us enough credit, boss,' he said. 'We all pitched in last night. Decorating is all finished and it looks great. We've now got *three* hampers for the Christmas raffle. All proceeds for the parish hall renovation. This morning Liz and Cook came up with all the menus for lunches and dinners until we switch to the Christmas menus. I don't know where we're going to put all the stuff we've ordered from George's, but at least there'll be plenty to choose from. I hope we get a load of people who enjoy a mince pie, or six, because we'll have a ton. Stollen for the morning coffee bunch. I love George's stollen. Custard tarts, Christmas cake with lashings of marzipan and royal icing. Pies and puddings, sausage rolls, pasties.' He rubbed his hands together. 'Of course, I won't be touching any of that. I've got discipline. Well, maybe a rum ball or two. I've got to keep my mind on my work.'

'You have what you like,' Alex said. She knew Lily would be feeding up Scoot and Kyle at James's house but, scattered and troubled as she was, keeping involved and active here was impor-tant to her. Working would keep her mind occupied.

Scoot put a hand on her shoulder and shepherded her before him and into the main bar. 'See,' he said, 'we're holding the fort and it's all looking good.' A glance at her watch showed the afternoon was all but behind them. Twinkling lights, cheery on such a gloomy day, adorned beams, the rows of shelves on some of the walls, the mantel, the stout wood pillars that supported the thick beam above the bar, and Alex could smell the tree, glimmering in its spot by a front window, from all the way across the bar. Brasses glittered, and the fire roared in the fireplace. More than anything, Alex wished she were sitting by that fire with Tony. She blinked fast.

'Alex, over here!' Harriet Burke, usually so soft-voiced, bubbled to stand at her seat by the fire, and Alex noticed that both Katie and Bogie were curled into a blissful heap almost completely on the hearth. Mary Burke stayed seated with her little Maltese on her lap but waved both hands.

Hugh Rhys, clearly anxious, but letting enthusiasm show through the dour expression, strode to clasp Alex's hand and steer her to the sisters. 'How are you, love?' he said, and his eyes smiled. 'Damn, but I'm so glad to see you. We all are.'

The affection she felt almost deadened the apprehension that coiled in her stomach. 'I'm going to move in here while Tony's in the hospital,' she said. 'I can't face that house yet. I'll have to gather up some things but that can wait a day or two. I've got enough upstairs in my room to get me through.'

As she reached her, Harriet clasped Alex's arm in both hands. 'Tell us how Tony is.'

While Alex gave the shortest possible report, the dogs scrambled to snuffle around her knees. She actually felt strengthened by the obvious fondness these people had for Tony. Even Major Stroud hovered, head averted in disinterested mode, but one ear cocked to catch what was said. Kev Winslet made no pretense of disinterest. He planted his feet apart and nodded repeatedly, a happy shine flooding his red cheeks. A bit of a hush in the room suggested these were not the only people straining to catch news of Tony.

As soon as she could, Alex pulled Hugh aside. 'I'm going to be in and out until Tony's on the way to recovery.' Her voice sounded positive and that made her feel tougher. 'How are we for staff over these next weeks?'

'Peachy,' said Hugh, and Alex smiled. 'And why is that so funny, Ms Duggins? I rather thought you'd be pleased.'

'I am.' Alex smiled at him again. 'I've just never heard you say *peachy* like that, before.'

'It doesn't take much to amuse you,' he said, with a rather straight grin. 'Anyway, everything's under control. Christmas bookings are about sold out and we're going to offer an extra seating for dinner. And, thanks to Leonard and Heather Derwinter, there will be a special snowball bingo game with a jackpot prize of five hundred pounds. The way things are going, we might get the parish hall renovated much sooner than we expected.'

Kev Winslet, the Derwinters' gamekeeper, did an ungainly soft-shoe shuffle, then stopped, looking bashful.

'This is really terrific,' Alex said, smiling in all directions, even as her eyelids wanted to close and her limbs turned to lead. 'Lovely. Thank you all. Will you forgive me if I duck out now?'

'You poor girl,' Harriet said. 'You'll want to get back to the hospital.'

Alex nodded and turned to the passageway that led to the restaurant and the upstairs rooms. This time she would take toiletries and something to read while she waited at the hospital.

Barely past the reception desk that Lily usually manned, Alex heard rapid footsteps behind her and turned to face Harriet – who was slightly out of breath.

'What is it?' Alex asked, vaguely alarmed. 'What's happened?'

'I'll be quick, my dear. I thought it might help you to hear how people all over the village are pulling together to do something special. You've got too much on your mind to bother with anything else, but we are all thinking about you and Tony constantly. We wanted you to know that Major Stroud bought ten of the little paintings as a set to raffle as a special prize on Christmas Day. He wants you and Tony to decide what to put the money towards, and the tickets are selling like hot cakes. We so want you to know you're in our hearts, Alex.'

'Major Stroud?' Alex said, bemused. 'I think that's bloody amazing.' She clapped a hand over her mouth.

When her mobile rang, Alex was standing on a chair to reach the small overnight bag she had just remembered storing there.

The mobile was on the chintz-covered bed and Alex scrambled down to snatch it up and answer. She took a moment to check the readout but didn't recognize the number and there was no name.

'Hello,' someone said, and she put the phone to her ear again. 'Alex, is that you?'

'Who is this, please?' She made a habit of not answering anonymous calls.

'Alex. Thank goodness.' The man sounded breathless. 'It's John Ross. I'm the one who—'

'Yes, I know who you are. Sorry, I didn't know your number when it came up.'

'Darn it. I'm sorry. I've got to fix that. I never was good with details. Are you somewhere you can talk? In private, I mean?'

Sometimes you knew, without having a real reason, that you didn't like someone. Alex could cope with that. It happened. But John Ross made her uncomfortable because she felt sorry for him without knowing why. She supposed she didn't exactly dislike him. 'I'm not with anyone if that's what you mean,' she answered him slowly.

'I'm making you nervous, I can hear that in your voice. I'm so sorry. I shouldn't have called but I'm at a loss to make a decision over something.'

'I'm not nervous about anything.' Perhaps he was one of those people for whom a foot in the mouth was his default reaction when he wasn't sure what he wanted to say.

He didn't respond.

'I can talk, John,' she said, annoyed with herself now.

'First, what's Tony's condition today?'

'Improving, too slowly for me but the surgeon seemed optimistic. Guardedly optimistic, I suppose they say. I sat with him for a while which felt good.'

'Thank God. Oh, I can't tell you how relieved I am. Do you remember how Tony went to the same school as Ricky Seaton? I did too, for that matter, which doesn't make me comfortable.'

'I remember. What do you mean by your not being comfortable?'

Several quiet seconds passed, and Alex sat in the small armchair in the corner beside the wardrobe.

'I don't know what I meant by that,' John said. 'I looked up the man, Edward Coughlin. His body was found near the cricket pavilion in the Playing Fields. St Edward's boys used to do a lot of sports there – in the Playing Fields. And Ricky Seaton's Phoenix Players performed in that tithe barn only a mile or so from where they played cricket and held sports days and so on.'

Alex had no idea where this was going.

John cleared his throat. 'I've got hold of some old clippings from the *Gloucester View*. They've got articles on happenings at St Edward's through the years. Surprised me. I didn't know they were putting those things in the paper. The *View*'s defunct now – like so many papers.'

'I see.' She didn't in fact, but he was so pathetically eager to share whatever was on his mind, she couldn't cut him off. 'You think these things could lead to finding out what's happening with all this violence? And why?'

She could hear him tapping the mouthpiece on his mobile before he said, 'I don't know why these things are happening, but I believe there's a link between them.'

'If you think you've got information that will help the police, you should go to them, John. Lay out what you've got and see what they say.'

'That's what I'm tempted to do, but I don't want to make a fool of myself.'

'You won't if you just . . . ask to see Dan O'Reilly. I've never heard him be rude to anyone who was straightforward with him.'

'I'm also afraid of drawing police attention. To me. Or causing them to be suspicious of me.'

Alex rubbed her eyes and looked with longing at the bed. 'You won't do that, John.'

'Stranger things have happened. You hear about people who come forward to try and help the police, then end up in an interview room . . . or a cell. And they can be held for quite a long time while the coppers twiddle about exploring every imagined lead. Then they tell you you're free to go and never a sorry is heard. Disgusting.'

'I can't say I know much about that sort of thing.' What she would like to say was that she wanted to go to the hospital, now.

'You know your way around dealing with the police, Alex.'

This suggestion had been made too many times before and it raised her hackles. 'How would you know that?'

'You're a legend in Folly. Harriet and Mary told me about your history. If I wasn't impressed, I'd be scared of you.'

She didn't respond and John was also silent. Finally, he said, 'If you took a look at everything I've put together since this started falling into place for me, then we talked it through, I think I'd know what to do. And then, if I go to O'Reilly, I'll feel more confident. If you could just look over what I've collected?'

Alex was torn. 'I want to get back to the hospital.'

'I'm so sorry. Of course, you need to get back to Tony. Look, don't give it another thought. I'll go through everything and decide what to do.'

'Well—'

'Just promise me you'll give me a shout when you have more news on Tony. And I apologize for rushing in where I had no right to be – at the hospital. I've had some difficult times recently and the memories are still too fresh. Forgive me, please.'

It wasn't so late. Should she try to see John? 'Where are you?' she asked him. 'I'm in Folly at the moment.'

'Cheltenham,' he said, and she heard hope in his voice. 'My photography studio is on Barrow Street, next to a horribly loud twenty-four-hour arcade.'

'You're a photographer?' She hadn't expected that but why should she?

'Yes. John Ross Photography. Original, right?' He chuckled. 'If you're on your way from Folly to Gloucester you can drive right past me.'

'All right, John. I'll do that, but I've got to be quick so get your facts lined up to make it easy.'

'You bet. And thank you, Alex. There's an alley on one side of the shop. Pull all the way in and park there, safer to get off the road after dark. I'll put out the closed sign, but the front door will be unlocked. Give the bell a ring and come on in.'

THIRTY

Dan poured Aberlour into the two glasses Calum had given him and held one out to Leon Wolf on the other side of his desk. He was coming to the conclusion that Leon felt comfortable with him now – perhaps that he had started to think of him as a friend. How strange was that, given their prickly encounters in the past? Today Leon had arrived smiling and revealed that he had come straight from a busy day in his consulting rooms to the Gloucester nick – to catch up on the case.

'I've heard you've used the parish hall in Folly before.' Leon propped the arm that held his glass on the desk. 'As a situation room. Bit informal, I should think, but you're the best judge of what works.'

'As you know, the area has had a rash of serious crimes over the past several years. Given the choice, I'd always prefer to work in the middle of the action.'

'Makes sense.'

'I think so. You remember Alan Dimbleby? He came here the first time you were in.'

Leon gave a short laugh. 'He who would be a guiding light on the county council? Yes, how could I forget? If I were hunting for new cases, which I'm definitely not, I might look in his direction. Interesting fellow. I wasn't inclined to believe much of what he said.'

'I wasn't either, but things have changed. It was him I was talking to LeJuan Harding about on the phone – at the hospital last night. I think I mentioned that. He changed his mind about being examined by our people.'

Leon sipped at his whisky with one of his eyebrows raised in question. 'You did say something about him,' he said.

'Seems he's probably got a cervical sprain. It can take a few days to show up apparently. Most likely caused by a blow to the back of the neck, which fits the MO of our killer.'

Leon frowned, fixing his gaze on the view from Dan's office into the squad room, where a group of intent officers was clustered around the whiteboards.

'You look as if you're trying to solve a puzzle,' Dan said. 'If it's our current one, think on – hard. We could use all the help we can get.'

'What did you make of John Ross last night?' Leon kept looking through the windows.

'You first,' Dan said, smiling. 'You obviously have some thoughts about him.'

'Bit of a puzzle. It's not a popular word to use, but I thought he verged on hysterical – or perhaps approaching hysteria would be more accurate. His theory about Tony Harrison trying to commit suicide because a friend had hung himself was farcical. It had already been established that Tony was beaten. He couldn't do that himself.'

Dan pushed aside enough papers to make room for his feet on the desk. He needed a day in the office to catch up, not that he could see that happening soon.

'Your turn,' Leon said. 'Thoughts?'

After a firm rap, the door opened and LeJuan stuck his head inside. 'Everybody working late, I see.' He wore one of his signature turtlenecks. He always looked as if he spent daily hours in the gym, damn him.

'Come in. We were just talking about John Ross. We're in agreement that, if nothing else, he's a bit over the top. How are you doing with him?'

'The information's a bit thin. Never been married, no kids that anyone knows of. He's a photographer – mostly portraits and has a bit of a name for working with pets. The man, Malcolm Loder, shared Ross's house for a couple of years before he died. He was also a student at St Edward's. It doesn't seem as if there was any particular connection between these men when they were at school. Ross and Loder would have been in a lower form from Seaton or Coughlin – and Tony. That's about all so far but I'm still on it.'

'Good work,' Dan said. 'It doesn't sound as if you had much to go on.'

LeJuan's mobile rang and he turned away to answer. 'Yes,

Longlegs. What have you got?' There was a short pause, then
LeJuan thanked Longlegs and disconnected. 'We should have
known this, boss. Alan Dimbleby was at St Edward's too. Year
ahead of Tony.'

'Bugger it.' How many boys were at St Edward's in any given
year? Did this mean some maniac intended to massacre a bunch
of them, one by one? 'We'll have to start out by tracking and
tracing everyone with any connection to our victims, including
the two who were attacked but aren't dead. This is going to take
lots of pairs of hands and the super will be yelling threats about
budget overruns all over the place. I can hardly wait.'

File folders began to slide from the desk. Dan made a grab
for them but only caused an avalanche. He squeezed his mouth
shut against a matching flood of expletives.

'Boss,' LeJuan said. 'Did you know you've got messages?'

'I'm damned!' No, he hadn't bloody well seen the message
light because there was too much crap waiting for his attention
and it had covered the phone.

Leon made a sympathetic noise but sensibly did not comment.

'Understaffed,' Dan sputtered as he stabbed at the machine. 'I
won't mention what else is lacking around here. Not enough time.'

> Hi Dan. It's Alex. Sorry to miss you. Nothing important,
> just keeping my promise to let you know if anything even
> slightly interesting comes up. I should have called earlier
> but I'm afraid I forgot. I'm on my way to John Ross's place
> because he thinks he's come up with a theory and would
> like my opinion. He's got something he wants to show me.
> I did ask him to go to you direct but he's unsure of himself.
> He really seems unhappy, Dan. I'll try to get him to call
> you. This is probably nothing, but I can't ignore anything
> that might help make Tony safe. I'll check in with you
> in the morning anyway. I can't spend long with John – have
> to get back to the hospital. Bye.

Stunned, he played the message again. 'Why would she do that?
I swear Alex would resuscitate a mass murderer if she felt sorry
for him.' He realized what he'd said and grinned sheepishly.
'Sorry about that.'

Leon put his glass down and stood. 'I'll get out of your hair.'

'Rubbish.' Dan waved him back into his chair. 'Finish your whisky. It's too good to waste. Have you got Ross's address, LeJuan?'

'Yes, boss. Any need for backup?'

'I'll know by the time we're at the car. Come on. Get on with it, man. It could be nothing or it could be a lot. Either way, she'll still get a mouthful from me. Yes, to the backup. They can meet us there. Naunton way, isn't it?'

'Yes. I know how to get there.'

THIRTY-ONE

Amusement arcade noise, runs of electronic buzzers, clangs, clatters, whistles, bells, and the thud of countless mechanical hammers blasted Alex the instant she opened the car door. Following John Ross's instructions, she had parked at the end of an unlit alley, flanked by his studio on one side and an undertaker's shop with flashing 'Welcome' signs on the other. John Ross Photography lay between the alley and the arcade, meaning his premises had better have triple-glazed windows and soundproofed walls.

She wrapped her coat tightly about her. What could he have to tell her? Getting Dan's answering machine had been lucky . . . she hoped. If they had spoken, he would have insisted she not visit John, and probably warned that he would come racing to head her off if she did.

'There you are,' a man said loudly as he popped from a side door to the gallery. Shocked, Alex slapped a hand over her heart and swallowed hard before realizing this was John Ross. 'What timing,' he continued. 'I thought I heard an engine, not that it's easy to tell one noise from another around here.'

'Should I come in this way?'

'Yes, yes. In you come out of the cold. I've just made some tea, or you're welcome to something stronger if you like.'

'Tea would be nice,' Alex told him, although she didn't want to waste any time when she could be back with Tony.

John led the way along a short corridor and into the showroom, where portrait photographs were displayed on the walls and on gilded easels. He ushered her to a table with several boxes piled haphazardly on top, pulled up a chair and waved her to sit. 'Be comfortable and I'll get that tea. Milk? Sugar?'

'Just milk, please.'

As he hurried away, a scratching sound overhead startled Alex. A shelf, about a foot from the ceiling, ran around the showroom and disappeared into the corridor leading to the back of the shop.

The lighting from above was not perfect. Alex squinted and soon saw the source of the sounds; a Siamese cat had positioned herself, long tail hanging as straight as a plumbline, where she had a direct view of the newly arrived human. Of course, this was the cat John had brought to the Black Dog a few days ago. Alex sat in the chair and stared back at the cat, who watched her with absolute concentration. And, in the background, the deepest arcade sounds thudded on.

It was only days since she had first seen John Ross. That didn't seem possible. The thought unsettled her, although she was not sure why.

'Here we go,' John announced, his voice a cheery singsong. 'Nothing like a hot cup of tea on a nasty night.' He ended on a giggle. His voice didn't match his appearance, which needed an athletic tenor or even a baritone – definitely not a mezzo-soprano.

'Tea? Alex?'

She jumped. 'Sorry, I was miles away.' He gave her a fine bone-china cup and saucer. 'I see a beautiful cat up there,' she said, indicating the shelf – *or should that be catwalk?*

'I should have remembered to warn you. Beatrix has to get a good look at anyone who comes in. Sometimes she helps make sales, but she may have lost me one or two. She gets lonely if there's no one around, you know. Then she cries awfully loudly to let you know she needs a cuddle. She's my most reliable friend.'

Somehow what he said made her sad. It was clear that John Ross led a rather quiet life. 'Tony says he believes animals are our most trustworthy companions.'

'And he's right!' John passed Alex a plate of chocolate digestive biscuits. 'Don't be shy. Have one or two . . . or more! How is Tony? Do tell me, please.'

The tea was lovely, but he sounded as if he thought they were settling in for a comfortable chat and that was definitely not on the cards. 'I've called the hospital several times since I left in the middle of the day. They say he's holding his own and he's resting more comfortably. That's code for something or other. They do the best they can to reassure you without giving unrealistic hope.' But there had been a touch of optimism from the nurse, hadn't there? 'I want to get back there as soon as possible now. He may be hearing more than we know and I'm hoping they'll let me sit and talk to him. He's going to come around, John – I know he is. And I want to be there when he does.'

'Of course you do.' He opened one of the boxes on the table and took out a handful of newspaper clippings. 'I don't want to take up any more of your time than absolutely necessary, so let's get down to business.' He scooped out more yellowing pieces and spread them. To this, he added photographs and printed booklets, or programs. 'You'll get the gist of this quickly enough.'

Alex's stomach curled. She had neither the desire nor the time to wade into this stuff.

The cat gave a long, sonorous meow, a full-throated contralto wail.

John showed no sign of having heard.

'That was good tea,' she said falteringly. 'I think you must have had a lot of practice.'

Once more he was completely distracted by sifting through the pile of paper and photos on the table and did not answer. He appeared detached, his mind somewhere else.

He picked up a photograph and looked at it closely as if his sight was poor. 'We were good kids. Good boys. We didn't deserve the treatment we got. Nobody did a thing about it. I couldn't go to my father. If my mother had still been alive, she would have put things right – not that I would have been sent there in the first place if she was. Oh, no, Mummy would have put a stop to that.'

Alex set down her tea and sat quite still, and quiet. The studio was warm – perhaps for the cat – and sweat prickled at her temples.

'Look.' John came around the table with the photo and thrust it into her hands. 'That's Malcolm with me, Malcolm Loder. You could never have met a sweeter boy, but that made him a target for the big, strong, *important* fellows. They bullied him even more than me. But I was stronger than him. I tried to help him, to stop them, but they only found ways to punish me, too.'

Alex looked at the two anonymous twelve- or thirteen-year-olds in the photo. A couple of skinny, ordinary kids, looking self-conscious, as children often did at that age when a camera was turned on them. 'Nice-looking boys,' she murmured.

'They hid our gym kits so when we went to get changed, we couldn't find them. They would appear again when those asses left the locker room but, by the time we got to the gym, we were late. But we never dared say anything because we knew they would get to us in some way. They were bloody scary, Alex. Take it from me.'

'I'm sorry.' And she was, but she didn't know what else to say to be helpful.

'All these newspaper clippings are from the papers back then. They recorded every so-called triumph of the St Edward's boys and it was always the same clique. They were the best at everything. Debate, drama club, music, art, sports, chess club. Boys like Malcolm and me, and boys like us, the also-rans, got dragged into being their fags and putting up with the punishments they doled out when it pleased them. They stripped Malcolm and tied him to a chimney pot on the roof one night. And they told him that if he made enough noise to bring one of the staff, the rest of his time at the school would be true hell. As if it wasn't hell enough already. They told him they wouldn't get into trouble. They had everything worked out. And we didn't have any of the power. We had to go along. Malcolm was ill after that. Pneumonia. And still he didn't squeal because he thought the bastards who did it to him could fix anything in their own favor.'

Why was he showing her all this? Telling her about it? His voice rose higher again as he became more agitated. And he was jerky, dropping papers on the floor and leaving them there while he continued to rail against his tormentors of many years earlier. Then he paused, took a pill bottle from his pocket and unscrewed the top. He swallowed a handful of pills, washed them down with tea. Perhaps she should make an excuse to leave.

'John,' she said hesitantly. 'You said you had a theory. About what happened to Tony, I thought.'

He stared at her, slammed both palms on to the table and dashed a flurry of paper and photographs into the air, allowing them to fall where they may.

She was afraid to get up, no matter how badly she wanted to leave. If she moved, he might become angrier and then what would it mean?

Suddenly he swept the boxes on to the floor where one tipped over, its lid flying open, and more confusion reigned. When John looked at her, she flinched. He moved his arms jerkily and it sounded as if he were crying.

What kind of pills had he taken? She could hardly draw in a breath. His eyes were stretched wide open, the pupils dilated, and his face was the color of wet putty.

'I can't explain it here,' he said, panting. 'You're all right. You're safe with me. And you're right that I know what happened to Tony – or I think I do. I can see you're getting scared and you can stop that right now. It's pointless. Don't be so melodramatic. I know things you don't know. If you do as I say, I'll tell you and you'll be grateful. Come with me. Now!' He finished on a hoarse shriek and caught her upper arm in strong, cutting fingers.

'That's enough,' Alex told him, trembling violently. She grasped his fingers and tried to pry them loose. 'Let go of me. What do you think you're doing?'

He only gripped her tighter. 'Come now!' he yelled again as he dragged her back into the little corridor, through a door he opened and which Alex hadn't noticed on her way in. This was probably where he did some of his work.

The door to the alley, and her Range Rover, was so close yet impossible to reach. Her stomach dropped sickeningly.

In a sudden move, he pushed her hard against a rack where a couple of coats swung wildly back and forth. Shoes fell from a shelf beneath the coats. She couldn't help crying out. A metal folding chair connected with her middle, forced pain through her ribs – winded her. Gasping, her eyes stinging, she slid to the floor. The room was so narrow she was sure she could touch both wetly shining yellow walls at its width. Everywhere there were heavy plastic bags, a few full but most empty and banded together in piles. All of the walls seemed covered with charts, joined by lengths of colored string. He didn't do his photography work in here.

He was looking at her – she could feel it. When she made herself look back, his eyes were doleful, moist, as if he were going to cry. Would he do that before or after he attacked her again? 'That was an accident,' he said, panting a little. 'I didn't mean to push you.'

In her mind she said, *liar.* He *had* meant to push her. Bile rose to the back of her throat. Something was the matter with him, but she couldn't guess what he thought that had to do with her. Perhaps what he said he knew was tied up with it – at least in his mind.

Her only chance was to get away from him. Scrambling, scooting backward, pushing the rolling clothes rack as she went and kicking men's shoes out of the way, she tried to put distance between them. No point. Nowhere to go. John stood, or crouched, between her and the door, which he elbowed shut behind him.

'Look around you,' he said. 'See up there?' He pointed to a wall. 'That is my command center wall. Think of it as the equivalent of the boards they use in police situation rooms – or whatever they call them. This is so much superior. I'm going to show you all the important pieces I've gathered here. It started years ago and for months now I've been pulling everything together. It was time, you see, time to start paying back old debts. And there are more who will pay the price for bullying and tormenting boys so much weaker than themselves. How your police friends would love to see this. They've made such a mess of their precious case and this could make it all come clear to them. But I won't be sharing, not with them. I don't trust them to do the right thing.'

'Why are you showing this to me? It's interesting but I don't know what it really means. If something awful happened to you in school, you can still bring it out into the light. These people's reputations would suffer for it. John, you haven't told me what you wanted me to look at before you decide whether to take it to the police. Is this it? The disgusting stuff about bully boys?' But he had just said he wouldn't take these things to the police. Her head buzzed and her jumper prickled against her damp back.

'Perhaps.' He pulled her up and sat her in the folding chair. She tried to shake herself free of him but that only made him bare his teeth and give her a good shake. 'I'm going to start with these,' he said, and in another swift move he grabbed her wrist and hauled her close to the wall. 'Look at these carefully and tell me what you see.'

A row of photos, extraordinarily bright and clear although she thought they had been taken in low light. He would know all about working with photographs to produce the effect he wanted.

He reached forward with the hand that gripped her wrist and pointed to the first photo. 'Edward Coughlin. Did you know him?'

'No,' she whispered. A man lying on grass, on his back, his face covered with blood and turned to the side to show a mashed wound to the skull. There was a cricket bat leaned against his damaged head. Alex swallowed. 'Why should I know him?'

'Tony does. And this is Ricky Seaton, perhaps the nastiest of the lot. Did you know him?'

Alex's gorge rose again. She wanted to look away but somehow thought John Ross would be pleased by that and get even more aggressive. The man he said was Ricky Seaton lay, face down, across what appeared to be a trunk. From the blood on his head, his shirt should have been soaked but it was almost clean. A knife protruded from his back. She thought this was taken on a stage with a painted backdrop of countryside behind him.

'Do you know him?'

'No!' she cried. 'This has nothing to do with Tony or me. What do you want from me?' Her skin felt icy cold. Her scalp tightened. There was no longer any doubt what he wanted to do . . . to her. Only how he wanted to do it was a mystery. Quaking took over her arms and legs, and she couldn't stop it no matter how hard she tried.

'I'll be telling you what I want from you shortly. Here, look. Coughlin's coat . . .' He pulled a leather coat from the rack and turned it to face her.

This was returned to its place on the rack and another hanger extracted. 'This was Seaton's.' When he turned this grisly thing around, the white wooly lining of a sheepskin coat, especially the collar, was caked with dried blood. 'He was wearing this when he died. Kept him nice and clean.' He jiggled on the balls of his feet.

'Where did you get these?' Alex asked.

'Wait, wait.' Fixing his eyes on her face, he ran his hands into his hair. 'Don't hurry me. I have to get everything right. I have to do it, you see? I've got to finish what I started after Malcolm died. That's when I knew it was my job. Only I could get justice for Malcolm – and for me.'

'Tell me about Tony, John. And show me what you're going to take to Dan O'Reilly. He's a good man, he'll help you.'

His face working, John reached for one of the plastic bags, this one large. He looked at a tag tied to the closed neck, slid it off and opened the bag. She didn't need explanation of what he pulled out: it was Tony's waxed parka, the one he had been wearing when they drove into Folly on the previous morning.

Speaking was impossible – Alex could scarcely breathe. Ross was so close she could smell his sweat.

'Yes, you know whose coat this is – I can see it in your eyes.' John put the coat back in its bag. 'You see, the rack is for graduates. Graduates get what they deserve – a place of honor to hang their coats. Tony's will belong there when he's a graduate. He will be very soon.'

Punching his face, pummeling him until he collapsed would feel so good. Doing something. Taking action. She had to take action. Her lungs expanded in short gasps. And he would beat her down . . . and silence her.

'I'll just put this back for a little while.' He grinned as he replaced the bag containing Tony's coat. 'Until it earns its permanent place in my exhibit. Look at this, Alex. This is so exciting.' He lifted a piece of cloth from one end of the table.

Alex straightened her shoulders and willed herself to stop shuddering.

'You see? The real cricket bat for the St Edward's cricket team captain, and the dagger for St Edward's true Macbeth.' He behaved like a magician, whipping the cloth behind him. 'You and I are the only ones to see all this. Next will come the tennis racket for a St Edward's tennis captain.'

'Let me go.' Pushing him was pointless. She used both fists and tried to force her way past him. He put a hand around her neck and squeezed – until she grew still, gagging.

Alex breathed through her mouth, the air searing her throat. When she could she said, 'I don't believe Tony ever did anything to hurt you or Malcolm. He's the kind of man who would help anyone in trouble.'

'And I suppose he's completely honest. Is he? Is he? Speak up and defend him, if you can.'

'I don't know what you mean. Everyone likes and trusts him. Say what you've got to say so I can explain what he's really like. He's so good.'

'Of course, he is,' John all but cooed. 'He includes you in everything he does, doesn't he? He shared every little detail of his life with you, no matter how much it may hurt – even frighten, you.'

'What does that mean? I think you're cruel. You're trying to hurt me with something you've concocted. Spit it out, or isn't there anything to say? Are you making up a story to try and frighten me? It won't work with Tony.'

John poked a finger into the soft base at the front of her neck. And poked again. She gasped and stepped back.

'He didn't share it with you, did he? Do you know what that means? You'd never be able to trust him to be honest with you because he'd keep secrets to himself.'

A pulse hammered at Alex's temples. 'What secrets?' She hated the way her voice sounded out of control. 'I need to go now. Let me know if there's a way I can help you and I'll do it. I think you're really upset and I'm sorry. I could come back later and talk some more.' But she wouldn't. She was babbling, but what else could she do but try to talk him down?

'Of course you will. And you think I'm a fool. You disappoint me, Alex, and just when I really need to know you're on my side. Tony has lied to you – by omission, but lied nevertheless.'

'No!' *Breathe slowly. Calm down and don't antagonize him.* 'We're both going through difficult times. But we could help one another.'

He studied her silently before lifting her hand and holding it between both of his. Alex felt sick. She held her tongue.

'You're a good person,' he said. 'I don't like to do this to you, but you deserve to know the truth about the man you think you love. If he'd told you what's been going on – told you everything about his time in Australia – you wouldn't be in this position now, because you'd have left him. He's not worthy of you.'

Could he possibly be talking about Tony's marriage? About what had happened between him and Penny?

'You don't know. I can see it in your eyes. You're puzzled and I hate him for treating you badly. I've told you he's no good. He didn't help Malcolm and me when we needed it so badly. No matter, it's all arranged now. I've followed everything about Tony Harrison, all the way through when he went to vet school and married Penny before they went to Australia. She disappeared in the ocean, or so he maintained. They didn't find her body. Imagine how he felt when he got an email from her and he knew it could mean the end of his plans to marry you. I think he believed he'd killed her, but he didn't do the job properly. Then the email came and he's been running scared. Didn't tell you any of this, did he? Didn't say if you married him it probably wouldn't be legal.'

Stunned, bemused, Alex stared at him, and kept on trying to think of ways to distract him from the nonsense he was spewing.

'You believe me, don't you?' he said. 'You should. He got an email all about Penny wanting to come back to him. But he's hidden it. You could never trust a man like that.'

Alex straightened her spine. She set her feet apart to steady herself. 'How could you know about it . . . if it existed? Let me go, please. We can forget any of this ever happened.'

'Really? And you would never tell anyone – definitely not the police – what I've told you and shown you? Of course you wouldn't. Yes, and of course you can just walk out of here and go to sit with Tony at the hospital. You wouldn't tell him or anyone about me, would you?'

She couldn't answer.

'You wanted me to tell you how I know all about that email? There really was an email – I didn't lie. And I know because I wrote it.'

Her mouth fell open. Again, she wanted to attack him. 'I don't believe you. You couldn't know everything.'

'That's what you think. Between me and a very good friend – who is a master at finding out secrets – I put everything together.'

The email was a hoax. 'What friend?' she asked quietly.

'Oh, I can't tell you that. It wouldn't make any difference anyway. I made Tony suffer and I'm glad. You still have to live with him being prepared to lie to you by not letting you know about it all. I've told you he's no good.' Suddenly, John stepped so close she could see veins bulging in his neck. His face had turned red. 'I'm in charge, do you understand?'

The words reverberated through her. She said nothing.

'I saw you put your keys in your pocket.' John's voice rose to a shout and he thrust a hand at her. 'Give them to me. This is taking longer than I expected. I'll have to move your car in case my undertaker neighbor needs to take some of his stock-in-trade in or out.'

She wasn't going to let him take away her one means of escape – even though she doubted she could ever get to it.

'Give them to me!' Again, the voice rose and his features twisted, but more in pain than anger. He was sick, mentally ill. She saw it clearly now.

But if he left to move the Range Rover, she just might be able to get to the street and run, to call the police. If she could grab her bag, with her phone, from the chair in the studio and get out through the front door, she would have a chance.

'Give me your keys, Alex.'

She pulled them from her jacket pocket and threw them at him. They bounced off his chest and fell to the floor. Her throat felt raw and dry.

Not loosening his grip on her wrist, he gave a nasty smile, scooped up the keys and pocketed them. Rather than make any move to leave, he flipped through a wad of photographs, selected one and showed it to her. 'Know who this is?'

'No . . . yes. I've seen him before but I don't remember his name.' Her heart was beating too hard and too fast.

'This should have gone better. I was caught off guard and acted in too much of a hurry. But, no matter. Does Alan Dimbleby ring a bell?'

'Not really.' Keeping her voice steady, pretending she was calm, took every bit of control she had. 'Is that his name?'

'He's running for the county council but I'm afraid he won't make it. Such a shame. And he has such a way with words. King of St Edward's debate team, he was. Such a promising fellow. Tongue like a stiletto, as long as he wanted to impress whoever he was talking to. But he'll be famous soon anyway. His photo will graduate to this wall and you know what that means. And dear Tony. I'm so glad he may recover. Such a strong man, but he may not be strong again for a very long time, and by then it will be too late.'

The next photo put in front of her was of Tony in front of their house. And at the open front door behind him – there she stood, wrapped in her bathrobe with Katie beside her knees. They both stared ahead, at whoever was taking this photograph, and how could it have been anyone other than John Ross? She hadn't known they were being photographed and neither had Tony. Ross had been following Tony, spying on him – who knew for how long?

The sound of a phone, ringing from elsewhere, brought a hunted look to Ross's eyes. Then he smiled at her. 'Your mobile? Of course it is. You left it in the shop, which was very wise of you because you won't need it.'

It didn't matter, she had no way of getting to it, or using it. It could be Dan. She felt jumpy, shaky. Dan could do whatever it was they did with phones to figure out where someone was.

'I can almost see you thinking,' Ross said. 'Is someone trying to reach you, someone who will gallop in and save you? Too bad Tony's lying unconscious in a hospital. He can't be your white knight tonight.'

She wanted to scream at him to leave Tony alone and let them both be. He had said he needed to move her car . . . but no, what he wanted was her keys to make sure she didn't try to get away in it.

John scrubbed at his face and pushed his hair back. 'I know more about him than anybody. I've thought about him for a long time, you know. He may have been better than the rest, but he wasn't good enough.

'Tony would never do the kind of things you're talking about these others doing. He couldn't be like that.'

'When I went to his clinic, I was testing him. The last test. And he didn't know who I was. He thought I was Malcolm. Just the same as when we were in school and we were nonentities. And not doing anything when you saw what was happening to us doesn't make a person innocent. Tony should have been on our side and helped us. He could have spoken up. He was looked up to by other boys and by teachers, but he didn't help us.'

There was no arguing with him. Whatever happened back then was long done, but she was certain Tony wouldn't have stood by if he had known someone was being hurt.

'I never wanted to harm you, Alex.' Suddenly his words were softly spoken. He took a step closer to her and she felt his physicality, his size. 'But you were suspicious of me when I talked to you at the hospital the other night. Everyone else was grateful for my concern for Tony, but not you. I can feel these things.' He pulled her to her feet and spun her to face away from him. When he took both of her wrists in one of his hands, she knew she had little chance of getting safely away from him.

Breathing through her open mouth, she leaned back against him, lifted her left foot and jammed it down on what she hoped was his instep.

He caught hold of her hair and yelled, 'Damn you! I knew I couldn't trust you.' He twisted her hair and tears of pain squeezed from the corners of her eyes.

Quickly, he bound her wrists together, sat her back in the chair and tied her to its back.

'I heard the suspicion in your voice again when we talked on the phone earlier. You only came here to further your own ends.'

'If I'd been suspicious of you, I wouldn't be here at all.' He was going to put her in the Rover and take her somewhere; she was sure of it. And she wouldn't be coming back. 'I don't have much room to bargain but hear me out. Get out of here. Leave and run because that's your only chance to get away now. I won't be able to leave until someone comes and that won't happen for hours.' Would telling him she had left a message for Dan, that he would know where she was, cause him to run as she had suggested, or make him hurry up and do whatever he planned to do to her?

'I don't need your escape plan,' said John. 'I've got my own, but thank you anyway. I'll just tidy up and get Beatrix, then we'll be on our way.'

THIRTY-TWO

*S*eeing that Range Rover parked in the alley had been like a punch to the gut. All he had been able to do was pull up close behind and open his own boot and doors wide to give some coverage. At least darkness was on his side now, and it was unlikely anyone driving by would even notice the other vehicle in front of his.

He had never been a team player, even less so as time passed. Nights like this reminded him why his instincts about not sharing, anything, were so good. You could only trust yourself to look after yourself.

The undertaker's seemed absolutely quiet. The photography studio's only windows fronted the street; no way to see in from this alley or from the arcade side. But that also meant there was no way to see out, which was heaven-sent in this situation.

Sounds blared from the arcade. Another piece of good luck, since he had a few unavoidable noises of his own to make. At the side door to the gallery, he dropped to his knees and put an ear to the keyhole, straining to hear anything that might tell him where they were inside. Nothing, the arcade racket made sure of that. All he had seen from the front as he drove by were portraits displayed in the window with the dim interior of the gallery behind.

Moving smoothly and deliberately, he fitted the key in the lock, turned it gently and winced when it clicked open. It had been easy enough to pilfer that key. He stayed still, waiting. Seconds passed, minutes. Next, he turned the handle and pushed a couple of inches. Once again, he waited, and froze. Inside and nearby, a door closed, and footsteps traveled fast . . . away from him, toward the shop. He visualized the layout in there; so useful to know. Whatever happened, he was ready, and this might be his best chance to grab a favorable vantage point.

All or nothing. Swiftly, he pushed the door open far enough to allow entry and, just as quickly, he eased it shut again behind *him. Through the gloom, he saw what had to be the door he had heard – the only door in a short corridor, other than the one he'd just used. A stroke of light shone at the bottom. To the right, there were boxes stacked against the opposite wall. To the left, in the gallery, torchlight swept upward, swept back and forth. He crossed the passageway and pressed his body in behind some of the boxes – and his foot hit a hard object that gave a hollow clang. Shit, shit, shit, a bucket.*

He waited, breathing shallowly.

'Stay where you are, then, silly girl,' *John Ross said in his 'kitty dearest' voice.* 'It'll be your own fault if you're lonely, Beatrix. I can't play games tonight.' *Rubber squeaked on the floor, then a creaking clatter followed, like something metal being closed up, or folded. Could be a ladder – sounded like that.*

Footsteps returned. The door in the corridor opened again – and smashed all the way back. 'Listen up,' *John said loudly.* 'You can make this easier on you, or . . . well, you can work out the alternative all on your own. We're leaving very soon. You have to cooperate and help me keep things clean.'

'What do you mean?' *Alex Duggins's unmistakable and shaky voice.*

'This isn't my fault,' *John shouted.* 'I told you all about what happened. It was those boys in school. They caused this and now I have to finish what I started. I can't go back – do you understand? And I'm not taking orders anymore – or putting up with being talked down to by someone who thinks he knows better. He doesn't, and he'd better keep his problems to himself. And deal with them himself. He tells me off like I'm a kid. You should have heard him go off about Alan Dimbleby, then Tony. I'm not supposed to think for myself, even when I know I'm right. He wanted me to wait, let him tell me when the time was right to go after them. To hell with that. My job is to settle things for Malcolm, no one else.'

Listen to John. The fool can't keep his mouth shut.

He took out the gun and held it, muzzle toward the ceiling, his elbow cocked. He braced the elbow on his opposite forearm.

Standing in near darkness while John and Alex were in full light, the advantage, the element of surprise should be his. Edging forward, around the boxes, he moved just far enough to get a

*narrow view – John with his back to the open door, Alex seated,
her hands behind her back and her eyes fixed on John.*

*The next breath he took cleared his head and cooled him.
He knew what he would do and the faster he was about it, the
better.*

'Leon!' When she saw him at the door, blood pounded at her
temples. She tried to stand but fell back on to the chair and all
but overbalanced. She had been working on the twine at her wrists
and it had loosened nicely. John was no expert at knots. 'Oh,
thank God you're here, Leon. John's upset. He needs to be reas-
sured that he can trust us.' The gun didn't engender confidence
in Alex, but Leon was her only hope.

'Hello, John,' Leon said, ignoring her and stepping into the
room. 'I thought I'd just drop in and ask how you're doing but
I can see for myself. Not very well, old son.'

'Get out,' John Ross cried, and he sounded frenzied. 'This is
nothing to do with you and I don't want more of your advice.
All those sessions with Malcolm, all the talk, and you couldn't
help him. He gave up on you and I don't need you.'

'I think you do. You've needed me for a long time. We agreed
on that and we worked well together – until you decided you
knew what was best. You didn't have the patience to wait until
I told you it was time to make a move. Look what that's done.
It's landed you here. You're in a corner and you won't get out
without help from someone who knows what to do. So, listen
and do as you're told.'

'You used us, you bastard! I didn't need you before and I
don't need you now.'

Leon smiled, a strange smile. 'So you've already said. But
you do and you always will. Just do as I say and everything will
work out the way we want it to.'

This man was a psychologist, Alex reminded herself. He knew
all about dealing with deranged people, and John was at least
that. Leon was Dan's friend, there was trust there. Leon was
working with Dan to diffuse all this, that's what was happening.
What could she do to help?

'You shouldn't have a gun,' John said. 'I've never needed guns
to do what had to be done. I don't like them.'

'This one's going to be very useful.' Leon's eyes flickered
to Alex and away again. 'What have you decided to do
afterwards?'

Alex closed her eyes and tried to calculate times. When had
she left the message for Dan and when had that call come in to
her mobile? Could it have been Dan trying to make contact? Had
he received her voice message? If he and Leon were working
together, did that mean Dan was nearby?

The twine slithered loose, fell over her hands. If she wanted
to, she could get free, stand up, make a run for it. And how well
would that work out with two men and a gun between her and
the only escape route? One of those men definitely intended to
kill her and get rid of her body? As yet, she wasn't sure whether
the other man was friend or foe. He did hold a gun, which meant
if he wasn't a friend, she could be dead.

'You can blame your friend Leon here for what's happening
to you,' John said, a mean expression on his face, his lips thinned.
'He was my friend's therapist for so long, but he only succeeded
in twisting him up worse than before they started together.'

'Shut your mouth.' Leon pointed the gun at John.

John took no notice. He looked from Leon to Alex. 'Instead
of dealing with what was done to Malcolm as a schoolboy, he
used him. He wanted to have Malcolm commit murders where
Dan would be involved. Malcolm told me all of it. Leon never
knew that, but he hated Dan. When Malcolm died, Leon thought
I would take over for him. He thought he was being so clever,
but I did what I wanted to do to get justice for Malcolm, and me.'

Leon was silent, aiming a pitying smile at John.

A flush washed over John's face and neck. He drew back his
lips from his teeth, taking loud, short breaths. 'Dan was supposed
to end up fired and disgraced for botching up the case. He' –
John pointed a finger at Leon – 'he'd meddled in other cases
Dan was on, trying to fix it for him to fail. All because his sister
died in a car crash forever ago.'

'Shut up, imbecile,' Leon said with a sneer on his face. 'Not
that it's going to matter. We just don't have time for this now
– or ever. We've got things to do. Let's get them over with.
You've had a bad time, John, and this night is more than any
man should suffer. Let's work together – help each other.'

'I've got a lot more to say.' John looked around with unfocused eyes.

'I'm about to change my immediate plans.' Leon advanced on John. 'Let me help you out and speed this up. Because when Constable Dan O'Reilly – as he was then – when he left my sister in a wrecked car while he pulled out her already dead boyfriend, my poor little sister died. She could have been saved, but she was dating a chief superintendent's son and good old Dan – he knew who the boyfriend was, it was the talk of the station – and he figured it would look good for him if he was reported as going above and beyond for the boy. It should never have taken this long to settle the score. His time was up years ago, but no matter. Now will be good enough. I'm going to finish him.'

Leon lunged at John. He jabbed the gun into his side. 'Get on the floor, flat on your face, and put your arms above your head.' And John subsided, did as he was told and lay there, unmoving.

Struggling, Alex yanked her hands free but kept them behind her back while she wriggled her arms, working to send blood through her numb flesh.

'Do as I say, and we'll be out of here and away fast. Just listen to me, John, concentrate on the sound of my voice.' Alex couldn't believe it – he sounded as if he was trying to hypnotize the other man. Leon knelt astride John, and started forcing his clenched fingers open. 'It's OK,' Leon said, cocking the gun, 'I want you to hold this for me. Just hold it, then I'll show you what to do next. Hold the gun, John. I said you could always trust me, and this proves it, doesn't it. I'm going to trust you with this gun. That's the way, old son. I'll help you. Fingers here, and here. We'll do it together. Two are stronger than one.'

Leon would help John kill her?

'We'll put her on some of those empty plastic bags and, when it's finished, we'll roll her up. No one's ever going to know. No one will hear anything or see anything – as long as we're very, very careful.'

Leon kept his hand over John's on the gun while he reached out and dragged a nearby pile of bags to spread on the floor.

'I want up.' John was crying now. He managed to wriggle and twist on to his back. 'What are you doing? Let me up.'

Alex closed her eyes for an instant, swallowing repeatedly. She wanted to scream, but she would not be heard. She wanted to run, but there was nowhere to go.

At least if they shot her while she was on her feet and not held down on their rotten plastic bags, her blood would go everywhere. That would make it harder for them. So what? God help her get away. She prepared to stand and saw something shift beyond the door. Darkness on darkness.

Surging to half stand, Alex propelled herself backward, crashed down on to the chair which collapsed beneath her.

A gunshot reverberated in the enclosed space. She screamed, and braced, expecting the impact of a bullet. She waited an instant and then she scrambled away, dragging the chair – it could shield her, couldn't it? She didn't know anything anymore.

Another shot sounded, and another.

'Stay still, Alex.' It was Dan!

She made herself be still, clutching the chair in front of her. Dan had taken the gun. Leon howled with pain. Blood soaked his back, ran on to John, and pooled beside them. With a little help, Leon collapsed to the floor and handcuffs, applied by LeJuan, reduced him to a squirming, bleating heap.

'Dan?' Alex started to get up.

'Just stay where you are and try to breathe deeply,' Dan said. 'You'll be fine.'

John Ross remained on his back, his eyes open; a long, grooved wound ran from his temple and across his forehead to disappear into a gaping wound in his blood-soaked hair.

'Are they alive?' Alex said. 'They're dangerous.'

She felt herself fainting. 'I want to see Tony.'

THIRTY-THREE

New Year's Eve

A single tap on the door almost blended with the sound of a passing hospital trolley. The tap became a patter – fingertips, Alex thought. She smiled at Tony, 'Early lunch?'

Dan leaned in. 'I may be in a service job, but I don't do room service. May I come in? I promise I won't stay long.'

'Come in, come in,' Tony said, rising from his chair. 'In case you haven't heard, I get to go home tomorrow!'

'I did hear something to that effect,' Dan said, and grinned. 'Yes, in fact, it was Alex who called me to share the news. I had to come by and tell you how chuffed we all are.'

Alex held up both palms. 'Slow down a bit. We're talking about going home to convalesce, not to start training for a marathon.'

The men laughed and Dan came around to perch on the side of the bed while Tony sat down again.

'They've been fantastic here,' Alex said of the hospital staff. 'And Tony helped by being so disgustingly fit to begin with. But he'll need a few more weeks of taking care and following instructions.'

'We're boring you, Dan,' Tony said. 'Sorry to warble on but, terrific as everything's been here, home is the most motivating word I can think of.' He looked at Alex and they smiled. She swallowed and rolled her lips together. This was an emotional day, following many emotional days.

Dan took off his coat and Alex realized she didn't remember seeing him in anything other than a suit before. Jeans and a polo neck suited him. 'Would you be interested in the latest news from my bailiwick?' After only a few seconds' pause, he added, 'I thought so. Leon Wolf is expected to recover – more or less. It's going to take some time before any trial can get underway.

'Close-quarters gunshots can do a lot of damage. He lost most of a lung. They've started shoulder reconstruction, but he'll never have much use of that arm. I could go on, but I won't. Gunshot wounds to shoulders may be made to look minor in fiction but in real life they frequently cause a lot of permanent damage.'

'Could have hit his heart almost as easily as a lung,' Tony said.

Dan shrugged. 'I suppose we could say he's lucky. But the only piece of luck I can see for him is that the clinical forensic people determined John Ross shot and killed himself, even though he was struggling with Wolf who was trying to take the gun away. These people are amazing. I'd take their word for anything.'

'Ross's hand was beneath Wolf's,' Tony said thoughtfully. 'Then Ross gets a shot off that smashes Wolf's shoulder and so forth, before Ross shoots himself. Deliberately or otherwise.'

'Yes.' Dan wrapped his hands around a raised knee. 'And finally I got control of the gun, thank God.'

Alex shifted in her chair. Going over this turned her cold. 'There were three shots.'

'The first one ended up among the coats,' Dan said. 'I was grateful it didn't hit you, Alex.' He was not making a joke. His direct stare spelled out how badly he did not want to meet her in a similar situation in future.

It won't happen if I can help it, Alex promised herself.

EPILOGUE

March

Tony:

M y Alex is one of a kind. I can't tell her that too often because she tries to turn it into a joke – but I can tell you, and me, of course. She is determined, caring, artistic, generous, maybe too often impulsive, and loving. The impulsive business will always be a worry since I don't expect her to change. She careens headlong into situations a more cautious person would run a mile to avoid. And some of her excuses for what I call bad decisions are maddening.

We were planning to be married on New Year's Eve but, given the circumstances, that had to be postponed. I've been out of the hospital over two months now and I understand from Alex that I look as good as I ever did – she says that's incredibly good – and no, I don't try turning that kind of a compliment into something clever. I like it when I get strokes from that woman.

By the way, I feel completely healthy and I wish the doc wouldn't keep saying I need to go easy on myself – at the practice – for another month or two.

This day is the best I've ever known. Our wedding day. Many times, I've feared it would never come. One of my first thoughts when they brought me out of the coma was that I might have missed our wedding! I had dreams, or maybe nightmares, of arriving on the day to find that Alex had just left the scene. Wild foot-races through places I didn't recognize followed, and I don't know if I ever caught up with her. Nightmares was the right word.

I'm so glad we went ahead with having the conservatory built. Alex wanted to halt the work when I came home from the hospital, but I made sure she knew who was boss and the construction continued. OK, so she is the real boss, but I played on her sympathy for my weakened condition and begged to get the construction finished. Honestly, she knew I was as strong as an ox after a couple of weeks, but I think she liked to pretend she must cater to me, look after me, and that included doing nothing that would upset my fragile mental state – like arguing with me.

That's another lie – the fragile mental state, that is – I've never been better, even if I do tire too quickly for my taste.

The conservatory had to be finished for today, and it's beautiful – not that I'm a man for the soppy stuff. But I can appreciate beautiful things, especially Alex. I've told her the bride gets pampered on her wedding day, but she's flitting about making sure everyone has a full plate and a full glass. Lily is backing her up and I swear, it's obvious where Alex gets her organizational prowess.

There goes Alex again. After today, I may buy her nothing that isn't green. She says her dress is a shirtwaist. Whatever, it's made of pale green silk and has a long, straight skirt. She told me she couldn't have a fuller skirt because she's short enough without making herself look shorter. Take it from me, she looks perfect and, more than that, she is perfect for me.

I'd better wander around and make witty conversation. It's just what I wanted, the two of us getting married, surrounded by good friends like Harriet and Mary, and tolerated familiars like Major Stroud, who has already overdone the alcohol consumption.

Katie and Bogie have been patient, but Katie's arthritis causes her issues if she sits too long, and Bogie becomes an issue if he doesn't get enough attention. Time to move. 'Come on, kids. Let's be sociable.'

Alex:

'Tiddly would be a weak description for the major,' Alex said, studying Major Stroud who looked unsteady on his feet. 'Look at him. It's amazing he isn't on all fours.'

'True to form.' Lily smiled and looked at a pale blue sky beyond the glass roof. 'You know Tony can't take his eyes off you, don't you?' she said, continuing to feign interest in the heavens.

'Really?' Alex glanced over her shoulder at him. 'Well, he's coming in with the dogs now, so let's not make any more comments like that. Don't you think he's seems really fit, Mum? I'm hoping he'll decide to keep Magnus Irving on permanently. He's done a great job filling in while Tony's been recuperating, but I'd like to see him stay, especially to help with the large animal work. The practice is growing and it's likely to keep on growing. And it's a very good landing strip for a new graduate like Magnus. And it could be he'd progress into a junior partner one day.'

Lily nodded. 'I won't be surprised if that happens, but don't expect Tony to give up his horses to anyone.'

There were footsteps and cheerful voices coming from the entry. Dan O'Reilly walked into the conservatory with Calum, who had kept his overcoat on. How did you tell a fifteen-year-old it was too warm for coats indoors?

'Alex,' Dan said, coming to put an arm around her. 'You're gorgeous. Sorry we're late, but we've been going through a bit of a fraught few hours. Tony, come and join us. You're just the man I want to see. Congratulations by the way.'

Tony grinned and nodded, but his eyes held a hint of confusion.

'Over here, and you, too, Calum,' Dan said, steering them into the breakfast room. Once inside, he closed the door to the conservatory. 'This wasn't in my plans but here goes. How do Katie and Bogie get along with cats?'

Alex felt her mouth starting to open.

'They're very good,' Tony said. 'They've been around so many animals I've treated, and they tolerate cats well. They'd have to if they wanted to be by the fire at the Black Dog with Harriet and Mary. But a lot does depend on the cat. If they mostly ignore the dog, there's no problem.'

'Well, if that isn't a perfect response from a man I trust implicitly.' Dan told Calum, 'Tony says it'll be just fine. What do you think of that, boyo!'

Never had Alex heard Dan sound more Irish.

Calum opened his coat, which she now saw was more likely to belong to his father. Someone she instantly recognized poked her head out, looking cross-eyed and not thrilled. But Beatrix pressed her face beneath Calum's chin and closed those beautiful blues.

Tony laughed. 'You soft devil, O'Reilly. Or am I misunder-
standing the situation and you haven't actually agreed to adopt
that amazing cat?'

'*We* are adopting her and full responsibility for her care goes
to Calum, here. Right son?'

'She's a corker,' Calum said, nuzzling the cat back. 'All I have
to do is get her to like Busy and I know he'll be a pushover.
He's a lover not a fighter.'

Alex smiled at Tony. She rose to her toes and kissed his neck
– then the corner of his mouth. They stared at one another and
she felt how ready they were to be alone.